Wedding at the Lakeside Resort

The Lakeside Resort Series (Book 4)

SUSAN SCHILD

Wedding at the Lakeside Resort
The Lakeside Resort Series (Book 4)

Copyright © 2020 by Susan Schild, Longleaf Pine Press

For permission requests, write to the author on Facebook at:
https://www.facebook.com/authorsusanschild/

Editing by The Pro Book Editor
Interior and Cover Design by IAPS.rocks

ISBN: 978-1-7328249-6-6
    1. Main category—Fiction>General
    2. Other category—Fiction>Women's
First Edition

OTHER BOOKS BY SUSAN SCHILD

Christmas at the Lakeside Resort
(The Lakeside Resort Series Book 1)

Summer at the Lakeside Resort
(The Lakeside Resort Series Book 2)

Mistletoe at the Lakeside Resort
(The Lakeside Resort Series Book 3)

Linny's Sweet Dream List
(A Willow Hill Novel Book 1)

Sweet Carolina Morning
(A Willow Hill Novel Book 2)

Sweet Southern Hearts
(A Willow Hill Novel Book 3)

For Bryan

CHAPTER 1

"ARE WE CRAZY TO GO for a boat ride in January?" Jenny sat in the first mate's chair, her voice muffled as her pink windproof neck gaiter came up over her chin and lower face and she had on a puffy coat with a high stand-up collar. Though it was thirty-four degrees and windy, she was toasty warm but knew she looked odd.

"Winter boat rides build character," Luke said with a raffish grin as he reached for the cleat, untied the boat line, and tossed it on the dock. "The leaves are gone so you can see the land and the houses better, and we have the whole lake to ourselves." Holding a gloved hand on the lever of the lift, he lowered the pontoon into the frigid waters of Heron Lake and stepped onto the boat.

"Plus, it means we are not getting old," Jenny said firmly. At age forty-four, she needed to do what she could to stave off thoughts of getting old. She still got her hair wet when she swam instead of floating around protecting her hairdo, never talked about her aches and pains, and always put the green sauce on Mexican food, though she'd started carrying minty antacids in her purse.

Luke's mouth quirked in a smile as he put the boat in reverse. He wore his heaviest winter coat, a red plaid scarf, and an insulated hat with a small bill on the front that she'd found for him at Country Supply in the section for hunters trying to stay warm in tree stands. She eyed him and smiled. The cap would make other men look like Elmer Fudd, but on her fiancé, it looked so manly in an original and not too perfect way. She didn't like too perfect men. Luke looked ruddy, handsome, and capable, like a Canadian Mountie on his day off chopping wood for his family's cabin.

Sighing happily, Jenny settled back in her chair as they smoothly glided away. With the higher altitudes of the mountains just thirty-five miles away, they'd had flurries and light storms that left inches on the ground for a few days, but no major snowstorms. It was cold today, though, and winter wasn't over yet.

Luke put the boat in forward, and they cruised off slowly, the boat's pontoons easily slicing through the choppy waves. Water gently splashed against the hull, making a pleasant, almost hypnotic sound.

As the boat drew away from the dock, Jenny admired the sight of her eight tiny cabins with their chocolate brown logs and forest green metal roofs. With their cherry red doors and green-and-white striped awnings, the cabins looked cozy, warm, and inviting. Jenny sniffed and caught the scent of the wood smoke that rose from the chimneys of several of the cabins. Though it was January, she had guests staying in four cabins. A poet from Virginia who was working on a new book was staying in her newest accommodation, the ten-foot-long 1956 Shasta camper model that fans affectionately called a "canned ham."

The day was a stunner, clear and sunny with blue skies feathered with a graceful white trail of cirrus clouds. Jenny settled back into the first mate's seat, still chilly despite her snowman's attire. She pulled a windproof blanket from the canvas bag she'd brought along and wrapped herself in it. She'd brought one for Luke, but he'd say he didn't need it, even if he was shivering. Men.

As they glided off, Jenny put a hand over her eyes to block the sun and gazed at the heavily wooded peninsula that sat to the left of her property. "That place has always intrigued me," she called to Luke.

He glanced over at it and pointed. "Look at that old fieldstone chimney. I never saw it before with all the leaf cover." Reaching under the console, he brought out a pair of binoculars and handed them to her.

Pushing her sunglasses up onto her head, Jenny took a moment to focus the binoculars and peered back at the neighboring land. "I heard there was an old home place there that burned down. It sure is a pretty point. Private and good height to the land," Jenny mused. "The owner always keeps that gate locked, and it's posted with *No Trespassing* signs," she added, trying to look pious.

"I'm sure that sign slowed you down," Luke said drily.

"I may have tried to walk down the old road or around the edge of the land, but the trees and underbrush are dense and full of briars. It looks snaky," Jenny admitted, trying not to think about stepping on copperheads or tromping down a shoreline and riling up a cottonmouth.

Luke nodded, guiding the boat down the shoreline until it came to a sandy point. He gave the land one last appraising look. "We should go meet the owner to find out what he or she has in mind for the property. If we ever decide to expand the resort, that would be good to know."

Jenny's heart lifted at Luke's use of the pronoun *we*. She loved being part of a *we* and having a future with this fine man. But then Jenny frowned, worried about a new trend on the lake that used to be primarily for families to get away. "Maybe we should do that sooner than later, Luke. What if the owner sold the land to a buyer who built a mega-house with twenty bedrooms to rent out to party crowds during the summer?" The tranquility of the Lakeside Resort would fly right out the window. "Let's track down the owner," she said with steely resolve and made a mental note of it.

But it was hard to hold onto dark thoughts when a wedge of Canada geese flew overhead, calling to one another, and a blue heron sat regally on a neighboring dock. Many birds had decided not to winter in Florida and were still on the lake. A loon, a low-to-the-water cruiser with a pointy beak, dove under the water and emerged after a few long seconds. Graceful birds, Jenny decided. They didn't say much during the day, but she'd heard their haunting calls in the evenings in the spring and summer.

"Hold on, girl," Luke called and nudged up the throttle. Now they were flying.

Jenny shut her eyes, inhaling the clean, cold air and relishing the feel of the speed of the boat. Heaven. How had she gotten so lucky as to have found this scenic lake and, after all the faithless, philandering, flat-out wrong men she'd chosen, found this gorgeous and kind man who wanted to marry her? Opening her eyes, she felt his eyes on her and looked at him. Luke flashed a pirate's smile as he gave her a thumbs-up.

In a quiet cove protected from the wind, Luke slowed, cut the engine, and dropped anchor. The winter sun warmed them, and they each pulled off their scarves and gloves.

Jenny reached into the canvas bag. The thermos had kept her homemade vegetable soup hot, and she carefully poured them each a mug. The air steamed over the rims as they sipped. Ah. Next, Jenny pulled out the still-warm roast beef sandwiches on crusty French rolls. She'd wrapped them snugly in foil and covered them with a fluffy bath towel to hold in the heat.

Jenny enjoyed a sip of flavorful soup and took a bite of the savory sandwich. Yum. She tilted her head and looked at Luke, who was balancing his soup on the dashboard and making good headway with his sandwich. "So, what was your week like? You're not big on the phone, you know." When Jenny asked how things were or what his day was like, he typically said, "*Good.*" It drove her crazy. If she pressed for more detail, he'd say, "Things are going along fine." The only way to get details from Luke was to talk with him in person and use phrases like "tell me more" and "speak in a mild voice like you use to calm spooky horses or jumpy dogs."

Luke rubbed his chin and looked off into the distance. "Zander's got personnel issues that need to be addressed, and he's brought people to the leadership team who are IT engineering brainiacs just like him." He shook his head. "Big mistake."

"Hmmm." Jenny took another careful sip of the hot soup.

Luke tucked a piece of roast beef that was falling from his sandwich back in and looked troubled. "He also isn't managing performance problems at the vice president level. Not good."

Though she'd never met Zander, Jenny had heard enough about him to feel like she knew him. Whip smart but arrogant, Zander counted on Luke to ground him, mentor him, and bail him out of trouble. Jenny just wished Peter Pan would grow up and stop bugging Luke.

Luke gave her an apologetic look. "I need to be back at the cabin at four for a phone call with Zander."

Jenny puffed out a quiet sigh of frustration. It was Saturday, their day to be together and relax. She'd hoped she'd have Luke to herself, but this was real life. Her appetite gone, Jenny carefully rewrapped the foil around what was left of her sandwich. "When we got home, I thought we were going to do our planning for the honeymoon."

"We will. We've got time to do that before the call."

Slightly mollified, Jenny couldn't let it go, though, remembering how hard it had been last spring to manage at the resort when Luke had traveled to Australia for almost two months to help Zander with a work problem. Jenny touched the smooth gunwales of the boat. With Luke gone and her having no experience with lake living, Jenny'd had to buy this used boat, learn how to tow it behind a truck, dock it, and operate it before her summer guests arrived at the resort.

Jenny knew her flare of resentment wasn't reasonable. Zander had needed Luke to go because he'd broken his hip and his femur and wasn't fit to travel, but knowing that hadn't made it any easier for Jenny to manage her own problems. The Lakeside Resort *could* have failed.

To add to the mix, Luke had also been away a lot to help his dad out after his strokes last year. Jenny understood it all but wanted, and *needed*, more time with him. Jenny blew out a breath slowly. "Is it always going to be this way? Your having to drop everything and help every time Zander gets himself in a bind?"

"I hope not. I'm trying to keep these kinds of issues from cropping up." Luke adjusted the bill of his cap. "But I can't let them down, I've still got a big financial stake in the company, and this is important to our future well-being," he reminded her. "The call won't take more than thirty minutes, I promise." Luke leaned over and kissed her cheek. "Promise, Jen."

"Okay." Jenny lifted her chin. "But Luke, we need time for this, too. We've got a lot of planning to do." She held up five fingers. "Five months, Luke. This is all happening in five months," Jenny reminded him. Though their plan all along had been for the wedding and honeymoon to be simple and low key, these things still took planning.

Luke gave her a conciliatory smile. "I came prepared. In addition to GPS, I got information about campgrounds from Good Sam, and bought real paper maps and a few colored markers. We can look at the big picture and plan the honeymoon trip in the Silver Belle."

Jenny gave herself a mental shake and gave him a crooked grin. "Sounds good." She gestured around at the glorious winter day. "But let's stay out a little longer. We've got a crystal blue sky and perfect sunlight. Let's do more riding."

Luke rose and leaned over to fold her into a warm, firm hug. "You're my girl, Jenny."

Leaning her forehead into his chest, Jenny closed her

eyes and breathed him in. Luke smelled like cedar, clean man, and a whiff of wood smoke. She could be patient. In just five months, they'd be married, living together, and setting off on the adventure of their lives.

Back at the cabin, Bear, Buddy, and her miniature horse Levi swarmed Luke like he was a returning war hero though they'd just seen him three hours ago. What was it with animals and men? "I'm divine until Luke shows up," Jenny muttered, but the dogs were busy doing figure eights around Luke's legs and Levi, who was rarely subtle, stood on Luke's foot.

Luke broke into a grin and spent a few moments scratching and rubbing them.

Jenny spooned cocoa powder into the milk warming in a pan, carefully measured vanilla extract and sugar, and added a pinch of salt. In a cabinet above the stove, she found a bag of marshmallows that she'd managed not to eat when she'd had a sweet tooth.

Luke goosed up the fire in the woodstove and stepped outside to grab an armload of logs.

The fire crackled and the cabin warmed up quickly. Jenny grabbed a small notepad and pen, and she and Luke got settled in side by side on the sofa.

Luke took a sip of his hot chocolate and raised his mug in a little toast. "Tasty, Jen."

"Good." Jenny sipped the chocolatey goodness, relishing it.

Luke quirked a brow. "Before we go full speed ahead on the honeymoon, let's decide what kind of wedding we're having. So, we were talking about a simple wedding, right?"

"Yes, and let's keep it small if we can." Jenny paused, considering it. "With just our families and closest friends, we'd have just twenty-five or thirty guests. How does that sound?"

"Suits me." Luke gave her a questioning look. "Are we having it here?"

"I like that idea. The cabins are where we met and fell in love," Jenny said happily.

With a James Dean smirk, Luke smoothed his hair. "Hard to resist my suave manliness."

"So true." Jenny patted him on the knee. "A summer wedding here would be rustic and picturesque." She pictured saying *I do* on a perfect, blue sky day. Ahhh. But the mental picture changed, and Jenny saw pitch-black thunder clouds roll in. Drenched guests would scream as they dodged lightning bolts and ran for cover. "It's too bad the new cabin won't be ready for the wedding."

"Agreed, but it's the best we can do. The logs get delivered by mid-February and the crew arrives in April. The log home company says to count on eight months for the build."

"Okay." Jenny was disappointed that the all-purpose

room they'd planned for in the cabin design wouldn't be ready in time for the wedding, but it *was* the best they could do. She jotted down the timeline. "We'll need to rent a tent like we did at Christmas." She chewed on the end of her pen "We can have big storms in early summer. The tents can handle heavy rains, right?"

"Yup. Remember what the tent man told us. They're waterproof, windproof, and have tip-over protection. We'll be fine."

But Jenny wilted, remembering how junky the resort had looked during renovations, a mud pit strewn with building supplies and adorned with a bright orange portable potty. Jenny sat up straighter and tried to see the bright side. Even with construction, the resort was a picture perfect setting for a wedding. "The Save-the-Date cards came this past week. We need to get them out and mail invitations soon." She tapped her pen on the note-pad. "I need your guest list."

"Okay." Luke cocked his head. "Did you get in touch with Paul about officiating?"

"I emailed him, but I haven't heard back." Their neighbor Paul, a retired Episcopal priest, was on a trip to the Galapagos Islands with his wife Ella. Jenny jotted down a reminder. "They may not have service, and I don't want to bug them on vacation. I'll call when they get home."

"So, we agreed the wedding is going to be an informal deal," Luke said, looking hopeful.

Jenny studied him with narrowed eyes. "You're hoping you can wear shorts, a Hawaiian shirt, and no shoes. Not that informal, buddy boy."

"Dang," Luke muttered, but he was fighting a smile.

Jenny pinched her lip. "How about no tux but a suit or just a coat and tie?"

"Done." Luke looked relieved.

"Why do men these days not want to get dressed up?" Jenny groused. "You all look so sharp when you do. Think about James Bond in *Goldfinger*, George Clooney in *Ocean's 11...*"

"Me at my first wedding," Luke said mildly.

"Oh, gotcha." Jenny gave him a quick look. Had she stirred up any poignant memories about his late wife? But Luke was whistling softly as he unfolded a map of the United States.

Luke pressed out the creases over Montana and Michigan. "Let's look at the big picture first. Where do we want to go, and how are we getting there?"

"So, we know we're visiting my friends from the *Small Hoteliers and Innkeepers Forum*." Jenny was so grateful to the innkeepers she'd met on the online site. Advice from forum folks had saved her bacon last year when she'd been dangerously low on guests, money, and ideas about how to succeed as the inexperienced owner of the Lakeside Resort.

"I did come up with a possible logical starting route." Jenny held up both hands. "These are just ideas. We can go any direction you want."

Luke gave an amiable smile. "It's a good idea to put pins in the map of places we know we want to go and build the trip around them. Tell me what you've got."

"What if we head south first?" Jenny glanced at her notepad. "Bertha runs an old-timey motor court made of vintage RVs in South Carolina. From there, we head to the mountains of Georgia, where a friend has the treehouses hotel. Next, St. Augustine, where two sisters operate B & B lighthouses. My friends from Texas run a motel made of twenty teepees, and my buddy Zig owns an old-timey motor court of chalet-style rooms near Yellowstone."

"Good. We head south and wind our way west." Slipping on the tortoiseshell readers he had hooked to his shirt, Luke studied the map spread across their laps.

Jenny arched a brow. "In those glasses, you look like a hot college professor."

Luke broke into a smile. "Focus, flirty girl. We've got a honeymoon to plan."

The phone rang promptly at four, and Luke sat down at the kitchen table to talk. Jenny did not want to listen. Rounding up Bear, Buddy, and Levi, she pulled on her warm clothes again and took all three boys out for a long walk. Bear and Buddy had a new habit of eating deer scat that she was trying to discourage. Levi was getting a belly on him from too frequent treats, and Jenny did a fast walk, jog with him to try to help get him back in trim, fit form. Just a little excess weight on a mini horse his size could cause real problems with bones and joints.

When they clattered back inside at 4:45, Luke was still on the call.

Inwardly, Jenny sighed. Calls with Zander often ran longer than expected, so she wasn't surprised, but Luke kept getting pulled back into the business that he'd said he wanted to leave. At times, Jenny just wanted to shake Zander *and* Luke. Jenny busied herself feeding the boys.

His brows drawn as he listened, Luke tried to wrap up the call. "All right. I think we've about covered it. So we need to look at every supporting document. Right. Right." He ended the call, and looked over at her, conflicting emotions passing over his face. "Sorry I ran late, Jen."

Needing to be busy to stay collected, Jenny took up the boys' bowls, hand-washed them, and set them in the drainer to dry. She gave Luke a cool smile. "So, what's happening?"

Looking weary, Luke rubbed the bridge of his nose. "We have other issues, too. We're applying for three business-process patents. The applications have to be done right." He scowled. "The draft that Zander and his team came up with was too technical by a long shot. All wrong."

Jenny had a sinking feeling in her chest. She knew what was coming. Crossing her arms, she leaned against the rough-hewn log post to the living room. "So, you're leaving again?"

CHAPTER 2

MONDAY MORNING, JENNY WOKE JUST after 6:00 AM and lay there in bed, feeling exhausted. Luke was leaving this morning. Pulling the covers over her face, she groaned aloud.

Jenny's sleep had been thin and restless, punctuated by crazy dreams. In one, Luke was driving to Athens, Georgia, by way of New York and, no matter how hard he tried to keep his truck on the road, it kept veering from one side of the road to the other.

Rubbing her gritty eyes, Jenny remembered part two of the dream, in which Luke had called Jenny from the road. She'd implored him to be careful and not drive north to go south, but he kept ignoring her, and his truck ended up sailing off a mountain. In part three, Luke FaceTimed Jenny and looked blasé as he told her that he loved being part of Zander's *dynamic team* and was moving back to *dynamic* Athens for good. He kept using the word *dynamic*. It's a *dynamic town. The work is dynamic.*

Bleah. Jenny was tired and ticked off at Luke for not

being a better driver and for wanting to be so *dynamic*. Mostly, she was mad at him for leaving.

Opening one eye, she glanced at the clock. She needed to get a move on. Luke was stopping by soon to say good-bye before he left. Rolling out of bed, she made herself get on the floor and do a quick Child's Pose and Bridge, trying to ease her aching back. Pulling on her robe, she trudged into the kitchen, let the boys out for a run, and brewed coffee. Catching a glimpse of herself in the micro-wave glass, Jenny grimaced. Her hair was flat on her head except for a poof on one side, and she had bags under her eyes. This was not the image she wanted to leave Luke with for the next few weeks. Taking a restorative gulp of coffee, Jenny called in the boys, fed them, and hurried to the bathroom to take a quick shower and spruce up.

Jenny felt better after her shower. Hot water and a second cup of coffee helped clear the cobwebs, and the bad mood hangover from her dreams was receding. Jenny fluffed her hair with a round brush and a hair dryer until the poof disappeared. But her wavy hairdo still listed a little to the left despite her best efforts. While brushing her teeth, she spied Levi walking around in a small circle. He breathed a happy chuffing sound. Buddy and Bear began play-fighting, almost knocking over two chairs. They were whimpering with excitement. All this happy frenzy had to mean Luke was at the door.

Jenny hurriedly slicked on raspberry lip balm and hurried to greet him.

Bringing a burst of cold, clean air with him, Luke stepped inside and folded her into a hug. "Morning, darlin'."

"I dreamed you were driving through New York to get to Georgia. Don't do that," she said grumpily as she reached up to kiss him. "Also, don't drive off a mountain or move to Athens."

"Okay. I'll just say no to all three," Luke said gravely and smoothed back her hair from her face. "Rough night's sleep?"

"Yup." Jenny looked at his indigo blue eyes and felt bereft. "I'm going to miss you."

"I miss you already, and I'm not even out the door," Luke said quietly and kissed her thoroughly.

For a long moment, Jenny let herself sink into the safety and comfort of being kissed and held on tightly to him, tears pricking her eyes. No need to get all emotional, she told herself. It would make it worse all round. Gently extricating herself from their embrace, Jenny handed Luke a mug of coffee and leaned against the kitchen counter. "How long is the drive?"

"Usually three-and-a-half hours, but it'll take five with the construction on the interstate." Luke pulled his cell from his coat pocket and pointed at all the red lines on his GPS. "They still haven't cleared the rockslide in the mountains, so I'll need to take back roads to avoid that mess."

Jenny pictured that part of her dream when Luke's

truck went airborne, and her mouth went dry. "Promise you'll be careful."

"I will," Luke promised. "I wish there were good flights but there are none. It would take me longer to fly than to drive."

She pinched her lip and thought about it. "If it takes five hours, I hope you aren't still thinking about driving home on the weekends."

"I really can't. It will take every bit of that time to straighten out the problems we've got," Luke said, looking regretful. "Zander has also planned team building activities for the weekends like going rock climbing and zip-lining."

Jenny enjoyed a mean thought, picturing Zander's zip line malfunctioning. Instead of gliding above treetops, he swung through thick bamboo fronds that kept whacking him the face. Zander would fall safely into a pile of leaves, but the experience would change him. He'd sit up and say, *I've got to get my act together, stop acting like an eighteen-year-old, and run this company so I won't need to keep calling Luke.*

"I hate to leave." Luke rubbed the back of his neck. "I really wanted to be here to help you with Valentine's weekend and…well…to be your valentine. I'll make it up to you," he said, his voice low and gravelly with intensity.

"I know." Jenny hooked her arm in his and leaned against him.

Luke glanced at the time on the clock on the stove and

winced. "I need to go. We've got an all-hands meeting at three."

"Let's get you on the road," Jenny said briskly. She pulled a muffin tin from the oven, scooped out several of the ham, cheddar, and egg cups that Luke liked so much, and wrapped them for him. "Be safe and text me when you get there."

"I will." Tucking his breakfast in his coat pockets, Luke embraced her fervently. "Love you, Jen."

"Love you right back." Slipping on a coat, Jenny walked outside with him and kept a bright smile on her face as she waved goodbye, but when Luke's truck disappeared from view, her eyes welled, and she brushed away the tears as they trickled down her face.

Maybe caffeine would give her a pick-me-up. Jenny brewed herself another cup and slowly sipped it. Instead of eating the protein-packed ham and egg cup she'd fixed Luke for breakfast, she'd fixed herself a microwave brownie in a mug. Excellent idea, she decided after her first spoonful, and so tasty with her smoky French roast. Jenny scraped the mug with her spoon when she finished so she didn't miss a smidge.

Rinsing her dishes and putting them in the dishwasher, Jenny realized her mood had brightened a bit. Raising her arms over her head, she did a little desultory stretching and rolled her shoulders forward and then back.

Taking a final swallow of her now cool coffee, Jenny gave herself a little pep talk. "Enough moping. You need to bite the bullet and put on your big girl panties. He'll be back soon. Let's be brave and get on with things."

All three boys woke from hard napping and looked at her with keen-eyed interest. Levi twitched his ears, seemingly heartened by her peppy words.

Grabbing her bucket of cleaning supplies and the new roll of biodegradable trash bags, Jenny slipped on her coat and headed out. She had cabins to clean.

When the fifty-ish poet with the shy smile and the ponytail tied back with a string of leather had checked out of the Shasta yesterday, he'd promised to send Jenny a copy of his soon-to-be-published volume, called *Dewy Morn with Geese Calling*. Jenny had thanked him sincerely, though poetry befuddled her. She always wondered if she'd gotten the meaning right or if she just wasn't deep enough to get it. Still, she liked the title and would give poetry reading the old college try. As she emptied the trash, Jenny grinned. The poet was a kindred spirit, another lover of the one-two lift of chocolate and caffeine. Apparently Hershey's chocolate kisses and diet Mountain Dew helped with meter and rhyme.

On to the Cedar, where the buttoned-up dermatologist and his pearl-wearing wife had also checked out. Jenny's eyes widened when she let herself into their cabin. Her theory was playing out. The tidiest, most proper-looking guests were often the sloppiest. Towels were strewn on the floor, bedding was half on and half off, and the blinds were higgledy-piggledy, with a few raised partway, crooked, and closed. As she stripped the bedding, Jenny glanced around, checking to make sure they'd done no damage to the room, though. Good. They were just messy. She remembered an All American-looking married couple with a small child who'd left large mustard stains on the bedding and broken a lamp, but failed to mention either to her when they'd checked out.

Jenny made quick work of the other three cabins. Though she'd finally come up with an efficient routine for freshening cabins, she'd be glad when she was sure enough about finances to hire a regular cleaning person. She fluffed pillows, straightened the quilt, and closed the door.

Jenny glanced at her phone again, but no word yet from Luke. He didn't text and drive, but he'd call her when he stopped for gas or a break. Pausing, she closed her eyes for a moment and sent up a prayer. *God, keep an eye on him. Protect him as he's driving. Let him arrive safely.* With a sigh, Jenny headed toward the laundry shed with a cart full of dirty sheets and towels, grateful for anything that would keep her distracted. Hard work was a tonic for almost anything, and she was not going to let herself mope for a month.

That evening, Jenny was in her flannel nightgown by 7:30,

snuggled on the sofa under a down throw with the dogs and Levi wedged warmly around her. The fire Jenny had built in the woodstove was glowing and crackling; she was sipping a glass of wine and had just cracked open the newest novel from her favorite author when the FaceTime tone sounded. Her heart ticked up a beat as she snatched up her phone and looked into the screen of her cell. "Hey, Luke," she said, sounding breathless in her pleasure.

Luke's face came into view, and he broke into a disarming smile. "Hey, Jen."

"How are you? How did today go?" she asked, her words tumbling out.

"It was good. The drive was fine, the meeting went smoothly, and we've gotten a plan for dealing with the patent issues." Luke scrubbed his face with a hand. "Tonight, we have a cooking class at an East African restaurant and dinner after. Turns out Zander and his team do all this social, fun, bonding stuff together several nights a week."

"What other things do they do?" Jenny asked. Luke had once told her he'd rather hang insulation in an attic in August than do after-hours socializing.

"Turns out trivia nights and axe throwing are old news. We're doing a Habitat project, a ropes course, and going to a comedy improv class." He gave a wry smile. "Hope this group works as hard as they play."

"Wow. That's a lot of work-related togetherness," Jenny said knowingly.

"Yeah." Luke rolled his eyes. "I don't need six new best friends. I've already got one, and that's plenty."

Jenny broke into a slow smile. "Miss you, baby boy."

"Right back at you." His gaze intent, he gave her a crooked smile. "What went on at the resort today?"

Normally monosyllabic on phone calls, Luke was talking up a storm on FaceTime. Jenny was enjoying hearing him talk. After she filled him in on her day, she saw how tired he looked and reluctantly ended the call. Seeing his face would make the month go faster, too. Jenny gave the phone a little pat and slid it back on the table.

The week puttered along. Late Friday afternoon, Jenny finished the online banking, reconciling and checking her bank statements and credit card charges for both the resort and for herself. After a hacker had gotten her business credit card last month and tried to charge $800.00 worth of video games, Jenny'd had a purchase alert set up on her phone and regularly checked her bank statements. All was well. They were even slightly in the black. Jenny rewarded herself with a mug of Earl Gray. As she dunked the teabag into her mug, a text tone sounded, and she glanced at it. Mama wrote:

Off to our Carolina Shag dancing class! So glad Lily the librarian got these kinds of classes going. So fun! How did we live in South Carolina so long and not learn this dance? Turns out Landis is a twinkletoes. Know you miss Luke. Have a relaxing evening. See you in AM.

Jenny smiled. Mama, like Charlotte, wrote lengthy texts, but the mode of communicating had proven to be a great way to check in with each other without intruding. She tapped out:

Have fun, you crazy kids. XOXO

When Mama and her husband Landis had moved permanently into the Redbud, the cabin less than thirty feet from Jenny's cabin, they'd both agreed to no dropping in and used texts for casual check-in's. Having them next door was not nearly as tricky as she'd worried it could be. Both Mama and Landis were good company. Mama was always up for a walk or an outing. Jenny felt comforted with them being there, and having them so close would help ease the loneliness of Luke's absence.

Jenny got up and searched the junk drawer until she found her very best black rollerball pen. Her pulse quickened with eagerness as she picked up the cellophane-wrapped stack of Save-the-Date cards. They were already late mailing these cards. The wedding etiquette site on the internet recommended they be mailed six to eight months before the wedding. Nothing to worry about. This was casual, she reminded herself, not an orchestrated, over-the-top wedding for young brides and grooms.

At first, Jenny had chosen a basic, no-frills design for the cards, but just before she clicked PAY NOW, she reopened the page and looked for more extravagant options. Their wedding deserved more than a generic message. It had taken her long enough to find Luke. Her wedding date would be the happiest day of her life, and she didn't want a fair-to-middling announcement. Sliding the cards out of their protective wrapping, Jenny exhaled with delight as she examined them. The photo in the middle was the best part.

With her cell, Mama had surreptitiously taken a photo of Jenny and Luke standing on the dock looking out at the water at sunset. The shot only partially showed their faces and was backlit. Both were dressed casually in jeans and boots. Luke had his armed draped around her, and Jenny had rested her head against his chest. Both of them looked relaxed and easy with one another, and the setting sun cast a luminous glow on them. The photo had caught them in a moment that was dreamy, poignant, and personal.

The message was simple:

Jenny Beckett and Luke Hammond are
getting married June 20, 2020!

The Lakeside Resort

Please save the date. We'd love for you to join us.

Jenny peered more closely at the graphic she'd picked. Instead of the typical garlands of magnolias, bunches of herbs, or roses, Jenny had found a dogwood tree branch with delicate white blooms that were the official flowers of North Carolina. On the branch perched two bluebirds side by side, a vivid blue male and a subdued gray-blue female. Jenny put a hand to her cheek and smiled.

Though she didn't tell this to people who might think her kooky, Jenny was sure the appearance of bluebirds was a way her daddy, Jax, conveyed messages to her from the other side. *I'm here for you. I'll love you always. You're my darling girl.* All the things that she'd wished he'd have said to her when he was living but never could.

Because she kept seeing so many bluebirds around the Lakeside Resort, Jenny had also read up on their meaning and found that they symbolized joy, happiness, cheer, and a happy future, all things she'd finally started to believe were possible after she'd moved to Heron Lake and met Luke. Since then, she'd put up a number of bluebird nesting boxes on the property to encourage their safely raising their broods.

The cards were perfect. Clearing a space on the turquoise blue Formica kitchen table, Jenny took a quick picture of one of them, adding a message of X's and O's, and texted it to Luke. He'd love it, and he'd get the bluebird connection.

Jenny unfolded the Bojangles' napkin Luke had handed her before he left. On it, he'd hastily written his guest list. Jenny blinked with surprise as she looked at thirty-four names he'd printed in his all-caps scrawl. There went their original *let's keep it very small* estimate. Glancing at the end of the list, she had to smile as she read his one-line explanation. *P.S. The list got away from me. We have a lot of people we care about. Okay?*

Jenny waved the note back and forth in her hand. Luke had more family than she did and had a lot of old friends from the community that he'd grown up with. Of course they could go bigger if that's what he wanted. Good thing she'd sprung for the larger box of announcements.

Putting her elbow on the table and her chin in her hand, Jenny started jotting down a list of friends and family she wanted to invite to the wedding. There was Mama, Landis, Charlotte, and Ashe; Luke's sister Alice and her husband, Mike; Charlotte's parents Beau and Nell; Paul and Ella; and Lily and her new beau, Tom, from the hardware store. Holy smokes. Before she knew it, Jenny had twenty-four folks she wanted to invite. Should she try to cull her list? Jenny nibbled on a thumbnail and made a decision. Nope. They'd go with it. Witnessing a wedding reminded people of their own love and made them hopeful. Everyone could use a dose of that.

Flexing her fingers, Jenny curled and uncurled them, shook them out, and leaned forward. Carefully, she began addressing the cards in her very best handwriting, incorporating a bit of the fanciness she'd picked up in a *Classy Calligraphy* class she'd taken at the Lake County Library.

After addressing them, Jenny affixed the elegant stamps she'd found with the bouquet of moss-green succulents and pink orchids. Pausing to shake out a cramped hand, she glanced at the clock. It was nine o'clock already. The boys needed one more outing before bed.

Jenny stood and stretched. Buddy and Bear wove their way around her legs, anxious looks on their faces like they worried this would be the day that Jenny would forget to let them out before bed. "Coming up, boys," Jenny called.

Jenny pulled on her coat and opened the door, but stopped still as she heard the rumbling roar of an engine in the distance. The road to the resort was dead-end and rarely had any traffic, but it sounded like that was coming from the road and coming closer fast. Buddy and Bear flew up and began barking ferociously. Even easygoing Levi looked worried.

Maybe a visitor was lost. Maybe it was a prospective guest who wanted to look at the resort before committing to a reservation. That happened a lot. But all of the guests had checked out, so Jenny was the only one on the property. That made her nervous.

The roar sounded similar to their friend Mike's big menacing-looking truck that had pipes on it that made it sound like it had no muffler. But Mike wouldn't make an unexpected visit. The sound grew closer and over the roar, Jenny could hear heavy metal music being played at an ear-splitting volume.

Jenny knew she was being a nervous Nellie, but pulse racing, she stepped back inside and locked the door. Scrabbling in the basket on the counter, she found the panic button for the alarm system that they'd just had installed. If she pushed her thumb down on that little button, that high-decibel shriek of a wailing alarm would sound both inside and outside the cabin. Strobe lights would flash, the sheriff would get notified, and two of their closest neighbors would hurry to the property, most likely armed.

Turning off the lights, Jenny shushed the dogs and eased back into shadows, breathing shallowly as she peered out the window.

CHAPTER 3

MUSIC BLARED AND THUMPED AS the moonlight illuminated a truck speeding past the cabin, spewing exhaust and blaring music. Jenny guessed he was going forty miles per hour on this narrow two-lane dead end. With giant tires, roll bars, and the frame lifted high in the air, the truck was similar to the ones Jenny had seen when she and Charlotte had tried to go to a craft show at the North Carolina fairgrounds but got the dates wrong and went to a Monster Truck Jam instead. Menacing-looking trucks like this one revved engines, flew airborne over hills, and crushed cars.

Opening the door a crack, she could hear the truck skid when it came to the end of the road. The truck's engine revved, and it sounded like it was driving off. But the only road at the end of the property was her neighbors' long driveway. There were no other open roads on the lot. The truck now sounded like it was crashing through underbrush. Then came the sound of tires squealing, and

Jenny guessed the driver was doing donuts in that cul-de-sac. Roaring back into view, the truck sped off.

Her fingers sweaty, Jenny tossed the panic button back in the basket and exhaled. Buddy and Bear had ridges of fur standing on their backs and were still showing their teeth and growling low and mean. "Good dogs." Jenny sank into the couch, trying to think it through.

Her cell sounded and made her jump, but she heaved a sigh of relief when Luke's face appeared. "Hey, Luke," Jenny said in a trembling voice. She was *so* glad to see him.

"Hey, Jen. How was..." Luke trailed off, his eyebrows in a V as he looked more closely at her face. "What's wrong?" he barked out.

"Oh, I had a little scare." Jenny leaned back, phone in hand. Feeling safer just seeing his face, Jenny filled him in, starting to wonder if she was being overly dramatic and if her response had been like Chicken Little. "I don't think it was much of anything. Once you get past our driveway, it's a state road. Anybody could drive down it, or maybe somebody got lost."

"I don't like you on the property alone. Getting security cameras up is the first thing I'm doing when I get home." Luke rubbed his jaw. "It could have been harmless, like a young guy cutting up and letting loose in a hot truck. But you think they drove onto the neighbor's property?"

"I think so, but I'm not sure." Jenny adjusted the pillow under her neck, relieved to be talking it through with Luke. "I'll ride down there in the morning and take a look."

"Take Landis with you," Luke said, the muscles in his jaws working.

"I will," Jenny promised. "We can see if the neighbor's chained gate is still intact. If they did any off-roading, we'll be able to tell, too. We had rain yesterday, and there will be tire tracks in the dirt."

"Good thinking." Luke looked thoughtful. "If it looks like they trespassed, I'll give Sheriff Tucker a call and let him know what you saw. They can always step up patrols down on our side of the lake."

"Good." Jenny recalled Luke had gone to grade school and high school with the sheriff, Ham Tucker, so that connection helped. "Let's not talk about it anymore. Tomorrow, I'm going online and try to find out the name and contact info of the property owner next door."

Luke nodded approvingly. "We wanted to find out their plans, and we may also want to give them a heads-up if they've got folks riding around their property."

"Good." Jenny gave Luke an apologetic look. "I haven't even asked how your day went."

"We're making headway," Luke said, but his brow was furrowed.

Jenny could tell he was still concerned and not up for *How was your day* small talk, but she wanted to keep him on the line longer. She needed his reassuring presence.

"Talk to me," she said. "I need you to keep me company for a little while longer."

"Okay," Luke said with a glimmer of a smile.

Jenny lay down on the sofa, feeling weak as the adrenaline receded. "I read up on Athens. Well, I glanced at a paragraph on the internet. It sounds like a great little town."

"It is. Since it's a college town, you get more artists, hipsters, and food lovers. Music is big in Athens." Luke still looked grim but was brightening. "We're all going to this cool iconic venue called the Georgia Theater to hear Aaron Watson."

"Oh, wow. You really like his music." Jenny knew he was a big fan.

Luke broke into a smile. "I do. I'm not complaining about that." His tone grew serious, and he gazed directly at her. "But, Jen, all I want to do is be back home with you."

Feeling a wave of pure love, Jenny blew him a kiss just as Levi jumped up and stood beside her on the couch. "Say hello to Daddy," she encouraged the mini and turned the screen toward Levi's face.

"Hey there, little man. I miss you," Luke called. "You men keep an eye on Mama."

Levi looked at the screen, blinked, and looked away. Heaving a sigh, he curled up in a ball beside her and closed his eyes.

Luke chuckled, and Jenny called over the other boys. "Come on up here. Daddy wants to say hello."

After a few moments of FaceTime sugar talk, Jenny ended the call, feeling safe again. Still, she had trouble falling asleep until she heard Mama and Landis come home and saw their lights go on in the Redbud. Sitting up, Jenny leaned on her elbow and tapped out a quick text to Landis. *"Everything fine here, but can you come by in the morning? I'd like you to go sleuthing with me. Kiss Mama for me, Mr. Twinkletoes!*

Early the next morning, Jenny was at the computer intent on finding out who owned the property next door. She tapped in *real estate ownership Lake County North Carolina.* Putting her chin in her hand, she leaned closer to the screen, trying to decipher what she found. The first result that came up was the official county website, but it was a one-pager. Squinting, Jenny looked at the only photo on the page, one of a fellow in a fedora and necktie behind the wheel of an old motorboat.

Luke had been tablet surfing vintage motorboats lately and kept showing her ones he liked and might want to own at an unnamed point in the future.

The boat in the picture looked like Luke's current faves from the 1950s and 1960s, an Eldorado and a Catalina aluminum boat. Jenny shook her head. Strange they'd put such a dated picture on the landing page. Update, people.

Update. On the landing page, Jenny kept clicking places where links should be but came up empty.

Backing out of that search, Jenny perused the other results of her first search. Nothing that didn't involve coding or metadata. No decipherable way to find out who owned that parcel of land next door. Tipping her chair back on two legs, Jenny chewed a thumbnail and thought about it. Hmmm. She wished Ella would hurry up and get home from her vacation to find out if she had any scoop. If she was going to get more information on the lot next door, she needed to go to the county office. After she and Landis did their reconnaissance, she'd do just that. No time like the present.

Landis appeared at her door at 8:15, and stayed cool and collected when Jenny quickly filled him in on the events of last night. "Let's go have a look," he said evenly and waved her over to his SUV.

The two of them wheeled down the road to the neighboring lot. The circle at the end of the road was covered with tire burnout marks. "I thought I heard a driver doing doughnuts," Jenny said.

Landis nodded. He put the SUV in park, and the two walked over to examine the entrance to the dirt road that led deeper into the abandoned property. The chain that had once been strung across the driveway was broken. A No Trespassing sign had been ripped down, run over, and was mired in mud. "Son of a biscuit." Landis took off his fleece cap and rubbed the back of his neck.

A cold knot of dread forming in her stomach, Jenny straightened her spine and walked closer, her eyes searching for the damage. Both sides of the driveway were rutted with deep tire tracks, and it looked like the driver of the truck had taken several detours off the road and through the underbrush. Landis stepped over a small sapling that had been run over and tried to pull it upright but it fell back down. "The boy had himself a little joyride," he drawled. "We'll have Sheriff Tucker swing by today and take a look."

As she thought about the driver's disregard for others' property, Jenny felt a slow burn of anger. Shaking her head in disgust, she pulled her phone from her pocket and carefully stepped deeper into the woods, taking pictures. "I'll send these to Sheriff Tucker."

Back inside the SUV, Landis held his key but did not turn on the ignition. He looked over at her. "Jen, this kind of thing can rattle you, but it happens. If the sheriff finds out anything, it's likely going to be that it was kids cutting up or a goober randomly trying out the new suspension on his truck."

Jenny crossed her arms and hugged herself. She looked over at him, reassured by his equanimity. "I know. I guess I always thought of the resort as a sort of perfect, quiet sanctuary where good-hearted people would come visit and leave all that jangling meanness of the world behind. And then the stupid people of the world bring their craziness and show up just a half mile down the road," she said glumly.

"The Lakeside Resort is still a quiet sanctuary. That won't change." Landis's voice was calm. "Our job is to deal with it the best we can and hold on tight to our sense of safety and peace." He gave her a rueful smile. "I did a few knuckleheaded things when I was a young buck."

"No." Jenny grinned despite herself. "You'll have to tell Mama and me about them over a glass of wine one night."

"I might do that," Landis said, then turned over the engine. "And if my mama and daddy's old neighbor from Aiken ever calls asking about an old tobacco barn almost burning down, you don't know anything."

Jenny grinned.

With a roguish smile, Landis turned the SUV toward home.

Back at the cabin, Jenny felt a surge of determination that was fueled by last night's scare. Now, for her detective work at the county seat. Though she always teased Mama for being old-fashioned for her advice about always dressing up when she dealt with public officials, Jenny pulled on her black dress pants with the hidden elastic waist, a crisp white shirt, and the boots with the little heels that made her feel taller. Buttoning herself into her black dress coat, Jenny grabbed the copy of her deed, filled a to-go cup with a strong dark Sumatra blend, and headed out the door.

An audiobook of Louise Miller's made the miles fly on the forty-five minute drive to the Lake County seat of Tifton. Jenny slowed to a crawl as she drove her little SUV into the heart of the small downtown.

The town looked sad, like the prosperity and resurgence of life that other luckier counties were enjoying had passed it by. Millie's Fine Women's Wear was deserted, a mannequin in the window still dressed in a floral shirtwaist dress, heels, and a flowered hat. Bart's Watch Repair had closed. The only businesses that looked open were a storefront church called *His Redeeming Word* and a vape shop with bright blue LED lights chasing each other around the store window. Those LED lights were popping up everywhere, even on boats on Heron Lake. Jenny knew she was old school, but she really didn't understand why people come to the lake to see nature and enjoy peace, and installed thumping stereo and bright blue LED lights on their boats. Cheerful, positive attitude, Jenny reminded herself, as she saw the Lake County Courthouse directional signs and turned onto Oak Street.

The scenery changed. In the block closest to the grand old courthouse, storefronts were freshly painted, windows were shiny clean, and several businesses were open and thriving. Professionally dressed men and women walked briskly along sidewalks, talking intently with one another or talking on the cell phones pressed to their ears. Lawyers, Jenny decided as she stopped at the one traffic light. The county seats always did better than the small towns out in the middle of nowhere. The professionals who did the legal and administrative work of the county all brought Tifton a bit of prosperity. The *Great South Diner* and the *Lickety Split Eats* were both doing a brisk business with the coffee and breakfast crowd. The *Get You Out Fast Bail Bondsman* was doing so well it took up two storefronts.

Spotting the sign for the Register of Deeds office, Jenny nosed the SUV into a parking spot. Gathering her paperwork, she stood straighter and headed inside.

When Jenny pulled open the heavy glass door and approached a high desk, she saw a haughty-looking young man with an aquiline nose, high forehead, and thin lips. He was tapping away rapid-fire at a keyboard and did not look up at her. The brass name plate on his desk read, *Bennett Carter*, and underneath was his title, *Senior Clerk, Register of Deeds*. On the wall behind him was a poster depicting a dapper, smiling fellow wearing a Clerk name tag handing a neatly bundled sheaf of papers to a grateful-looking older couple. The caption underneath read, *It's always our pleasure to serve the citizens of Lake County!*

Jenny waited patiently for a minute or two, but felt her blood pressure start to rise. Even if the Senior Clerk was right smack in the middle of important work and needed just another minute, the least he could do was acknowledge her. Jenny's feet hurt in her chic-looking boots. She cleared her throat. Still no response from the very busy, very important man. Patience thinning, Jenny said, too loudly, "Good morning. I'd like help."

Bennett Carter's brow creased in annoyance, and he held up a finger.

This move made Jenny want to pinch the man *hard*. She spoke more loudly and clearly. "Good morning. I'm Jenny Beckett."

"Beckett?" He looked up, his eyes bright with interest. "Are you one of the Conway county Becketts from Finley county, tobacco, cotton, pigs, banks?"

Jenny blinked, confused. "Ugh, no." She suddenly got it. A few old-school Southerners still used questions to place you. *Who are your people? Where are you from? Where do you go to church?* These questions could help determine if you were related, which was highly likely in the old days. It could also help them learn if you were a Yankee or *from away*. Jenny thought about telling him she was a Beckett from Winston, Jefferson, Carter, and Wiley counties, and that her people were in petered-out gem mines, failing karaoke laundromats, unwise real estate speculation, and blazing hot poker hands. But really, why bother?

Impatient now, Jenny made a show of studying the poster of the helpful and cheerful clerk on the sign behind him. "*It's always our pleasure to serve the citizens of Lake County!*" she read aloud slowly. "Such a great motto," she said in a saccharine voice.

But Bennett tip-tapped out a few more words, put

his chin in his hand, and stared at her. "How may I help you?" he said curtly. "And let's make it quick, because my lunch hour is in ten minutes at twelve noon. After that, we'll be closed for the rest of day for staff development."

No point in trying to make this man act right. "I need to find out who owns the property beside mine at the end of Bluewater Road," she said crisply.

His eyes hooded, he waved vaguely to his right. "Over here, vital records. births, deaths, marriages, military discharge, etcetera, etcetera, and etcetera." With a world-weary sigh, he pointed to his left. "Over there, register a business, real estate instruments, deeds and trusts, satis-faction instruments, plats." He tilted his head to the wall behind her. "There, additional subsequent instrument index references and notary public commissions." His job done, he turned to look back at his computer screen.

"I need to research real estate records," she said firmly.

"Okay," he said flatly, but made no move to stand.

Jenny looked at the massive books on the wall of shelves. "Are your records computerized or are they all paper?"

"Computerized from 1990 to the present, paper be-fore." He gave another vague wave.

"Can I photocopy documents to take home?" Jenny was scanning the shelves behind him, trying to figure out the exact section she needed and how to find the records in nine minutes.

"Of course." Bennett clasped his hands together and gave an obsequious bow.

Now the man was acting right. Jenny had a flash of buoyant hopefulness.

"Our copying rates have gone up to $48.00 for the first three pages and $10.00 per page after that. No checks or credit cards." Folding his hands, Bennett Carter gave her a sly smile.

Jenny gaped. Were public servants allowed to be that snippy? Opening her purse, she found her wallet and looked at the contents. As usual, she'd let herself run low on cash. She glanced at the clock on the wall. No way could she find an ATM machine in such a short time. Giving him a baleful look, Jenny hurried over to Real Estate records but had just started to get the hang of it when Bennett clapped his hands sharply and kept clapping them.

"11:59, people," he called loudly. "Closing time." He shooed the grumbling patrons out the door. Stopping, he turned around to look at Jenny as she clomped toward the door. He gave her a hard smile. "Funny. You're the second person this week who's asked about that property."

The second person. Who else was inquiring about the neighbor's property? Was the neighbor planning to sell? Would a buyer who didn't love the land as much as she and Luke beat them to the punch and buy the place? Her stomach churned.

But she couldn't let Bennett Carter think he'd gotten

away with such meanness. Jenny paused and took a picture of the clerk with a sour expression on his face sitting beneath the *It's always our pleasure* poster. He glared at her, but she just gave a big fake smile and a finger wave. "This picture will be great for my online review."

As she buckled into her seatbelt, Jenny felt better. She'd not post a bad review, but she hoped she'd give Bennett Carter heartburn and make him think twice about acting rude.

But Jenny heaved a sigh of frustration. She'd wasted a whole morning. Pulling out of the parking lot going a little too fast, Jenny stepped on the brakes as she saw a policeman watching her from his patrol car parked right beside the 15 MPH sign. Yikes. A ticket was not what she needed. Jenny slowed to a snail's pace. A snowy-haired woman who could barely see over the wheel of her old Buick followed her too closely, gave her a pitying stare as she finally passed Jenny, drove over a curb, and tootled off on her way.

Back home, Jenny felt immediately better when she'd wiggled off those boots. She pulled on fleece pants, an old sweatshirt, and sneakers and got behind her computer. Quickly, she set up an email distribution list group with the members of the *Small Hoteliers and Innkeepers Forum* who had been especially kind to her when she'd been struggling so to get cabins booked. She wrote:

Hey there, my dear friends,

It's Cabin Gal. Hope your websites, phones, and reservation systems are jumping with guests with lots of money and grateful, happy attitudes who love to give five-star reviews.

Thanks to you all, the Lakeside Resort is up and running with actual paying guests. I'm not booked solid by any means, but I'm getting the hang of it. We threw a Fabulous You All Gal Fitness Week last fall that went well. The writing workshop was a crowd-pleaser and the yoga and relaxation weekends draw a calm and happy Zen crowd (who also drank a lot of red wine). This summer, we're doing swim lessons, a birdwatching weekend, and a fun program for the young adults on the Autism Spectrum and their families.

I've got big, joyful news! Though I wasn't looking to get hitched again, I met a great guy named Luke, and I'm marrying him!! For our honeymoon, we're taking our old Airstream on a cross-country trip. I'd love to plan two-night visits with each of you if you have rooms available.

Would you please let me when you have availability for two nights after June 21? Bertha, was hoping to start with you; head to see you, Cooper; meet you lighthouse sisters; and make our way west, ending up with you, Zig. We are flexible about dates and will travel for two months!

Can't wait to meet you all in person.

Your grateful friend, Jenny Beckett (Cabin Gal)

CHAPTER 4

O N TUESDAY MORNING, JENNY STOOD in front of the bathroom mirror with a comb and an elastic hair tie in hand. Her phone was propped on the tissue box on the counter and, for the third time, she was watching and trying to follow along with the young woman deftly twirling locks of her hair on her YouTube tutorial on *Easy Peasy Updos for Medium-Length Hair*.

Jenny had looked at the clip to try to get ideas about how her hairstylist, Star, could fix her hair for the wedding, but since it looked so easy, Jenny thought she'd try on her own to do the half-up, half-down twisty chignon. Biting a lip in concentration, Jenny managed a fat, uneven French braid before she gave up and gathered the rest of her hair in a ponytail.

The dogs began their happy yipping. Poking her head into the living room, Jenny saw her mother approaching, a stainless steel coffee mug in her hand. Dressed for the chilly weather, Mama wore her amethyst-colored down coat and a purple beanie cloche adorned with a fleece flower over her head. Her long, silvery-blonde braid was glossy and romantic-looking. Jenny grinned. Mama looked casually elegant, and she'd probably done that braid while she was staring dreamily out the window, imagining her next painting.

Jenny swung open the door and gave her a hug. "Morning, Mama! The temperature dropped fast, didn't it?"

"Twenty-six degrees." Pink-cheeked, she shivered. "Yesterday was mild, and today we're back to full winter." Mama leaned closer, studying Jenny. "Your hair looks precious."

"Thanks. All this hair stuff is harder than it looks." Jenny gave her a wry smile. "I'm almost ready. Can I top off your coffee?"

Claire tilted her coffee mug back and forth and sat it on the counter. "No, I'm done. I've had just enough caffeine to think picking up trash on the side of the road is going to be fun."

Jenny smiled. "Believe it or not, it is kind of fun, especially when we see how pristine the road is on the walk back." Though the road into the resort was not that heavily traveled, if you didn't pick it up two or three times a year, it started to look unsightly.

Eyes bright, Claire rubbed her hands together. "I'm ready."

Giving Mama's arm an affectionate pat, Jenny quickly put away breakfast leftovers so the dogs wouldn't make bad decisions. She couldn't believe she'd had even one concern about Mama and her husband Landis moving to the resort full time. After temporarily staying in the Redbud cabin while their new home near Asheville was being built, Mama had decided she wanted to stay in their tiny guest cabin and live full time on the lake. Turning off the coffee pot, Jenny remembered Mama tearfully blurting out the truth she'd been hiding from all of them, including Landis.

Here's another thing I didn't like about Laurel Vista. It was manicured and safe just like our house in Summerville was. But I want a life that's different, wilder, where I can have new adventures. I want to start painting classes here. I want to plant a fragrance garden and grow all sort of flowers for cutting. I want to go to church fish fries and start hiking. I want Landis to teach me how to drive the boat.

Jenny gathered garbage bags from under the sink and found work gloves for them both. Mama and Landis were always there to help if needed. She and Luke wouldn't even be able to consider an extended camping honeymoon if Landis and Mama hadn't insisted on taking over the innkeeping responsibilities while they would be gone.

While Mama scratched Levi's back and told him how good-looking he was, Jenny pulled on her heaviest windproof parka and a hat and was ready to go. To keep the boys from mooning dramatically about being left, Jenny tossed carrots to all three of them, and they started enthusiastically crunching. "Let's hustle, Mama, before they know we're gone."

They each stepped into their cars. "See you at the end of the road," Jenny called. It was several miles out to the end of the road. They'd leave Mama's car at the end of their route, drive Jenny's car back to the resort, do their trash pickup on the way out, and drive home.

Back home, the two set off at a brisk pace.

"How's that sugar-pie husband of yours?" Jenny handed Mama a garbage bag.

Claire sighed happily. "He's wonderful. You know Landis. He always has to be trying new things and learning. The latest hobbies he's trying out are making beer and smoking meats."

"I could see Landis getting good at both." She reached for a soda can.

"Sort of." Claire smiled wryly. "He exploded a six-pack of beer yesterday. Glass everywhere, and Landis says the smell lingering in the kitchen is *hoppy,* whatever that means."

Jenny chuckled. "How about the smoking?"

Claire pushed up her slipping sunglasses. "His brisket was chewy, but the turkey he smoked was tasty and tender. I'll bring you a sample later today. Amazing."

"I'd love to try it."

Claire looked at her. "You'll never guess who Landis keeps up with. Remember Coy Thompson?"

"Of course. We called him and his wife *the fighting*

couple when they first checked in." Jenny gave an exaggerated shudder. "If I'd have kept a good iron skillet in their cabin, no telling how that story could have ended."

"Remember when his wife jumped out of their canoe and swam ashore because she couldn't stand being with him anymore?" The corners of her eyes crinkled with humor.

Coy had been such a grouch at first, but he'd shaped up and ended up falling back in love with his wife. "So, Landis and Coy email each other?"

"Like BFF's or whatever the kids these days call it." A smile played at the corners of her mouth. "Coy grills and smokes, too, so they give each other tips on sauces and rubs. Anyhow, Coy and Neecy are coming to stay at the resort this summer for two weeks. I took their reservation and entered it into the Welcome Inn system," Mama said proudly.

"Good job." Jenny snagged an empty fertilizer bag.

With a gloved hand, her mother picked up two beer bottles and slipped them in her bag. "I wonder if the domestic beers or the imports are most popular with the litterers."

Jenny grimaced as she reached for an empty bucket that had held fried chicken and stuffed it in her trash bag. "I try to not get grossed out or get mad at people when I do this. I know a lot of the debris blows out of the back of trucks when folks go to the dumpsters up the road, but people still just toss the trash right out the window."

"There's a whole crowd that thinks others should pick up after them. Just big ole babies and people who just weren't raised right," her mother mused as she reached for an empty French fry box. "You're on the right track with your attitude, though."

"It helps," Jenny admitted. "Every time I pick up a piece, I think to myself, *There. The decent people of the world are winning.*"

Claire broke into a smile as she reached for a balled-up paper bag. "Ha. Take that, you littering baby."

Jenny smiled and turned around to admire the clean stretch of road behind them. She tilted her head, noticing the sepia-colored field of golden brown grasses frosted and glittering in the early morning sun. "Pretty."

"Very." With an artist's eye, Claire admired the view, a hand on her hip. "The color hues in winter are more subtle than other seasons, but just as bewitching." She pointed at the field with a gloved hand. "I wish I had my paints and easel and could capture that, but my fingers don't work well when it's this cold."

"It's too cold to stop moving." Jenny pulled her gloves on tighter as the two resumed walking. "Anything else new with you all?"

Claire gave her a questioning look. "Have you noticed anything about Landis? I mean, about his appearance?"

Jenny tilted her head. "Not really, but he's been bundled up every time I've seen him."

"He's started not shaving except once or twice a week.

It's growing so salt and pepper and it's not that appealing." Claire wrinkled her nose. "Also, he's wearing these baggy sweatpants around the house. He always used to wear those nice khakis or at least a tidy pair of jeans."

"Landis has always been a sharp dresser. Casual but put together," Jenny said.

"Not anymore." Mama raised her eyes to the sky. "Those fellows down at Gus's Gas-N-Git have a dress code. They all look like they rolled out of bed, decided against combing their hair, and put on yesterday's clothes. He's starting to do the same."

"Maybe it's a phase. Remember Luke's scraggly goatee? I bit my tongue, though, and he shaved it off."

"Hmmm," Claire said thoughtfully. "When I talk with Landis about it, he brushes me off. He's getting that from his cronies at Gus's, too. He gets a philosophical tone and talks about dressing for comfort, country living, and *athleisure wear*." She shot Jenny an exasperated look. "What is athleisure wear?"

Jenny looked at her. Mama was partial to flowy dresses and had a boho, hippie-chic style. Yesterday, she'd just had golden highlights added to her long gray-blonde hair and always wore fun earrings. For today's trash pickup, she wore a blue-and-white flowered tunic top over jeans. Her nails were polished a teal green. "You always look pretty, Mama. You make an effort."

"Thank you," Mama said with a gracious nod. "I try."

Jenny unzipped her coat a few inches, getting warm

from the walking. "Charlotte's mama complained about her husband, Beau, going to seed after he retired. She called it the Sweatpants Syndrome." She tried to remember the whole story. "I think Charlotte said he spruced right back up once he got into his retirement groove. He started doing woodwork and got into genealogy and stamp collecting."

"Well, Landis has been retired for a while now, so that can't be his excuse. Honestly, he can look like a hobo." She gave an exaggerated shudder. "That look does not inspire romance."

"I'm sure." Jenny winced inwardly, spraying imaginary Windex on her brain so she could stop picturing Mama and Landis getting romantic. "He'll come around. One thing I know about Landis, he wants to make you happy."

Claire nodded as the two paused to close their full trash bags and tie the tops in a knot. They left them by the side of the road to be picked up when they'd finished and shook out fresh bags.

"How's Luke?" Mama got a fond look in her eye whenever she said Luke's name.

"He'd doing well. I miss him," she said glumly.

"I'm sure." Claire raised a brow. "He's with that fellow that needed him in Australia last summer for two months?"

"That's him."

"The man that was his ex-business partner." Claire tucked a green beer bottle in her bag.

"It's complicated." Jenny bent over to pick up a can of chewing tobacco. "After Luke's wife got sick, he sold his shares of the business to Zander. Last year, Zander need-ed capital and Luke's steadying hand, and asked him to buy back his shares and stay on as a silent partner in the business. But Zander acts like Luke is still involved in the day-to-day operations of the company. When he gets in a bind, he expects Luke to pull a project from the fire."

"I see." Her mother shot her an inquisitive look and reached for an empty cigarette pack. "What's Zander like?"

Jenny thought about it. "Zander's not that great with people, but he's basically a good guy." Scanning the weeds for trash, she spotted a green bottle cap and picked it up. "He's helped make the business as successful as it is, and he's still one of Luke's best friends."

Her mother nodded her understanding. "These busi-ness owners are always under a lot of pressure. When there was all that trouble in banking, Landis worked fourteen-hour days trying to make sure the doors stayed open. Not only did the poor man worry about our finan-cial future, but he also had the financial future of all the people who worked with him, the shareholders, and the customers. That's a lot of responsibility. If the bank had failed, hundreds of people could be in a far different position than they are now. We would have been, too." Mama shuddered delicately.

"If the company goes south, Luke and Zander's employees could be out of work, and we could lose his life savings and retirement," Jenny said slowly, the enormity of that realization sinking in. She was sad because she didn't have a valentine while Luke was trying to fix problems that could affect the futures of many people. Serious business.

"I was worried he was going to have a heart attack or stroke," Claire confided, then put both hands on her lower back and arched backward to get rid of a kink.

Yikes. Jenny's stomach clutched. When was Luke's last physical? How was his blood pressure and cholesterol? She'd keep a much closer eye on that. After it had taken so long to find such a decent man, she didn't want him keeling over on her.

"I know you miss him like crazy, but it sounds like Luke is wise to step in," Mama said.

"I think so, too." Jenny gave her a grateful look. "Thanks for the perspective, Mama. It helps. Luke is a hard worker, and we have a lot at stake. I'm going to work on being more understanding." Jenny kicked at a rock with her boot, a little ashamed of her neediness. "This is silly, but I wish he could be here for Valentine's Day."

"It's not at all silly," Claire said firmly. "Of course you'd like that." Mama linked an arm through hers, and the two walked on companionably, carrying garbage bags.

A battered blue pickup truck approached and slowed. The burly, bearded driver must have realized their litter pickup efforts and rolled down the window to call out to them. "Thank you very much, ladies," he boomed out as he passed.

"See? The decent people of the world appreciate us." Jenny patted her mother on the back, and the two of them smiled, appreciating the compliment. As the two watched the blue truck accelerate away, several paper fast-food wrappers floated up from the truck bed, hung gracefully in the air for a few seconds, and floated lazily to the ground on the stretch of road they'd just picked up. Jenny groaned aloud.

Wide-eyed, Claire touched the sides of her head with the back of her gloves.

The absurdity of it hit them, and they got the giggles. Each fueled by the other, the two laughed so hard that Jenny wished she hadn't had that tall glass of water before she'd left the house. It felt good to laugh like that.

They resumed walking. Mama gave a last snort of laughter that got them giggling again.

"We're almost at the end of our road. The state does pickup on the main road, so we're done." Jenny put her hands on her thighs and leaned forward with a straight back for a stretch.

"Good." Mama took off a glove and pushed back a

lock of hair that had escaped her hat. "Landis and I plan to help with Valentine's Day. I'd like to shadow you. I think I know the ropes, but I want to makes sure. Plus, we need to get up to speed for when you and Luke are rolling down the highway on your honeymoon."

Jenny gave her a grateful look. "I don't know what I'd do without you, Mama."

"I feel the same way, sugar pie." Kissing Jenny on the cheek, she whirled off home.

Later that afternoon, Jenny was gimping around the cabin as she tidied up, trying to decide whether to take an anti-inflammatory or not. She should have known that the repetitive leaning over might result in a seizing, breathtaking back spasm when she stood a certain way. If she didn't get on the couch with an ice pack soon, she'd regret it.

Settling onto the cushions gingerly, Jenny propped up her tablet so she could read proposed menus from the three catering companies she'd contacted for quotes. Pimiento cheese bites; crunchy fried green tomatoes; caprese skewers; warm ham biscuits; a barbecue bar where guests could choose from pulled pork, smoked chicken, or a vegan option with seven different choices of sauces and buns; bourbon cocktail meatballs; prosciutto-wrapped melon; flatbread pizza with fresh basil, sundried tomatoes, mushrooms, and grilled zucchini. Holy Moses. Jenny's mouth watered just reading about the food. She'd pick a few favorites and run them by Luke.

Jenny gave her body a cautious wiggle. Did her back feel better, or was it just frozen? Wincing, she lifted her hips and pulled out the ice pack. She'd defrost for a while.

Checking her email, Jenny broke into a smile. Every one of her innkeeper friends had responded to her note.

Bertha, who owned the vintage RV court, wrote, *Hello, camper! I have a special little baby that I keep as a guest house for friends and family, a 1965 Frolic that's adorable. Come see me."* She'd attached a picture of a pale yellow and white number with jalousie windows. Bertha had added a P.S. *I adore later in life love stories. I met my man at sixty!!!*

Cooper wrote, *Greetings from the treetops. Come anytime. I'll leave the porch light on.*

Ahoy! Love to have you come see us in early July, wrote one of the lighthouse sisters.

Trevor replied, *Congrats on nuptials, Cabin Gal! I highly recommend marriage! My wife and I want you to come see us in the Lone Star state. We have a teepee with your name on it.*

Zig, who owned an old-timey motor court of chalet-style rooms near Yellowstone, wrote, *Cool beans. Anytime, little lady.*

Ah. Jenny sat back and smiled, clasping her hands between her knees. Finally, their honeymoon was starting to take shape.

The FaceTime tone sounded, startling Jenny. Luke didn't usually catch up with her until later in the day. "Hey, sweets." She tucked an arm behind her head to see him better.

"Hey, Jen. I only have a few minutes but just wanted you to check this out." He grinned and showed her his seat, an orange fabric chair shaped like an egg. "This is my sound-insulating personal capsule for thinking deep thoughts. All the high-tech companies here have them."

"It looks like a George Jetson chair," Jenny said, bemused.

"It does." Luke's face grew serious "How did it go at the Clerk of Courts?"

Jenny blew out a sigh. "It was a bust, but I have more tricks up my sleeve. I'm not letting an uncooperative public servant slow me down."

"You'll figure it out." Luke looked regretful. "Sorry, Jen, but I need to get going. We've got another problem-solving meeting and then another team-building deal."

"Don't go yet." Jenny's pent-up words spilled out. "I'm sorry I've been upset about your being gone. I know you're trying to keep the company healthy for every-body's future."

Gratitude and relief flitted across Luke's face. "Thank you, sweetheart, but you don't need to apologize. You've been understanding, and I'm grateful for that."

Jenny gave a shaky smile but thought about Mama's words. "Have you had any heart palpitations? Is your blood pressure okay?"

"Everything is fine, darlin'," Luke assured her. "I need to run. After the meeting, we're going skydiving at an indoor place."

Jenny's heart hammered as she pictured Luke clutching his chest in cardiac arrest while being buffeted around in a wind tunnel. Her words flew out of her mouth hard and fast. "Luke Hammond, if you hurt yourself, I'll jerk a knot in your tail. Then, I'm coming for Zander."

"That's my sweet girl," Luke said, his eyes twinkling with amusement.

CHAPTER 5

I T WAS TWO DAYS BEFORE Valentine's Day, and Jenny was in her kitchen baking up a storm. The radio was on, and Jenny was singing along with the bluegrass classic, Boudleaux and Felice Bryant's *Rocky Top*. Jenny wore the apron that Charlotte had bought for her for twenty-five cents at a yard sale, a vintage 1950's number that had cherubic cupids flying all around it with drawn bows. Tomorrow was Valentine's Day, and guests would be arriving soon. The treats she was baking were for a love- and romance-themed welcome basket she was preparing for guests. Ooh-la-la.

Jenny had a full house booked for the weekend. Two couples were arriving early, extending their weekend getaway. Never mind that she would be without her man on Valentine's Day. She'd press on. Jenny turned on the oven light and peeked in the glass door. Her cookies were browning nicely. Refrigerating the dough ahead of time had helped them hold their shape and not spread. Good.

Hands on her hips, Jenny paused to breathe in the aroma of butter, vanilla, and cinnamon in the air. Heavenly. Baking always centered her and put her in a good mood.

Bear whimpered piteously. She shot a look at the dogs and Levi, whom she'd barricaded in the living room with two lounging lawn chairs turned on their side. The boys gave her the full guilt treatment for their banishment. Bear gave her the sad eyes, Buddy gave her baleful looks, and Levi turned his head, just so hurt that he that couldn't even make eye contact. Jenny shook her head. With all that acting talent, those three needed to be in Community Theater. "Sorry, guys. No pet hair in the air while I'm cooking and no animals underfoot."

The timer dinged, and Jenny pulled the last batch of heart-shaped, red velvet sugar cookies from the oven. With a spatula, she carefully placed them onto a cooling rack and added red sprinkles she'd found online that were made from beet juice so there were no artificial dyes or coloring. No guests having allergies or food reactions on her watch.

She'd made twelve dozen homemade sugar cookies from a recipe her grandmother had called True Heart Sugar Cookies. She'd nestle them carefully in the red-and-white striped boxes she'd found at the Just a Buck store.

Guests seem to really appreciate the personal touches. It meant extra work for her, but had won her rave reviews online about their stays at the Lakeside Resort. Many guests had gone into great detail about their stay. *Low-*

key, rustic retreat with all the comforts of home! Reconnected with my husband over board games and hikes! Canada geese, osprey, and even eagles will fly right over you! None of us used devices all weekend, and it was the best vacation we've had in years!

Jenny thought about it as she ran hot water in the sink and let the cookie sheets soak for a minute. Those reviews drew the kinds of guests she liked best, the ones who wanted peace, nature galore, a jaw-dropping view of a gorgeous lake, and rustic living quarters. The vacationers who wanted nightlife, a party scene, or nonstop planned activities like you'd find on cruises could read the reviews and, hopefully, pick accommodations that better suited them.

As she finished scrubbing the mixing bowls, her cell rang, and she smiled as she saw Charlotte's number.

"Hey, girly girl!" her best friend chirped, sounding upbeat as usual.

"Hey, sweets." Jenny held the phone to her ear with one hand as she slipped the cookie sheets in the bottom drawer of the stove and closed it with her foot. "Where are you?" Jenny could hear the road noise in the background of the call.

"About twenty miles away. I'm working this week at a job in Shady Grove helping a woman update the house she won in a divorce settlement from a husband who is *a lying, cheating sack of worms.* Her words, not mine," Charlotte said cheerfully. "I'm headed home to Celeste."

"Do you have time to stop by and visit?" Jenny asked hopefully. It had been too long since she'd seen Charlotte.

Charlotte hesitated. "I don't have much time. I need to get home to cook supper for my husband."

Jenny couldn't help but smile. Her friend sounded so proud when she spoke of Ashe, her husband of less than three months. "Can you take a half-hour detour? To save you from coming all the way from the main highway, I can just run up to meet you at Gus's Gas-N-Git. We can just have a cup of coffee and say hello."

"Sure. I'll meet you there in..." Charlotte paused, probably fumbling to put on her readers to glance at the navigation system on the phone, "twenty-six minutes."

Jenny put the still cooling cookies up on top of the refrigerator, high enough that the dogs, who could win Olympic gold in high jumping, wouldn't get any ideas. Shrugging on her heavy parka, she grabbed her purse, tossed the boys treats to keep them occupied, and headed out the door. Wow. Quite a shock to step from the cozy warmth of her cabin into the biting cold of the February air. Jenny puffed out a breath just to watch it freeze.

Feeling a buzz of anticipation, she pulled out of the gravel driveway and tooled off toward the only convenience store within a ten-mile radius of her Lakeside Resort. Not only was she excited about seeing Charlotte, but she was also excited about seeing the new coffee shop and bakery that Gus had just opened. The fact that the new place was technically connected to the gas station and convenience store did not dampen her enthusiasm.

Here in the country, the first day of hunting season was a buzzworthy event, and the churches' fish fries and chicken suppers were marked in red Sharpies on people's refrigerator calendars. Jenny's weekly visit to the county library was a treat. Her jaunt to the only decent grocery store in a town thirty miles away was kind of a big deal. Jenny would take all the excitement she could get.

A few minutes later, Jenny was shivering, though she'd had the heat on high. She gave a resigned sigh. Her trusty SUV was finally showing its age. The heat was tepid. Her two eighty-plus-pound dogs' claws and Levi's sharp little hooves had been hard on the upholstery.

And here was an indignity, Jenny thought as she slipped on new driving glasses. In the days following her forty-fourth birthday, her vision that had always been 20/20 had started to get blurry. She could sure use the backup cameras and side cameras that the newer cars had. When she'd ridden with Mama in her newer SUV, the seat warmers were like rolling down the road sitting on a heating pad. Ah, heaven. Jenny patted the steering wheel. She wasn't quite ready to say goodbye, but she was starting to think about it.

Slowing, Jenny wheeled into the parking lot of the convenience store, right beside Charlotte's older four-door that had a basketball-sized dent in the side panel and a crack in the windshield that looked like a map of

Africa. Despite her friend's mind-boggling wealth that came from the Berkshire Hathaway stock her parents had bought her for every one of her forty-six birthdays, Charlotte happily drove this beater of a car, and was proud to be a thrifty gal.

As Jenny released her seat belt, she looked at the newly updated sign on the convenience store and started to chuckle. Under the Gus's Gas-N-Git sign hung a rider that read: *Fuel, Fine Wine, Live Minnows, and Posy's Sweet Shop!* Yup. Gus had covered his bases.

Jenny stepped inside the brightly lit store and got a cheery wave from Gus, who was at the cash register with a customer ringing up his gas and Doritos. Glancing around, she spied a white sign with red lettering that read, *Posy's Sweet Shop.* Jenny stepped tentatively into a back room that had probably once been a storage area and gasped quietly as she got hit with the delicious aroma of fresh-brewed coffee and the heady, homey smell of fresh-baked bread. Glancing around, she didn't see Charlotte but saw a coat that looked familiar hooked on a chair at a bistro table. Her friend had probably popped into the Ladies' Room.

Jenny put her purse on that table and spun around, slowly taking it all in. Acoustic Americana folk rock drifted from small speakers on the wall. Strings of softly lit Edison bulbs gave the room a warm glow. An architectural glass brick wall separated the convenience store from the coffee shop, and large potted plants had been used to create even more privacy. Jenny walked over to investigate the large glass display cases filled with tempting-looking baked goods with neat, handwritten labels propped in front of them. Streusel-Topped Blueberry Muffins, Petite Chocolate Eclairs, Snickerdoodles, White Chocolate Chip Cookies, and Blondie Brownies. Holy smoke. This place could give any big city bakery a run for its money.

Charlotte waved wildly at her as she wove her way around tables and hurried over.

In a plum-colored cashmere turtleneck that Jenny would bet a dollar had been a score at the Episcopal Women's thrift store, Charlotte looked luminous, relaxed, and happy. Marriage suited her. The two women hugged, and Jenny breathed in the familiar scent of the lemon hand cream Charlotte used.

"Isn't this just the best?" Charlotte twirled a hand around the room.

"It's charming, and we could walk seven steps and buy a half-gallon of milk or a pickled egg from a jar on the counter," Jenny said with a grin. The two sat down.

Charlotte looked intrigued. "How did such a perfect spot happen in a gas station?"

"I've got the scoop from Landis." Jenny's stepfather drove up to Gus's every morning to get a paper, have a cup of coffee, and shoot the breeze with his buddies, a group of retired men who had the same routine. "This is Gus's daughter's new venture." Jenny spoke softly. "Posy dropped out of college and worked a bunch of different jobs but couldn't find a fit. She's young, you know? Anyhow, she'd always loved baking and coffee and talked Gus into letting her open this shop."

Charlotte put the arm of her reading glasses in her mouth and pretended to look thoughtful. "As a former cosmetic consultant, soy candle saleslady, real estate agent, etcetera, the path to my current success has been a bit of a..." She stared off into the distance to find the right word.

"A zigzagger," Jenny finished helpfully and laughed. "But look how well you turned out, Ms. Successful Stager slash Designer."

"Right." Charlotte gave her a cheeky grin. "I hope this is the perfect fit for her and that this shop is a success."

A fresh-faced young woman, who wore a maxi dress and had her hair tied back with a colorful scarf, approached their table and handed them menus. "I'm Posy. Welcome to my coffee shop," she said, a slight tremble in her voice betraying her nerves. "My breads, cookies, muffins, and pastries are all baked from scratch daily, and I only use super fresh, high-quality ingredients."

"Sounds delicious." Jenny quickly scanned the menu. "I'd love a cup of decaf and a blueberry muffin. I'm Jenny, and I live just up the road a ways, and this is my friend Charlotte."

"Pleased to meet y'all." Smiling shyly, Posy shook their hands.

"This place is just too cute for words, and your baked goodies look scrumptious." Charlotte gave Posy an encouraging smile. "I'll have a caramel latte and a blondie."

Flushing with pleasure, the young woman nodded and hurried off.

"How are you, sweets? I've really missed having you stop by." Jenny leaned forward over the green-and-blue paisley tablecloth. "It's already February, and I haven't really talked to you since Christmas. That's not right," she groused.

"We'll fix that," Charlotte promised, pushing back her glossy black bangs. "You got a

full house for Valentine's Day?"

"I do, plus I've rented the campers." She shook her head wonderingly. "The cabins have always been a draw, but guests are lining up to stay in the campers. Five couples called or wrote, asking to stay in the Shasta, and its only ten feet long. The Airstream is my best booked room."

"Ka-ching." Charlotte rubbed her thumb against her fingers.

"So true." Busy times tided Jenny over during scarily slow times.

"How's Luke doing in Athens? I know you miss him like the dickens."

"He's making headway, and yes, I'm missing him." Jenny reached over to give her friend's hand a squeeze and held it for a moment to admire her rings. "How's married life?"

Charlotte gave a radiant smile. "I adore it. Ashe is just the best husband. The amazing thing is that he thinks *he's* so lucky that *I* married him!" she said, shaking her head.

"I love that!" Jenny clasped her hands together. Charlotte had been convinced her plus size meant that she'd never find a good husband, but with a little match-making from Jenny, her friend had found true love. "What have you been up to? Fill me in."

"I've been getting settled into Ashe's house. He bought it years and years ago from an elderly couple and never did any updating." She wrinkled her nose. "It had original, dust-packed carpeting, old appliances, and a musty smell. The house still had the wallpaper from forty years ago with crushed velvet swirls, antique cars, and poodles. Now, it's out with the old and in with the new."

"I'll bet the house looks great. All modern, Swedish, clean-lined, farmhouse glam." Jenny knew her friend's aesthetic. "How's Ashe?"

"Being mayor keeps him busy, busy, busy. He and the town council are working to keep a developer from building cheap-looking, ticky-tacky apartments over near the historic district."

Unobtrusively, Posy delivered their orders. Both women tasted their baked goods and sighed with pleasure. Jenny pointed at Charlotte with her muffin. "You were saying?"

Charlotte patted her mouth with her napkin and continued. "I've been busy with house fix-up, but I'm also crazy busy with work. I'm Marie Kondo-ing boomer clients who are downsizing to smaller homes and helping new lake homeowners decorate their homes," Charlotte said proudly. She sipped her latte. "Yum. Perfect."

"Have you come up with your First Lady of Celeste platform?" Jenny had given her that nickname, and it had stuck. As wife of the mayor, Charlotte said she wanted to *do more than kiss babies and gaze at Ashe adoringly.*

"Not good. Will you help me with it? You're so good at marketing the resort." Charlotte leaned forward. "I want to make a positive impact, but I'm not sure how." A cloud passed across her face. "The FLOTUS already has dibs on the anti-bullying campaign. That was a good one."

"It was." Jenny mulled it over. "Can you try to get people to stop body-shaming others?"

Charlotte held up a finger and finished swallowing a sip of her frothy drink. "I love that idea, but it might be a little close to home. Let me think about it."

"Okay." Jenny savored another bite of the delicious muffin bursting with blueberries.

"How's the wedding planning? Have you all decided on your honeymoon itinerary?"

"We're getting there, slowly." Too slowly. Jenny feigned pulling her hair out. "We have so much to do by

June." She took another swallow of her coffee. "I'm nervous," she admitted.

Charlotte tilted her head "About what, girl?"

"We still have too many cabins that aren't booked. Mama and Landis don't know social media, so how are they going to post or grow the business while I'm out?" Jenny shook her head.

"Can't you pay a person to do it? Does Lily the librarian know anybody?"

Jenny mulled it over. "I could ask."

"Why not?" Charlotte narrowed her eyes. "What else is bugging you? Spill."

Jenny looked at her friend. "I feel...guilty. I've never taken so much time off in my whole life. I mean, who takes a two-month honeymoon? Luke and I will be sitting by campfires and exploring charming little towns while Mama and Landis are working..." She trailed off.

"So, you feel lazy and guilty gallivanting around while others are working their fingers to the bone." Charlotte put her chin in her hand and gave her a knowing look.

"Maybe," Jenny muttered.

Charlotte raised her eyes to heaven. "You have been working hard as long as I've known you, and you have given Lakeside Resort a ton of work since you inherited it. Am I correct?"

"You are." Jenny chewed her lip, unconvinced.

Charlotte tapped a finger on her lip. "Just to make sure I'm following, Luke has had a tough year and a half dealing with his daddy's health, running the store, heading over to Australia for Zander, and helping you with the resort."

"True." Too often, Jenny had worried about Luke's tired eyes and the heavy step.

"So he needs a getaway too." Charlotte eyed her. "And this trip will be an economical one if I know you. You'll cook most of your meals. You'll stay at nice campgrounds, state parks, and you'll boondock a bit, correct?"

"Correct." Jenny sat up straighter, feeling heartened.

"And we have established that Luke is loaded, too, haven't we?" Charlotte asked.

"I don't know about loaded, but he's comfortable. I just don't like wasting money." All those years of living on her own had made Jenny always careful about spending.

Charlotte popped the rest of her blondie in her mouth and studied her. "As you know, I got a little obsessed with honeymoon plans before I met Ashe."

"I do recall that," Jenny said mildly.

"I researched it. The average honeymoon costs about $5,000. A luxury honeymoon is $10, 000," Charlotte said knowledgeably. "Y'all won't spend close to that camping."

"True." Jenny did the math in her head. They'd be well under the $5,000 mark.

Charlotte wagged a finger at her. "So, little missy, stop it. You're going on the trip of a lifetime with a hunky man who you love to pieces. Let's not turn this into a Greek tragedy."

Jenny smiled ruefully. "You're right. I need to work on my attitude."

Charlotte finished her latte. "I've got to run. I love this new gas station-coffee shop-bakery. This could be our new favorite meeting place besides the resort."

The two settled up with Posy and headed out to the parking lot.

"Ashe is headed out of town on Monday for the Southeastern Mayors' conference. Can I come for an overnight visit while he's gone? Do you have room?"

"I do," Jenny said, cheered at the prospect.

Charlotte beamed and did an exuberant little jump in the air that only she could pull off. "Oh, fabuloso. I've missed you all. Pat the boys and give Levi a big ole kiss on the nose for me."

"See you soon, girly. Give that husband of yours a pat for me." Jenny hugged her friend and headed home.

CHAPTER 6

O N THE DRIVE BACK TO the Lakeside Resort, Jenny took it slow. Just past dusk, the deer were on the move. Jenny kept her high-beams on, ready to brake with any glint of the shiny eyes of a deer in the headlights. Up ahead, her pulse quickened as a doe stepped out from the woods, glanced at Jenny's car approaching, and trotted across the road. Not even a near miss, thankfully. Jenny braked and waited. Her friend Ella was seasoned at country living and had cautioned her about deer and the rule of threes. If one deer crossed, it was likely that two more would follow right behind. Just up the road, Jenny smiled as she watched two fawns step tentatively into the road and follow their mama into the woods. Whew. Jenny accelerated cautiously.

Back home, Jenny let the animals out to air. The clouds must have rolled in because a sliver of a moon cast a weak light. She rubbed her arms to keep warm. The temperature had dropped at least ten degrees since earlier in the day. Jenny crossed her fingers that the bad weather would hold off until all of her Valentine's guests arrived, enjoyed themselves, and left for home.

Supper was chips, guacamole, and salsa, a delicious and possibly nutritious combination. After Jenny washed up, she arranged a production line on the kitchen table and counter. Nestling her red-and-white boxes of cookies inside her guests' welcome baskets, she added chocolate kisses and splits of bubbly, one of sparkling cider and one of Prosecco. As a final touch, she'd added a little pack of retro-looking valentine's cards from the Just a Buck Store. The small cards featured ole-timey cartoon couples staring soulfully at one another with little captions like, "*My heart beats true for you*" or "*You're heaven sent.*" They were darling and whimsical, perfect for adding a personal message and tucking into a loved one's pockets or leaving on a bed pillow.

Later that night when Luke called her, Jenny thought about the miles and miles between Heron Lake and Athens, Georgia, and felt a wave of bleak loneliness. All day, she'd been imagining happy couples arriving tomorrow, cooking supper in the cabins, laughing, reminiscing about their first date, and maybe exchanging small gifts. Suddenly, Jenny found she was blinking back tears. "I sure wish you were here tonight," she blurted out, her voice shaky.

Luke nodded gravely. Pulling the phone in closer, he gazed at her. "Tonight, I was thinking about just when it was that I started falling in love with you."

Jenny stared at him wonderingly. Luke never talked like this. "And?"

"When I met you at the hardware store and came to see you about putting in that dog door for Levi, I thought you were a nice woman. A little lost, a little odd, but nice."

Jenny gave him a look meant to bring him in line, but grinned despite herself.

"When I first came out to the resort to see what kind of help you needed, I thought you were going to be a high-maintenance type who'd seen too many HGTV shows and thought the cabin fix-up might be a *fun little project*." The corners of his mouth twitched. "But then I noticed how dang pretty you were, with your cinnamon hair, and big eyes, and open face. Then, you smiled, and I fell hard. You were *dazzling*." Luke trailed off, smiling at the memory.

Jenny's breathing was shallow, and she didn't want to say a word that would slow him. She wanted…needed… to hear every word he had to say.

Luke looked away, remembering. "It was a cold, clear winter day, and the lake was just so blue. You were an original. You had that banged-up Airstream and that bad attitude about men. You had Levi, the big dogs, and the big ideas. You were sitting in the sand, blowing on a fire to get embers to catch. You had that old aluminum coffee-pot percolating. I remember looking at you and thinking, this day, my life is going to change. I want to be with this woman forever."

Their eyes locked, and Luke gave a slow, heart-melting smile.

Drawing a shuddering breath, Jenny put a hand to her heart. "I love hearing this, Luke. You've just given me the most perfect Valentine's Day gift ever."

Luke shrugged but his eyes glowed with the depth of his feelings. "I mean every word."

"I'm so glad," Jenny said softly. Pausing, she eyed him. "This is a conversation that will tide me over until you get home," she said briskly, instinctively knowing that asking for any more from Luke might traumatize the man and cause him to clam up for the rest of his life.

But as Jenny tried to drift off to sleep, she kept replaying the words Luke had said and just couldn't stop smiling.

The next morning, Jenny had a to-do list as long as her arm, but she didn't feel a bit overwhelmed. Humming as she did chores, Jenny was upbeat, energized, buoyed by Luke's words. Having him reveal what was in his heart had left her feeling elated and cherished.

Shrugging on a warm coat, Jenny hurried to the laundry shed and put in another load of wash. One thing she hadn't known when she'd dived head first into innkeeping was just how much laundry the cabins could generate. Pulling the still-warm sheets from her favorite appliance ever, the magic, high-capacity, always reliable stainless steel washer and dryer she'd splurged on last year, Jenny paused to inhale the barely there scent of the organic lavender laundry detergent she'd been using. Ah. The soothing scent was subtle, but it was there.

As Jenny folded towels, she thought about how well she was doing with her New Year's resolution for 2020. Usually, she resolved to be an all-round better person. She'd vow to improve her posture, not be so judgmental, and stop keeping bags of chocolate on hand for emergencies. This year, Jenny had resolved to try to do better environmentally, and she was making headway. Steadily, she and the resort were getting greener.

Jenny had switched to organic products whenever it didn't break the bank. Her trash bags were biodegradable, and she was working on using rags instead of paper towels. Gone were the water bottles in guest's cabins. She'd bought stainless insulated drinking cups, put water filters in all the cabins, and shared with guests her desire to not use any plastic if at all possible. A lot of people had thanked her for her efforts.

The dogs barked, and Jenny glanced out the laundry shed window. A delivery van with *Beautiful Blooms* emblazoned on the side lumbered up the driveway. Maybe they were lost. Loading the last freshly folded towels in the basket, she rested it on her hip and hurried to her cabin. A fellow in a green uniform was knocking on her door, and he held a huge spray of flowers.

"May I help you?" Jenny put hands over her eyes to shield them from the sun. They must be for an arriving guest, maybe a good husband had arranged delivery for his wife as a surprise.

"These are for Ms. Jenny Beckett from a Mr. Luke Hammond," he called cheerfully.

Jenny put a hand on her cheek. "That's me." Luke was not usually a flowers guy. Sending her these on top of all those heartfelt words, her fiancé was turning into a regular Romeo.

Holding up a finger, Jenny ducked inside amid the din of barking dogs and pulled a few bills from her wallet. As the fellow presented her with the flowers and a card, Jenny tipped him and he rattled off in his van.

Holding the bouquet out so she could look at it, Jenny admired the colorful and fragrant arrangement of lilies, iris, tulips, hyacinths, and freesias. Burying her nose in the blooms, Jenny inhaled the heavenly scent and laughed aloud with pleasure.

Jenny fumbled as she opened the card, a large, over-the-top valentine that had probably cost too much. Though the message inside was one created by the card company, it included phrases that seemed exactly suited for their relationship. *You are my love and my best friend. Too many times, I don't tell you how I feel, but I'm working on it. You are the center of my world.* Touched, Jenny put a hand to her mouth, her eyes pricking with tears. Luke had not just snatched this card off the shelf with all the other spouses racing through the drugstore on February 13. Luke had carefully picked this card, and it said exactly what she knew was true but needed to hear. He'd added a handwritten note:

> Jen, you said the resort needs a lot of landscaping. See enclosed. Hope you like it. I'm going to have them install this in spring. Much love, Luke.

Wonderingly, Jenny pulled another piece of paper from the envelope and examined it. Luke had had the master gardener prepare a detailed landscape design for the whole property.

Twice more, Jenny read the card and studied the rendering. What a thoughtful gift. Sighing happily, she headed inside to find water for the gorgeous flowers.

Mama texted her at 11:30, and the two of them made their rounds, delivering gift baskets and making sure each cabin was spic-and-span. Mama smoothed the down comforters and plumped bed pillows. Jenny spritzed Murphy's cleaner on a cotton rag and wiped the dresser and wood surfaces one last time. "I can't believe how much dust accumulates in just a week."

"I know." Karate-chopping the couch cushions to crease them, Mama sniffed the air. "I love that smell of Murphy's Oil. It brings me back to my childhood. It just smells like home."

"I agree." Beside each gift basket, Jenny propped up

a welcome note that she'd had printed on stationary that featured two black Labs sitting in a red canoe.

At the Hydrangea, mother and daughter stood side by side, hands on their hips, and proudly surveyed the tidy cabin with its cotton-boll wreath, twig baskets, and bright red-and-white striped wool blankets at the foot of the quilted bed.

"All ready for a cozy weekend," Jenny said softly. She hooked her arms in Mama's, and the two headed home, ready for their guests to arrive.

Mama tagged along with Jenny as she checked in the first guests to arrive, Misty and Burt, a couple from New Hope, North Carolina. The two looked to be in their late forties, wore pleasant smiles, and were dressed comfortably in jeans and heavy down coats. Jenny and her mother greeted them warmly and led them to the Camelia.

Chatting with them about their drive as they walked to their cabin, Jenny realized they were both dressed in royal blue fleeces and black jeans. Trying to be surreptitious, she glanced at their footwear. Yup. Almost identical black lace-up boots. When she was younger, she didn't understand why couples started dressing alike, but now she did. They were showing solidarity, dressing like members of the same team. These days, she thought it was adorable.

Misty looked around the Camelia and clasped her hands together. "This place is just precious." Whipping out her phone, she began taking photos. Posing with her mouth parted in the open-mouthed smile movie stars used, Misty took several selfies.

"Let me take a couple of shots of you and Burt," Jenny offered and snapped off a few.

"Thank you. I'll post these so all our kids can see them," Misty said, pink with pleasure.

Mama briefed them on operating the wood stove while Jenny looked on approvingly.

Another car crunched into the gravel driveway. Mama made her apologies and scurried off to greet other arriving guests.

After Jenny handed the couple the map of the property, she pointed out the hiking trails and spots for the best views. "Is there anything else I can do for you?" she asked.

"Not one little thing," Misty burbled.

"We're good." Burt gave his wife a tender look and gently patted her back. "I've been married to this beautiful lady for twenty years. How I persuaded such an exquisite creature to marry me, I'll never know."

Jenny smiled. Misty had even features, a strong nose, and an easy smile. She wore no makeup and was average in size; her hair was cut in the same bowl cut that Mama used to give Jenny with the kitchen drawer scissors when they were too tight on money to pay for a haircut. Misty had expressive eyes and a pleasant face, along with the faint wrinkles around her eyes and mouth that came with age. But when her husband gave her that still-besotted look, Misty's face lit up, she glowed, and she suddenly became a beauty.

Blushing, Misty waved him away. "Hush, you daft man," she said but her eyes were shining with affection, and she reached out to clasp his hand. "I was the lucky one."

"How did you all meet?" Jenny couldn't help but ask.

"In sixth grade, I was so shy that I hardly spoke to anyone, especially boys," Misty said.

Burt rubbed the top of his balding pate, remembering. "So, I played it cool. Sat with her at lunch. Poked her arm. Brought her boiled peanuts. That kind of thing."

Misty patted his arm. "It was those boiled peanuts that got me."

Jenny smiled, charmed. "Well, you two have a great time. Call us if you need anything."

Chase and Allison, a couple who looked to be in their early twenties, shyly told her they'd gotten married the day before in Lynchburg, Virginia. As they unpacked their small hybrid and walked toward the Magnolia, they exchanged jubilant looks. Their hands and arms stayed entwined, even as they carried their duffle bags. Bearded Chase's head was shaved except for a shock of hair at the crown of his head. His bride wore a wispy pale pink dress, ripped fishnet tights, and macho-looking boots that hit her leg mid-calf. Allison looked winsome, charming, and just plain breathtaking.

"Let me see those rings." Jenny waved her fingers in a gimme gesture.

Shyly, the two thrust out their left hands, and Jenny held them, admiring the intricately detailed tattoos that were their wedding bands. "These are very special," she said, feeling a pang of envy. In their early twenties, these two had their whole lives in front of them, and marrying in their forties meant she and Luke would miss out on twenty years of each other's company. But at least they'd found each other. Be grateful, she reminded herself and felt better.

"Congratulations," Jenny said sincerely, and walked back to her cabin with a light step.

Jenny checked in a young woman who had just passed the bar exam and was celebrating by spending a weekend in the Shasta. She saw Mama leading a little family toward the Mimosa.

Clifton and Janis from Hickory arrived in their minivan. These two had booked five nights in the Hydrangea, and from Janis's excited tone of voice when she'd spoken to Jenny to book their stay, this extended getaway was a big deal for them.

As she greeted them, Jenny saw a number of bumper stickers that adorned the back of their van. *Proud Parent of Honor Roll Student. Chess Rules. Marching Madness.* "Looks like you've got accomplished kids," she said pointing at the stickers.

"We've got five kids between us," Janis said blithely. "Second marriage for us both."

Clifton gave a rich baritone laugh. "It's a Brady Bunch madhouse."

"My parents are babysitting." Janis heaved a happy sigh. "Six whole days without kids barging in on me in the bathroom, expecting meals, or needing their fights refereed."

"Or having drama with their friends." Clifton shook his head slowly. "We have five girls, and there's always drama."

"We're so glad to be here." Nabbing a canvas tote from the cargo area, Janis hoisted out the bag of books and lugged them along, pausing to do a happy dance.

Clifton chuckled as he wrestled out the extra-large-sized roller bag.

Jenny hefted a rolling cooler bag and tried not to puff as she struggled to keep it upright. The cooler contained weighty items, cinder blocks or maybe small anvils.

Clifton gave her a sympathetic look. "Leave that bag right there. I'll come back for it."

"I've got it," Jenny insisted and tried to be quiet about her huffing and puffing.

"Show her what's in the cooler, hon," Clifton said to his wife.

Janis's eyes sparkled as she unzipped the lid and lifted the ice packs and showed her rows of neatly stacked casserole dishes. "Ta-da! Twice a year, our church has a fundraiser and sells homemade, just frozen meals for twenty dollars a pop. The casseroles go like that." Janis snapped her fingers. She pointed at one neatly packed supper and then the next. "I brought chicken and sausage jambalaya, curried turkey pot pie, black-eyed peas and ham, a lemon artichoke chicken dish, and a squash casserole." She put a hand to her chest, sounding as fervent as Scarlett did when she vowed to *never be hungry again.* "I will not have to cook for days."

Chuckling, Jenny tapped a finger on the side of her head. "I like the way you think."

Janis gave Clifton a radiant smile. "I just want us to sleep in, relax, eat great food, and remember who we were before we became parents of five."

"I love that plan. Let us know if you need anything." Jenny waved and headed home.

A Volkswagen bug pulled up with two sisters. Jenny quickly got them settled in the Silver Belle. Mama got another couple ensconced in the Azalea. Counting in her head as she trudged toward the Dogwood, Jenny figured they'd filled five of the six available cabins and both campers. All her guests were accounted for except for one.

A glossy white sedan wheeled into the driveway so fast that it threw up gravel. Jenny jumped back hurriedly in case the car slid. This had to be her missing guests from Charlotte.

Jenny put a smile on her face and approached the car.

She'd hung around her gearhead fiancé long enough to know that the T logo on the front meant the car was a Tesla.

Jenny tried to take a mental snapshot so she could tell Luke about it. As soon as the car rocked to a stop, Jenny saw the driver, a women with swingy, sleek blonde hair, chandelier earrings, and a rosebud mouth. She was tapping at her phone almost frantically.

Waiting for the woman to look up so she wouldn't startle her, Jenny held up a hand and called to her, "Hey there. I'm Jenny Beckett. You must be Astor Warren." She gestured to the woman's phone. "Not great reception out here."

The blonde lowered her window and wrinkled her nose. "This place is in the sticks."

Jenny made herself not say what she often thought when guests complained about the resort being in the country. *We thought about putting the lake in town convenient to a Pottery Barn and a Starbucks but decided against it.* "Our guests come here to get away from it all."

Astor sniffed and held an inch of air between her thumb and forefinger. "I came this close to hitting a deer, and I think I saw a bear," she groused, and looked at Jenny accusingly.

"Glad about missing the deer, and that probably *was* a bear," Jenny said mildly.

The woman's mouth twisted. "Nowhere. I'm in the middle of nowhere," she muttered.

"My husband, Trey, will be here later tonight. He had a board meeting run late, and it was essential he be there. He's the chairman and a very busy man."

"We'll keep an eye out for him," Jenny said neutrally. "May I help you with your bags?"

Astor waved imperiously for her to move away, and Jenny jumped back as the doors rose like the unfurling wings of a bird. Jenny had only seen doors like that in movies. Astor jerked her seatbelt off and stepped out in a tight red pencil skirt and black high-heeled boots.

Jenny grabbed two of the six bags from the trunk. Astor reached for one pink leather train case and patted her hair as she waited for Jenny. Humping the bags toward the Gardenia, Jenny decided she had a two-bag carrying limit. Miss Priss could schlep in the other bags on her own.

Inside the cabin, Astor glanced around, looking unimpressed. "It's frigid in here."

"You'll be toasty in just a few minutes." Jenny lit the fire she'd meticulously laid. The flames crackled as they caught the kindling, the fire popped as it grew stronger, and bone-warming heat emanated from the robin's egg blue stove.

Astor took off her black leather gloves and just glared at Jenny, brows in a V. "So we need to keep a fire going for four days? We came here to relax, not become pioneers."

Ah. She was a charmer. Jenny gestured to the split unit

on the wall. "This unit heats as well as cools, and here's how you set the temperature." Jenny showed her how the remote worked. "You can use this the whole time if you'd like but lots of folks like a fire."

Astor looked skeptical. "Seems like a lot of work. Trey can handle it when he gets here."

"Well, I'll let you get settled." Jenny headed for the door, breathing a sigh of relief as soon as she stepped outside. Her glamorous guest seemed like a spoiled, self-involved wench. But had she caught a glimpse of sadness in Astor's remarkable violet eyes? Jenny shivered.

Astor Warren seemed a very unhappy woman.

CHAPTER 7

SATURDAY MORNING, JENNY GLANCED IN the mirror as she brushed her teeth and blanched. She wore the slightly ratty-looking, oversized terrycloth robe she'd had for fifteen years. The nose spray she needed for year-round allergies hadn't kicked in yet, so she had pouches under her red, itchy eyes. Her hair was haphazardly pulled back with a claw clip. She looked nothing like the glamorous Astor with the swooping eyeliner, pillowy scarlet lips, and smooth, white blonde coif.

These days, Jenny was a low maintenance gal. Jeans, boots, and fleeces suited her life, and she was generally okay with that. Luke seemed to like how she dressed. Jenny patted her mouth dry with a hand towel. Luke would be confused if she started getting dolled up, but maybe she should be making a bit more of an effort.

Jenny twisted off the lid of her gummy multivitamins and gnawed off a bite that she estimated might be her daily dose of two. The gummies had congealed after she'd accidentally left them in the car during a hot spell in September and instead of replacing the $16 bottle, Jenny was determined to finish them. Luke did not need to see this sort of thing or the bloom would quickly be off the rose. She was going to have to clean up her act when they married.

As Jenny unloaded the dishwasher, she tried to recall what it was like to live with a man full time. How comfortable did you let yourself get? She thought about Mama's complaints about Landis's "leisurewear" and weekend stubble. During her first marriage to a workaholic, she fruitlessly tried to get him to pay attention to her by dressing in clothes he liked to see her in, eating too many salads, and always being upbeat and interested. She'd gotten up before him in the mornings to brush her teeth and put on subtle makeup. She'd worn scratchy, uncomfortable but supposedly sexy underwear and nightgowns. It hadn't worked, he'd left her, and it had been exhausting.

Jenny thought about her ex-fiancé Douglas and began putting silverware in the drawer with more vigor than was necessary. She'd tried to be as perfect as possible with him, and he'd left her too. By the time Luke had arrived in her life, Jenny was tired of twisting herself into a pretzel to keep a man's attention and, miracle of miracles, Luke seemed to love her just the way she was. Jenny shook her head and smiled as she dried her hands on a dish towel. She was done aiming for perfect, but she didn't need to get sloppy and let herself go, either.

Luke would be calling soon. Hurrying back to the bathroom, Jenny fluffed and smoothed her hair, and slicked on lip gloss. She could make herself look just a tad more alluring.

"The flowers and the landscape master plan were amazing. Luke, you are a sweetheart," Jenny said as she adjusted the camera angle.

"I'm glad you liked them." Looking embarrassed, Luke's face colored.

Jenny's mouth quirked up, liking that he was a bit shy about his romantic gesture. "It was so thoughtful. Thank you."

"All the guests arrive safely?" Luke asked hurriedly, ready for a change in subject.

"They did. No problems, even with folks from the western part of the state. They were supposed to get snow showers, but didn't."

"Good." Luke took a swallow of his coffee. "All happy campers?"

Jenny sipped her peppermint tea. "All but one. She would be happier at a Four Seasons or a Ritz-Carlton, but she may come around when her husband gets here."

Luke gave a half-smile. "You can handle her."

"You'll never guess what she drives."

Looking intrigued, Luke rattled off a few of the cars on his dream ride list. "A 1967 Corvette Stingray, a 1964 Pontiac GTO Tri-Power, a 1965 Shelby Mustang GT350?"

"No, a Tesla with the doors that go up like an osprey's

wings." Bending her elbows, Jenny raised her arms to demonstrate.

"Gull-wing doors? A Tesla Model X. What a cool design," Luke breathed, looking reverent. "Man oh man. I'd love to see that or, better yet, drive it."

Jenny enjoyed watching him salivate over a car.

"A few of those Teslas have a Ludicrous Mode that gives an extra kick to the acceleration, so those cars can go from 0-60 mph in under 3 seconds. An electric car, mind you."

"Amazing," Jenny said drily, wondering why she would ever need to go that fast. An urgent trip to get her highlights done? A one-day sale on chicken breasts at the grocery store thirty miles away? "What are you up to today?"

"We were at work at eight. We got the patent applications done, and they're good. Zander and I got together and hammered out a plan for him to be clearer about expectations for his top people and to hold them accountable. I think he's finally seeing the light."

"Good." Jenny tilted her head. "But it's Saturday and you met at eight?

"Yeah," Luke said wearily and rubbed his eyes with his fingers.

"Are your co-workers married? Do they have families?" Jenny would be ticked if Luke was gone several nights a week with work-related stuff and then worked on a Saturday.

"Some are married, some aren't. Interestingly, more than a few are in the middle of divorces." Luke grimaced. "The lack of work-life balance and the excessive togetherness is a topic I'm talking about with Zander."

"Good," Jenny said.

"I'm meeting everybody again in a half hour. We're team-building by racing go-carts," Luke said, his face lighting up.

He looked so much like a twelve-year-old boy that Jenny burst out laughing. "Promise not to get hurt."

"I promise." Luke held up three fingers in a Boy Scout salute, grinned, and signed off.

Jenny was not a snoopy Mrs. Kravitz kind of innkeeper, but from the side window in her kitchen, she couldn't help but see the other cabins as she did her morning chores. Clifton and Janis had wood smoke coming from their chimney, so they were relaxing. Good for them. The newlyweds had bundled up and set off on a walk, holding hands and pausing every ten feet to smooch. Sickening, but cute. The newly minted attorney ambled out of the Shasta with a large-lensed, expensive-looking camera draped around her neck and took shots of the campers, the cabins, and the lake. The Warrens' cabin was quiet, and there were no new cars in the parking lot. Heron Lake had no Ubers or taxis, so unless the very busy and important Trey Warren had been whisked in by an ultra-quiet corporate helicopter, he hadn't yet arrived.

When she heard a cabin door slam, Jenny peered out

the window and squinted. Wearing an expensive look-ing leopard-print walker coat and knee-high black boots, Astor stalked to her car and flung herself in.

Carrying walking sticks and wearing water bottles strapped to their waists, Misty and Burt were coming back from an early morning hike, laughing and chat-ting with each other. Without looking right or left, Astor peeled out of the parking lot. The Tesla came too close to the hikers. Startled, the two jumped back, shook their heads, and headed back to their cabin, but Jenny felt a slow burn of anger. If Astor wanted to be dramatic, she could do it on her own time. Jenny was not going to allow her to drive recklessly on resort property and endanger her guests. When the woman came back from her errand, Jenny was going to have a little chat with her. Taking a few deep breaths, Jenny willed her blood pressure down.

Jenny saw the Tesla glide into the parking lot, and Astor stepped out, carrying orange plastic grocery bags from Gus's Gas-N-Git. Quickly throwing on a coat, Jenny hurried outside and began walking in step with her guest. Astor must have been intent on her own thoughts because she hadn't heard Jenny approach and looked startled.

"Good morning, Astor." Jenny said pleasantly. "Can I help you carry your groceries?" she asked, reaching out a hand toward the bag with the Cheetos sticking out of the top.

"No," Astor snipped out and then looked a bit

abashed. "No, thanks. I've got it," she clipped out, accelerating her pace.

"Sure." Jenny walked faster to keep up with her. "Your husband's not arrived yet?"

Astor's mouth tightened into a hard, thin line. "No. He's...been delayed."

"Well, I'll keep an eye out for him," Jenny said.

Astor just looked more annoyed. At the door, she scrabbled hurriedly in her purse and finally pulled out her cabin key. Astor turned to face Jenny. "Is there anything I can do for you?" she demanded. The woman's face was stony, and her eyes blazed.

Jenny lifted her chin. She was not going to be cowed by this woman. "Would you please drive more carefully when you are here on the property? Today, you came too close to hitting two of my other guests when you drove off," she said in a tone that said *I mean business.*

Shock and remorse flashed across Astor's face before she turn stony again. "I will." Turning around, she jammed the key in her door and strode inside, shutting the door firmly behind her.

Jenny turned to go, her thoughts racing. The bags from Gus's were translucent. If her Nancy Drew skills and eyesight were up to par, one bag contained slim brown paper bags, probably wine. The other two bags were full of comfort food—chips, cheese puffs, chocolate chip cookies, and ice cream. The signs were there. Astor was in the middle of sadness or heartbreak. There was trouble in Paradise.

That afternoon, Jenny got a text from a Raleigh area code. It was from Astor Warren. *I'd like to extend my stay through Monday. Is this an option?*

Yes. Cabin not booked and happy to have you, Jenny tapped out.

Sunday morning, Jenny waved goodbye to the last departing guest, satisfied that all her guests had had a happy weekend. Clifton and Janis were staying on, as was Astor Warren. Still no sign of her MIA hubby.

Jenny took a long walk with the dogs and Levi. The phone in her pocket dinged and she smiled when she saw the text from Charlotte.

Girly girl, Had genius idea for my first-lady platform. I'll run it by you tomorrow. See you around six. Bringing big ole bottle wine. Kiss, kiss, kiss!

Jenny felt her spirits lift. She was lonely without Luke and sick of her own company. *Can't wait. I'll make faux fried (baked) chicken in my new pressure cooking air fryer. Hope I don't blow myself up. Vino sounds perfect.*

The next evening, Jenny was carefully timing the depressurization of the pressure cooker when she heard a car arrive. With one last double-check of the instructions to make sure she was doing everything safely, she gave the machine one final worried glance and hurried outside.

Charlotte stepped out of her sedan and waved gaily. "Yoo, hoo. I'm here," she caroled.

Jenny hurried over, admiring her friend's sense of style. Her glossy black hair twisted into a messy bun, Charlotte wore a black, military-inspired coat, slim cut red pants, a cream-colored Angora cowl neck sweater, and sharp-looking high-heeled boots. "Yowsa. You look beauteous *and* professional."

"Thank you very much. I gained four pounds over the holidays, but I'll get back on track."

Charlotte's newfound confidence in herself was evident. Before Ashe, she would have beat herself up about a minor weight gain.

Jenny enveloped her friend in a hug and gestured up to the sky where a giant, buttery-looking moon cast a soft yellow glow from where it hung low in the sky. "Can you believe this gorgeous full moon? I'll bet it lit your way on the drive in."

"It did! For a minute, I turned off the headlights to see if it was bright enough to drive by," Charlotte said blithely.

"Was it?" Jenny asked, genuinely curious.

"Nope. Hit a little underbrush on the side of the road, but no harm done." Charlotte fondly patted the new scratches that ran down the side of her car. Reaching into the passenger seat, she thrust a large bottle of wine into Jenny's hands and lifted a flowered duffel from the back seat. "I've been in dressy clothes all day. My feet and back can't take these shoes anymore. I'm going to change into comfy clothes, and I'll see you in just a few." Holding up a hand in a wave, Charlotte headed to the Silver Bullet, her home-away-from-home whenever she visited Jenny.

Comfy clothes sounded perfect. Jenny wriggled out of her jeans, and slipped on fleece pants and her red cowboy boots when Charlotte gave a perfunctory knock on the door and swept in. Her puffy coat atop a plush robe, she wore flannel sock monkey pajamas and Uggs.

After enjoying a deliciously moist chicken dinner and crispy zucchini fries, the two sat and sipped their wine, the dogs lounging on the couch between them. Jenny filled her in on all her news about Luke's trip, the mystery truck guy, and her Valentine's Day guests.

"Never a dull moment around here." Charlotte tenderly stroked Levi, who stood beside her leaning his weight into her with his eyes closed dreamily. "You're my little sugar booger, snickerdoodle, tootsie-wootsie." Levi sighed heavily, and put his head in her lap.

Jenny rolled her eyes. The boys were faithless. Charlotte showed up, and Jenny was old hat.

"That Astor is mysterious. It sounds like a husband problem," Charlotte mused, looking like the avid self-help aficionado that she was. "I have been in that particular try-to-numb yourself phase before. Classic first reaction to heartbreak. It passes with time, though."

"I remember that phase, too." Jenny grimaced and

moved on to happier topics. "How's your First Lady of Celeste platform coming along?"

Charlotte shrugged. "I've gotten nowhere. I was going to do some Lady Bird Johnson roadside wildflower fields, but Celeste already does that. They have a horticulture program at the community college, and that's what they do. Biological diversity, restoring native plants, seed collecting and banking, blah, blah, blah. Darn progressive town," she said grumpily.

"What a shame," Jenny said drily, but Charlotte just nodded her agreement.

"All the good ideas got taken," her friend said, sounding discouraged.

Jenny swirled her wine around in her glass, thoughtful. "I liked your *Drive Friendly* idea. This week, I was coming home from the grocery store, and a car zoomed up behind me and tailgated me so closely that he was inches from my bumper. I was going above the speed limit. He had a clear lane to pass but he just stayed stuck to my bumper." Jenny's heart thudded just remembering. "It scared me. I finally pulled off at Gus's store just to let him pass."

Charlotte nodded so hard that her bun bobbed. "I pulled out in front of a truck that was going faster than I'd thought. The driver just laid on the horn and yelled at me when he passed. Now, there was just no need for that. Hasn't he ever misjudged another driver's speed?"

Charlotte asked primly. "It didn't use to be like that. People drove more courteously."

"I agree." Jenny thought about it as she leaned down to scratch Buddy's belly. "Maybe it's the big influx of newcomers. People move here because the pace is a little slower and the people are more polite. Then they bring their hustle-bustle and bad driving habits with them. Then, natives get their backs up and start acting snippier, too. It's a vicious cycle."

Charlotte nodded vigorously. "You know that bumper sticker I had made and put on the back of my car that says, *Drive nice, darlin'!* You wouldn't believe how many drivers have given me a thumbs-up when they see it. I've had three different women stop me when I walked to a store from a parking lot and tell me that it's a great idea."

"I think you're on to a good thing, girl." Jenny leaned forward, excited about the idea. "The rudeness is contagious, but so is the courtesy. This week, I had to drive to Charlotte to pick up a part for the Silver Belle. Traffic was bad, and a fellow slowed down and flashed his lights at me to let me know I could pull out in front of him. I waved at him. Later that day, I let a car into traffic in front of me. The politeness is contagious."

Charlotte gave a little whoop that caused Buddy and Bear to raise their heads, check for any problems, and then drop their heads back down with aggrieved sighs. "I think I've got my platform." She tilted her head, a glint in her eyes. "Could I have rude drivers arrested? Maybe sentence them to jail, and let them split rocks like on the old chain gangs?"

Remembering the ten big bags of trash she and Mama had picked up so recently, Jenny grinned. "They could do roadside litter pickup in August when it's hotter than blue blazes."

"I love that." Charlotte's eyes were wide and glowing. "Realistically though, we *could* get law enforcement to crack down on aggressive driving, but we'd also need to have a big campaign about driving courteously. Make it a real town of Celeste effort."

Jenny shook her head. "Sweets, you have found your platform."

"I'm so glad." Charlotte put a hand to her heart. "I love Ashe so, and I've grown to love Celeste. I'd really like to make a positive change."

"With this campaign, you could." Jenny glanced out the front windows. That moon had risen in the sky and now shone a golden path across the water of Heron Lake. She pointed. "If you can believe it, that full moon has gotten even more luminous and amazing."

Charlotte turned and took it in. "Wow. Just wow."

Jenny gave Charlotte a mischievous look. "Let's go sit outside and build a fire."

"I'm in." Charlotte gave the animals a few more pats and extricated herself from the sofa.

"Oh, it's cold." Jenny opened the door to the frigid night. Coats pulled tight around them, the two stepped out while they still had the nerve. Jenny put a match to the kindling in the fire pit, and the two sat in lounge chairs wrapped in blankets watching the fire and the moon.

"It looks like the yellow brick road," Charlotte said dreamily. "You know what? We haven't talked about the special populations weekend. What are we planning?"

Jenny rubbed her chin. "You're the one with the experience with autism."

"Not so much now," Charlotte said. "My cousin Cody and his folks moved to Raleigh. We keep up on Facebook. He's quirky and awkward socially but has a good heart."

"Okay," Jenny said, not sure where to go with that. "What else should I know?"

"His mama says he doesn't have many friends, and when he's not working, he plays too much X Box, watches YouTube, and stays on Facebook," Charlotte said. "What if we go for the outdoor adventure angle? Maybe we could try to encourage a device-free weekend?"

Behind them, a figure appeared. Jenny gasped, her heart racing, until she realized it was Astor. Clutching a white down comforter around her, Astor's hair was messy, her mascara was smeared, and she looked like she'd been crying. "Terrible idea about no devices," she called out brusquely. "Push that idea, and they'll revolt and want to leave an hour after they get here."

CHAPTER 8

"Astor!" Jenny put a hand to her pounding heart. "You scared me to pieces."

"Sorry," Astor said flatly and flung herself in an empty lounge chair, pulled the comforter tightly around her, and stared moodily at the fire.

Charlotte shot Jenny a questioning look.

Not sure what to say, Jenny fell back on manners. "Charlotte, Astor is staying in the Gardenia. Astor, this is my friend Charlotte."

Without making eye contact with either of them, Astor raised a hand and let it drop. She pulled her hair into a haphazard bun and let it go. Her hair looked like an untidy bird's nest.

Charlotte's eyes widened as she registered the woman's words about devices. With a knowing look, she pointed at Astor. "You have a relative with autism."

Astor gave a glimmer of a smile. "My younger brother, Nick."

"Ah." Charlotte touched her chest. "My cousin Cody's on the spectrum."

Astor fixed her gaze on Charlotte. "How's your cousin doing? What's he up to?"

"For three years now, he's been a bagger and stocker at a grocery store," Charlotte said proudly. "He just got an award for perfect attendance and got commended for being such a hard worker."

"Good man." Astor moved her chair so she could see the girls better and readjusted her comforter. "Nick works in IT at Freddie Mac."

"Good for him," Charlotte said warmly.

Jenny enjoyed watching the two women connect. Although there was subtext she didn't get, Charlotte and Astor seemed to instantly *get* each other and their relatives with autism.

Astor looked at Charlotte and cocked her head. "Any areas of special interest?"

"Cody can tell you every detail, date, and battle of the Civil War. He knows everything about each president of the United States." Charlotte held up a finger and began chuckling.

"Oh, and *Designing Women*. He loves reruns of that show."

"I loved that show, too." Astor broke into a delightful open smile. "Nick is into World War II planes and American gold mines. He's encyclopedic about both."

"Smart guy," Charlotte said. "You must know a lot

about this. We want to plan a special needs weekend and focus on younger adults on the autism spectrum. Maybe you could help us." She gave Astor a curious look. "Why did you say that about the no-devices idea?"

"You could set up special times for phone and device use, but I wouldn't try to ban them altogether. That would cause too much anxiety. Your ideas about outdoor activities are solid. You'll also need a few quiet places set up so folks can go and decompress. "

"Good idea," Charlotte said thoughtfully. "Cody does need his down time."

"We had a writer's workshop here last summer and have already set up private seating areas outside around the property," Jenny added. "Would that work?"

"It would." Astor looked off into the distance. "If you did that weekend, you'd be hitting on one of the biggest problems. Individuals on the spectrum need help making friends." Her elbow on the arm of the chair, she rested her chin in her hand. "But here's another problem. The parents or caregivers, especially the ones who have their adult children living with them, can get burned out and rarely get a break. Could you invite both groups out here and plan different activities for each group?"

"We could." Jenny sat up straighter, exhilarated at the possibilities whirling in her head.

Astor tucked her feet up under her. "Nowadays, one in forty is diagnosed with autism, more boys than girls, and about a third have an intellectual disability on top of the autism, too."

"You know a lot about this, Astor," Jenny said, impressed with the caring in her voice.

Astor shrugged. "My degree is in Special Education, and I'd planned on working with people who had developmental disabilities, but then I met Trey. He wanted a wife who stayed home. So *stupid* of me to go along with him," she said bitterly and pressed a finger to her temple.

Charlotte shot her a sympathetic look. "You got man troubles? Tell us about it, sister, because we've been there."

Astor shook her head, and tears began to course down her cheeks.

Jenny pulled a handful of clean tissues from her coat pocket and handed them to Astor. "You don't have to talk. Just sit with us. It's a gorgeous night, and we can just enjoy the moon."

Astor hesitated, looking like she was weighing staying or bolting. Suddenly looking very young and fragile, she blotted her tears. "My husband and I were supposed to have this getaway because his work had been so intense and we've...well, we've been hardly communicating."

"We're with you so far." Charlotte nodded encouragingly.

"Trey accidentally pocket-dialed me on Friday afternoon. He was supposed to be here that night," Astor explained, her voice tight. "The phone was in the bottom of my purse and when I picked it up, I could hear him talking to a woman, and it didn't sound like talk between two colleagues." Her eyes flashed. "Trey called her *sugar*, which is what he calls me. I heard them laughing in a sort of intimate way."

Jenny felt a burn of old anger, recalling the moment when she'd discovered her ex-husband was having an affair. She wouldn't wish that feeling on her worst enemy.

"So I FaceTimed him." Astor dabbed at her nose. "He answered, all peppy and innocent. He said his meeting was running late and that he'd be up Saturday morning. I asked him point-blank about the call. He gave me this condescending, almost pitying look, the one he uses with me a lot," Astor said, fire in her eyes. "He was gaslighting me. One of Trey's favorite techniques." Suddenly sounding weary, Astor went on, "He said he was in a conference room waiting for colleagues to get back from break. But Mr. Smart Guy wasn't holding his phone up high enough. In the mirror behind him, I could see a bed and a woman in a red silk nothing of a nightgown who thought she was out of range of the camera. But she wasn't." Astor tried to give a wry smile but couldn't pull it off. She started to cry again.

Charlotte gasped. "Oh, the dirty rat."

"What an awful discovery," Jenny said, steamed for Astor.

Astor's mouth twisted. "I believe he's cheated on me for most of the sixteen years that we've been married. I used to confront him when I suspected he was having another affair, but each time he denied it. He'd say I had an overactive imagination or was under stress." Astor stared moodily at the lake. "Usually, he'd say work was intense. When he got through with that woman, he'd act super devoted, give me jewelry, and take me to Bermuda or Portugal or another luxury destination. It would be smooth sailing again, until the next woman." She looked at each of them and shook her head slowly. "The affairs make me loathe him and loathe myself. It's past time I put an end to it all."

"We're so sorry, Astor," Jenny said.

"We are," Charlotte said softly. She pointed a thumb at Jenny and then at herself. "We've both had rat husbands. My ex talked me out of a bucket load of money before my daddy ran him off. Two months later, he married a doctor named Keith that he met in a hip-hop class." She held up a finger. "This explained a few miscommunications we'd had in the boudoir."

Astor gave a wan smile and turned to Jenny. "What's your story?"

"My ex-husband said he needed to *find* himself but really he'd *found* his skinny, young, mean-as-a-snake boss, Natalie." Jenny shrugged.

Charlotte elbowed Jenny. "Tell her how you figured it out."

Jenny rubbed the back of her neck, remembering. "When he moved out, I couldn't find a few pieces of clothing. I was missing a red sweater with a roll neck like

Audrey Hepburn used to wear, my green vintage cowboy boots, and a pair of old earrings that looked like a bunch of grapes that my grandmother gave to me."

Wrapping her arms around her knees, Astor was looking rapt. "Go on."

Jenny grimaced, remembering. "I thought the things would turn up after he moved out, and I got settled in without him. Then, I saw a work picture that he'd posted on Facebook. His boss was standing too close to him and her arm was around his waist, sort of possessively. She had this smug expression on her face, and she was wearing my missing clothes."

Astor shook her head in disgust. "That's trashy behavior. Shame on them."

Charlotte held up a hand. "But here's the bright side. Her ex married his mean boss and gets scolded all day every day. My ex got divorced again, married again, and is going through another divorce. So, it all turned out happily," she said cheerily.

Jenny rolled her eyes. "The *happy* part is that both Charlotte and I found men that are so much better for us."

"That's what I meant," Charlotte said primly and looked at Astor. "What are you going to do now?"

"I'm going to end this charade and get what's mine." Astor's voice was steely. "Yesterday, I hired a private investigator. I already had an attorney on retainer because I guessed this was coming. She's got all the banking information and will protect my assets. I need to get back to town and start mopping up this mess."

Jenny could only imagine what Astor had in front of her, guessing she'd have a battle about money. Though Jenny and her ex didn't have a lot of money to fight over, the emotional aftermath had been hard. For months after he'd moved out, she'd walked zombie-like through her days, feeling like the biggest loser in the world. "Let us know if there's anything we can do for you."

"Astor, think about helping us with the autism weekend. We need you," Charlotte said with a twinkly smile.

"I'll think about it," Astor said with a nod. "Y'all have been kind despite my crankiness." She gazed at Jenny. "I've been self-absorbed and mad at the world. I'm sorry I was rude to you."

Jenny waved away her apology. "No need. I get it."

With a grateful look, Astor rose from her chair, adjusted the drape of her down comforter, raised a hand, and walked back to the Gardenia. "Good night, women. I'm grateful to you."

The next day was gray and drizzly, and Jenny's mood matched the day. Both Charlotte and Astor cleared out early and, though she had guests in three cabins, the property was quiet. Astor's story had dredged up old sadness for Jenny about her own losses, and she was missing Luke so. Feeling empty and lonesome, Jenny promised herself that once she got the most important chores done, she'd stoke the fire, get snuggled in on the couch with the boys under the afghan her grandmother had crocheted for her, and spend the afternoon reading.

After chopping carrots, garlic, celery, onion, red potatoes, and peppers, she scraped them into the slow cooker and poured in two quarts of chicken stock. Adding three chicken breasts she'd cut up, Jenny sprinkled in herbs and put the lid on. If she let it cook on low heat all day, she'd have a comforting, healthy supper and leftovers to freeze.

As she put away her ingredients, Jenny glanced at her Horses of America calendar she'd taped on the refrigerator and felt a blossoming of hopeful happiness. Luke would be home in just a few days. Leaning against the counter, she paused to sip her peach-ginger tea and let herself feel buoyed as she imagined that homecoming. Jenny would have his solid, warm bulk to hug most any time she wanted. The video chats had worked better than calls, but there was nothing like having Luke's love in person, his comforting conversation, his sincere interest, and the commotion and energy and brightness he brought with him. Jenny's mood brightened just thinking about having him home.

But Jenny looked more closely at the calendar and saw the notes she'd scribbled to herself. Two dates for the delivery of logs for their new cabin had come and gone. Both times, she'd called to follow up with the log company and gotten what felt like blasé responses. There were

problems with machinery at the sawmill, parts that needed to be shipped from far away, a truck that broke down.
She'd be first on their delivery calendar, they claimed, but
still no logs. Making sure the materials got here was the
one thing she'd promised Luke she'd take care of.

Jenny felt a rush of resolve. She'd make that call and
get those logs out here as soon as possible.

But cell in hand, Jenny paused before entering the
number. If she sounded too frustrated about the two
missed dates, she'd bet there would be more delays in the
delivery.

Whenever Luke had to make himself heard with other
men, he got a good response. He'd drawl, *"You boys
headed this way Tuesday?"* And, most times, the contrac-
tors would show up pronto. In this neck of the woods,
men seemed to respond better to men, especially about
construction-related stuff. She considered calling Luke
in Athens and having him handle the log guys, but she
didn't want to fall into the trap of always needing Luke to
handle things for her.

Jenny gave herself a pep talk. She'd managed on her
own for years and was no helpless female. She'd make
the call, but try to do it in a way that didn't get their backs
up. The main goal was to get the logs delivered as soon as
possible. Jenny scrolled through her contacts, took a deep
breath, and made the call.

The next morning, Jenny was up early checking her Welcome Inn reservation system. Brow furrowed, Jenny saw too many open nights on the books. Maybe the weather had been too cold for people to think about spring and summer getaways. Jenny mulled it over. Time to write a newsletter, she decided. Today, she'd take pictures and shoot a brief video clip. Including those always got the phones ringing and the online bookings humming.

But just after seven, she heard the deep rumbling of a large vehicle and tensed. Was it the monster truck guy? The dogs started barking, and Jenny flew to the window.

Landis was already outside, striding down the driveway toward the road. Quickly, Jenny grabbed a coat and hurried to catch up with him, her phone clutched in her hand.

As the rumbling grew louder, Landis raised a hand to shield his eyes from the sun and stared down the road. Turning to her, he beamed. Jenny skipped to catch up to him, catching his excitement. "What?" she asked. "What's going on?"

A giant semi rolled majestically down the driveway, followed by a second truck. The driver slowed as he approached them and stopped with a hiss of air brakes. Lowering the window, he lifted his chin in greeting and looked at Jenny. "Mornin'. You the boss lady?"

"I'm the boss lady," Jenny said with more confidence than she felt.

The fellow looked at her with grudging respect, and stuck a toothpick in his mouth. "I brought a load of fine-looking logs for the Hammond project. Show me where I'm headed."

Jenny shot a video of the orange forklift machine cruising nimbly around, scooping up and lifting heavy logs as if they were light as Tinker Toys. His truck now empty, the fellow at the wheel gave Jenny a two-fingered salute and a crooked smile as he trundled off. The driver of the second truck maneuvered in, and before long, their logs and lumber were neatly stacked in the spot beside the foundation.

Back inside, Jenny sent the photos and video to Luke, feeling proud of herself for getting the job done. Jenny did a quick check of email and saw the note from her South Carolina friend, Bertha. The subject line was, *We're rolling down the road.*

Hey there, lady. Big news. We are looking for new digs. The state is putting an on-ramp to the interstate right next to us. All that traffic noise! There goes bucolic. Good news, though. We found a great place to relocate. Moving vintage campers is tricky but doable. Thank goodness we didn't own a brick-and-mortar motel. We'll be just fine and ready for guests by June. I'll text you our new address when I know it. Can't wait to meet you and the new hubby.

Jenny scrubbed her eyes with her fingers. Could that happen to them? What if the land next door changed hands? Could a commercial property go in there? Jenny's stomach clutched as she imagined a dirt bike track, a music venue specializing in heavy metal, a neighbor with a shooting range. Her life savings were invested in this resort, and they were about to build an expensive cabin that was even closer to the neighbor's property line.

Jenny tried to do her deep breathing, but had trouble calming down. Twice, she dialed Luke but both times her call went straight to voice mail. She tapped out a text. *Call me when you can. All okay, but need your calm perspective. XOXO.* Willing the phone to ring, Jenny waited for a call, but none came. Where was he when she needed him?

Slumping on the sofa, Jenny thought about it. When she got wound up like this, Luke always said, *Do what you can and let go of the rest.*

What could she do? Jenny had to find out who her neighbor was and talk to them. Galapagos or no Galapagos, Jenny sent a text to Ella. Phone in hand, she mulled over other ways to get answers to her questions.

Jenny sat up straighter. She'd go back to the county office and be there when it opened. If that snooty, work-dodging Bennett Carter tried to stonewall her, she'd raise a ruckus. But when she pulled up the website to check the hours of operation, she groaned aloud as she read a yellow banner spread across the homepage. *The Lake County Register of Deeds Office will be closed for an undetermined period of time. Broken pipes upstairs have caused extensive damage. We appreciate your patience and will reopen again as quickly as possible.*

Enough fretting. A long walk would clear her head. Calling up the boys, Jenny threw on a coat and headed out. Hopefully, the neighbor was going to keep their land the way it was forever.

But Bertha and her husband had hoped their property would always stay bucolic, and look how that had turned out. If the neighbor ever decided to sell, she and Luke needed to be the ones to buy it.

CHAPTER 9

T HE NEXT MORNING, JENNY HUMMED along to the radio as she fed the boys. Her mood had lightened. Last night's conversation with Luke had been reassuring. He'd reminded her that, even though the zoning was not as strict as it was in more developed areas, the county still had jurisdiction and would be unlikely to approve a property that could be a nuisance. Jenny was also heartened by a two-sentence response she'd gotten from Ella. *Be home tomorrow. We'll sort this out.*

Still, Jenny was glad she had a busy day. That would keep her from getting back on the hamster wheel of worry.

The farrier was coming by at 8:30 to trim Levi's hooves. Jake came out every six to eight weeks to keep the little guy's feet healthy. After he finished, she needed to make a run to the recycling center to empty the big cans of glass, aluminum, plastic, and cardboard that the resort had accumulated over the past few weeks.

As the farrier pulled away in his big dually truck,

Jenny gave Levi's rump one more scratch of appreciation for being so well-mannered with Jake. When her phone rang, she perked up even more when she saw Charlotte's number. "Good morning, girl."

"What are we doing about the wedding dress? We're running out of time," Charlotte said by way of greeting. She'd taken to using the royal *we* when talking about any activities relating to Jenny's wedding. "Are we going traditional or modern? Do we want to go vintage? Long, short, or tea length?" Her voice was tinkly and bright. "Are we leaning toward white, ivory, or another fabulous color? Brides are wearing floral gowns now."

"Ah." Overwhelmed, Jenny sat on the steps of her porch and ran a hand through her hair. "I don't know. I've had so much going on that I haven't thought much about it. I looked at a few online, but I'm having trouble getting interested in my wedding dress," Jenny admitted.

"I think it's hard to get a feel for a dress online. Let's go to town and look at wedding dresses. We'll have lunch and make a fun girls' day out of it," Charlotte said.

"Okay," Jenny said glumly. She disliked shopping anyway and dreaded the pressure of shopping for the perfect wedding dress. For her, the day would not be a *fun girls' day out.*

The two made plans for Thursday. Inside, Jenny wrote it on the Horses of America calendar. Maybe they'd get a blizzard and she couldn't go.

Back to chores. Jenny lifted a new bag of Bear and

Buddy's kibble to pour into the air-tight pet food storage bin and yelped in pain. Without bending her knees or contracting her core, she'd just tried to heft up a fifty-pound bag like she didn't have a tricky back. "You are foolish," she scolded herself. The back spasm was mild, but if she tried to push it today and wrangle those giant cans to the recycling center by herself, she'd regret it. Jenny hated to do it, but she picked up the phone. "Morning, Mama. May I borrow Landis?"

A half hour later, Landis stepped out of the Redbud, beamed at her, and gave a hearty wave. In a parka and red wool beanie, the big man looked peppy and cheerful.

Jenny rubbed her gloved hands together to warm them as he trotted over to her. "Good morning, you nice man," she said warmly.

"Morning, young lady." Landis leaned in to buss her cheek.

With a wry smile, Jenny touched her palms to her lower back. "I'm decrepit today. I feel old, not young."

"I understand. I've got a trick knee from playing football. From time to time, it just gives out on me." Landis pulled work gloves from the back pocket of his jeans and slipped them on. He tilted his head toward the Redbud. "After we get loaded up, your mama wants to ride along with us. I promised to buy her a cup of coffee and a muffin. I'll treat you to the same."

"Great." Jenny considered it, realizing how glad she was to live in a place where going to the recycling center and getting a cup of coffee was considered a pleasant family outing.

Companionably, the two walked toward the laundry shed where she stored the fifty-gallon rolling recycling cans. Pausing to admire the glittering indigo lake, Landis shook his head. "I hope I never get so used to living in such a pretty spot that I don't stop to take it in." He clapped his hands against his chest. "It's a great day to be alive."

"It is," Jenny replied, then patted his arm and the two walked on. Too often, Jenny let a breathtakingly glorious day just sail on by without really noticing it because she was focused on getting things done or caught up in needless worry. She really needed to work on that.

Hands on hips, Jenny felt a bit of pride as she looked at the six large trashcans containing the recyclables they'd generated at the resort for the past few weeks, including the Valentine's weekend. Before she'd made an effort encouraging guests to use less plastic and go greener, they probably would have filled ten big trash cans in the same time frame.

They worked as a team. Jenny pulled the locking pin on the utility trailer, and Landis easily lifted the tongue of the trailer and rolled it over to line it up behind his SUV. Hopping inside his vehicle, Landis opened the cargo door so he could see behind him and slowly backed up a few feet to line up closer to the trailer, Jenny directing him decisively. Her weak hand signals, which Luke had later described as looking like *fluttering and confused birds*, had almost resulted in his backing his truck over a bulkhead and right into the lake last year. Jenny exaggerated her *come on, a few more inches* and *stop* gestures until the trailer hitch was close to being directly over the trailer ball.

Landis stepped out and gave her a thumbs-up. With a *thunk*, they connected the trailer's hitch to the ball and lowered the metal gate. Landis rolled and manhandled the bulky trashcans into the trailer. The two of them strapped and bungeed them in securely so they wouldn't tip over and leave a trail of empty cola and beer cans along the road to the county recycling center.

Claire came around the corner in a bright red coat, her long silvery blonde braid over her shoulder and poppy-colored lipstick brightening her face. "Morning, darling." She gave Jenny a quick hug and a mischievous look. "My timing was perfect. Y'all finished the heavy lifting."

"Morning, Mama." Jenny looked more closely at her mother, saw a dab of blue paint under her chin, and smiled as she reached to scrape it with her fingernail.

"Come on, lamb chop." Landis held open the front passenger door and gave Claire a steadying hand as she slid into the seat.

In the back, Jenny turned the seat warmer on high and felt the soothing heat on her sore back and rear end. Ahhh. Best invention in the world. "How's the painting going, Mama?"

"Splendidly. I've been working on a still life with Red

Anjou and Asian pears, but after that spectacular lunar light show Sunday, I'm experimenting with capturing moonlight. The brightness, the glow, the iridescence..." Mama trailed off.

Jenny's mouth quirked up as she caught Landis giving Mama a doting look.

At the recycling center, the three of them made quick work of emptying the cans and bottles into the separate dumpsters. Jenny and Mama got so enthusiastic about tossing the wine empties into the glass area that the attendant gave them a stern look.

After they'd motored back to their side of the lake, Landis glanced over at Jenny and Claire. "If you gals don't mind, I'd like to make a pit stop at *Country Supply.*"

"Sure." Jenny loved wandering the aisles of this store.

Landis flipped on his turn signal, and rolled into the parking lot of the store.

Mama rubbed her hands together. "This spring and summer, I'm getting into gardening. No staying stuck behind the easel," she said firmly. "I'll get seeds and seedlings and put them in that front window with a grow light."

"Good, darlin'." Landis gave his wife a little pat and unbuckled his seatbelt.

Jenny clambered out. Mama and Landis's cabin was already tight on space. Mama's mini-greenhouse might be a stretch, but Jenny wasn't about to spoil her fun.

Inside, Mama made a beeline for the garden area,

pausing only to admire a pen teeming with baby chicks cheeping happily under a heat-emanating red brooder lamp.

Landis winced as he watched his wife bending down to coo baby talk to the yellow downy babies. "Please don't fall in love with a chicken," he muttered under his breath and heaved a sigh of relief as she straightened and headed toward the garden shop.

Jenny and Landis meandered up and down the aisles. Jenny enjoyed looking at everything: the feed bins, worming products, farm machinery and implements, grass seed, and hay grapple hooks. The next aisle displayed cast-iron cookware, nutcrackers, and smokers. At times when cabin fever struck, she and Luke would drive all the way to *Country Supply* and cruise the aisles. Jenny liked learning what the products were and how they were used. Having grown up in a family hardware store, Luke knew the answer to almost any question she asked. Fighting a pang of longing for him, Jenny ran her fingers through a barrel of cool feed corn for deer.

Beckoning Jenny, Landis picked up a box, slid readers on his nose, and peered at the directions. "I'd like to see what wildlife we have on the property." He gave Jenny a Cool Hand Luke kind of smile. "It's also just the ticket if our late-night trespasser comes back."

Jenny studied the picture on the box and broke into a grin. "I like it."

Landis held up his hand, and she gave him a high-five. The game camera they picked, the Outdoorsman's Covert Cam, was hidden in leafy camouflage and could be mounted in a tree so it wouldn't be easy to spot. This model had no-glow infrared LEDs that made flashes invisible.

As they tooled toward home, Landis pulled in at Gus's Gas-N-Git. "The place is busy."

Lowering her sunglasses on her nose, Mama stared. "Is this a bingo game or a meeting?"

"Gus always has a steady morning crowd, but nothing like this." Landis gestured toward the crowded parking lot. "His daughter's bakery is bringing them in."

No wonder. Jenny fondly recalled that tasty blueberry muffin with the streusel topping.

As the three of them headed inside, Jenny spotted Ella Parr's familiar dusty white car. Just the woman she wanted to see.

Mama and Landis stopped to talk with one of Landis's buddies and introduced Jenny to Lewis, the retired surgeon from New Bern. A fit, green-eyed guy with a stubble of beard and disarming smile, Lewis's khakis were spotted with black paint. His glasses were taped in the middle with gray duct tape, and both his tennis shoes had gaping holes in them near his little toes.

Mama caught Jenny's eye and surreptitiously pointed from Lewis to Landis. For the first time today, Jenny really looked at her stepfather. His khakis were two inches too short and had pale bleach spots on them. His face was unevenly shaved. Hoo, boy. Lewis and Landis both looked sketchy. Jenny was starting to get Mama's exasperation with the retired gents' casual dress code.

Leaving those three to chat, Jenny approached the counter and ordered a coffee and an eclair. Spotting Ella, she wove through the crowd to her café table. Ella looked up from her coffee, smiled, and stood to give Jenny a quick half-hug, half-pat on the arm.

"Hey there, stranger." Jenny had missed her no-nonsense neighbor while she was gone.

"Hey, yourself." Ella pointed at the chair. "Sit a spell. Take a load off."

Jenny slid in across from her. Taking a bite of chocolate-topped custard, she sighed happily. "How were the Galapagos? Give me the synopsis."

"Wildlife out the ying-yang. Cormorants that don't fly, albatrosses with eight-foot wing- spans, wild penguins, and giant tortoises, which blessedly are making a comeback because of the environmentalists. Paul had a big time. Took a thousand pictures. That's the sum of the trip."

"It sounds amazing." Jenny sighed wistfully. "I'll add that trip to my bucket list."

Ella took a large bite of cruller and chewed it slowly. "Now, what was your question about your neighbor, and what's all the urgency about?"

Jenny lowered her voice. "Who owns the property next door?"

Ella pinched her lip. "I don't know who owns it. We've lived here for a long time, and that property has always just been there."

"Dang," Jenny muttered. "Luke and I may want to buy it. We might build more guest cabins later, and we'd also like to not get bad neighbors. I've been hearing more about people building fifteen-bedroom houses and renting them to crowds in the summer." Jenny shuddered inwardly, imaging her guests being disturbed by drunken parties and loud music late at night.

Ella leaned forward with her coffee mug in both hands. "It steams my grits. The county needs to start to make zoning decisions to regulate that mess. It's too loosey-goosey now."

Jenny nodded. "I tried to get information at the county office but ran into a brick wall." She quickly filled Ella in on her visit. "The clerk at the County Register of Deeds office was...less than helpful. Public service may not be the field for him," Jenny said wryly.

Ella snorted. "Bennett Carter thinks he is special because his family settled here a while ago. Did he ask you who your people were and put on airs like an old South aristocrat?"

Jenny smirked. "Yup."

Ella snorted. "The Carters were hard working farmers, not old money blue bloods." She gave Jenny a canny look. "I've got a Women's Guild meeting at the church coming up. I'll scratch up info on your neighbors. Church is the place to get the real dirt around here."

"I'd be grateful." Jenny was relieved knowing Ella was looking into it. "Did Paul get my email about the wedding?"

"He's tickled about getting you two hitched and it's on his calendar," Ella assured her.

Jenny let out a breath she didn't realize she'd been holding. "Oh, I'm so glad. I didn't want to even think about anybody but Paul marrying us."

Ella took a large bite of a second cruller and patted her mouth with a napkin. "After we recover from our trip and Luke gets back, let's have supper at Slowpoke's Diner and nail down details. Paul likes to do that with folks he's marrying, even if they're our friends."

"Good. We'll look forward to that." Jenny noticed that Mama and Landis looked ready to go and rose. "Thanks in advance, Ella. Call me." Patting her friend's back, she headed off.

Back home, Jenny and Landis made quick work of unloading the recycling cans and putting them away. After effusively greeting the animals, Jenny had just put a mug of water in the microwave for a cup of tea when her text sounded. Jenny was bemused to see it was from Mama, whom she'd just left four minutes ago. It read:

Honey, I hope you noticed how Landis was dressed this morning. Do you see what I mean? You met Lewis, the ringleader of the gas station cronies. I got a group text going yes-

terday with a few of the wives of the cronies. We all agreed that what's good for the goose is good for the gander. While you're doing your wedding dress shopping tomorrow, I'll be doing a bit of clothes shopping of my own. I'll give you a fashion show soon. Stay tuned. Love you, Mama.

Jenny grinned as she texted back a series of x's and o's. She wasn't sure what Mama was cooking up, but Jenny had a feeling it was going to be fun.

When Luke called that night, he looked harried and sounded tired. "Hey there, Jenny."

"Hey, sweets," Jenny said warmly and glanced at the time. "Let me guess. You ate out with the team and had a fun team-building activity. What did you do tonight?"

"We had a lesson on how to make an ice sculpture with a chain saw. A few of the others wanted to try it afterward, but Zander and I said no." Luke rolled his eyes. "What's new on your end?" He pulled a bottle of beer from his hotel room refrigerator and opened it with one hand.

"Poor you. You missed a trip to Country Supply..." she teased and filled him in.

"Hmm," Luke said thoughtfully and tilted up his beer to take a sip. "There's lots going on but you're staying on top of it. Keep me posted."

"I will." Jenny pointed at the screen. "You must have had a frustrating day because your hair is standing up in a few places." She knew Luke raked his fingers through his hair when he was stressed.

Luke grabbed a clump of hair and feigned pulling it out. "I'm babysitting here. Zander wants me here to advise him, but he won't listen to me."

Jenny settled back in her chair, getting comfy. "Tell me."

"Zander's top two guys undermine him. When they're face to face with him or in a meeting, they act like solid team players. But they talk about him behind his back and even criticize Zander to customers." Luke's mouth tightened. "They don't do the quality of work they should and miss deadlines. They're the reason for the mess with the patent applications."

"That's not good." So much for team loyalty. Jenny felt a little sorry for Zander.

Luke continued. "Zander needs to get rid of them, but he's got a blind spot and doesn't see it. He thinks they're his buddies. They're part of the crew that socializes together all the time." Luke scowled. "I've talked with Zander about it, but he just can't believe it."

"But you both have a big financial stake in the success of the company," Jenny said.

"Exactly," Luke said evenly. "The problem needs to be fixed, and we'll get there."

Jenny opened her mouth to offer a sage piece of advice about a business she knew nothing about but caught herself just in time. She was working on not offering advice. Jenny smiled sweetly. "You'll figure it out. You're the smartest man I know."

CHAPTER 10

THE NEXT DAY WAS SUNNY and mild. Jenny was riding shotgun in Charlotte's car as they sped down the interstate headed toward the Queen City. According to a readers' poll her friend had read in *Today's Bridal Style* magazine, the city of Charlotte, North Carolina, had the best shopping for bridal and bridesmaids gowns in the South.

Charlotte tended to trust every survey, poll, and study she read, but Jenny was skeptical. The readers responding to the poll were probably dewy-skinned twenty-four-year-old bridesmaids, who couldn't wait to ride around standing in the open sunroof of a limousine, drinking tequila shots, yelling *woo-hoo*, and pointing at their bride-to-be friend and screaming, *"This one's getting married!"*

Depressing. Sipping a cup of coffee, Jenny tried to remember the pep talk she'd given Charlotte not that long ago. Many brides are not in their twenties. Many women were getting married and remarried in their forties, fifties, and sixties. Her hair stylist, Star, had told Jenny she had an eighty-one-year-old client who'd lost her husband and recently married a beau she'd lost touch with after high school.

Charlotte was humming along to the radio and was just a titch too cheery for Jenny this early in the day. Staring out the window, Jenny tried to tune her out.

When Charlotte saw an opportunity to let a driver ahead of her into her lane of traffic, she waved them on with a gallant hand-rolling gesture that said, *after you.* When someone let her into their lane, her friend waved extravagantly in thanks.

"What's with the super-friendly driving?" Jenny stared over at her. "Next thing, you'll be blowing kisses at them."

"Okay, Ms. Grumpalicious. Just drink your coffee." Charlotte patted her knee. "I'm doing a social experiment for the *Drive with Courtesy* campaign I'm about to launch in Celeste. If I drive extra courteously, will the people I am kind to pass it on?" She pointed with a shiny black fingernail with nail art on it that looked like the Big Dipper. "I let that fellow driving the white Honda in, and he then let the silver Nissan in in front of him. I used my turn signal way ahead of time for this last exit and the pickup behind me, who did not have his blinker on, turned it on." Charlotte looked at Jenny, her face animated. "I think I'm on to a good thing."

Jenny had to smile. "You could be right." Adjusting her too-tight seatbelt, Jenny jumped when she felt a sharp jab in her rear end. What in the world? She put a hand under her bottom, searched around, and felt a sharp metal point. Shifting in her seat, she finally saw it. "Charlotte, a metal spring is sticking up from your car seat and poking me in the bottom."

"Oh, that." Charlotte gave a gay little laugh and pointed. "I put washcloths in that glove box. If you fold one in a square and put it on it, it won't hurt one little bit."

Jenny grinned and shook her head. The sedan only had 150,000 miles on it. Despite being a jillion-aire, Charlotte would never buy a newer car until the odometer on the sedan hovered at 200,000. Jenny carefully folded the washcloth and sat on it. Sure enough, it worked fine.

Jenny went back to stewing and knew she needed to make herself stop. She *would* find a dress that suited her perfectly. "I don't need to go all white, beaded, and lacy, right?"

"You do not," Charlotte said firmly as she gave a very friendly thank-you wave to the fellow behind her who'd let her slip into the lane in front of him.

"I *could* do that if I wanted to, though, right? Just because I'm forty-four and not a first-time bride doesn't mean that I can't, right?"

Charlotte shot her an exasperated look. "Don't you remember the pep talk you gave me just a few short months ago, when I was having the same qualms about my wedding and my dress?"

"Maybe I was just being glib," Jenny muttered, picking at a loose thread on her black slacks.

"You were not," Charlotte huffed indignantly. "You were being perfectly sensible." She shot her a beady-eyed look. "You know what your problem is?"

"What?" Jenny suddenly wished she was back in her cozy bed in her flannel nightie with two dogs. Maybe she'd be drinking a coffee laced with Bailey's Irish Cream and watching re-runs of one of her favorite shows, *Hart of Dixie.*

"What's wrong with you is the same thing that was wrong with me." Charlotte's look was kind. "When it gets down to what to wear for the big day, we just keep buying into the image the media portrays of a bride who is young, exquisite, and size four. Many brides are that way, but many are *not.*"

Jenny nodded. "A good number of us have gray hair coming in and a few wrinkles we've earned, but still look darned good for our age."

Charlotte chimed in. "A lot of us older brides have fluffed up a bit too, but who cares? Look at the older men. Not a lot of princes left out there with all their hair and six-pack abs." She shot Jenny an impish look. "Beside Ashe and Luke, of course."

"Of course," Jenny agreed wholeheartedly.

Charlotte wasn't finished. "Every day, older women are falling in love with stellar men and marrying."

"Amen, sister." Jenny raised her stainless steel mug

in a toast and took a sip of her now-cold coffee. She grimaced at the sludge but, in a show of solidarity, swallowed it anyway.

Charlotte threw up a hand. "We need magazines and TV shows about older brides. You know how much I adore Hallmark channel, but they absolutely need to do shows with older heroines and older couples falling in love and marrying." She pointed out the car window. "That's what's out there happening in the real world."

"I so agree." Jenny paused, recalling all the years she'd been on her own and maybe a little lonely but not withering on the vine. She would have had a perfectly fine life had she not met Luke. "Or how about shows where women fall in love, fall out of love, and still live happily ever after without any spouse?"

"Yes." Charlotte hit her hand on the steering wheel to emphasize the point. "Now, those would be shows worth binge-watching."

Jenny felt better, her funk having evaporated. "You are so right, girl. I need to brace up, find a dress I like, and shoo those expectations right out of my head."

Charlotte lowered all four car windows and let the wind blow hard inside the car, whirling their hair around their faces. "There you go, pumpkin. Let all those dated expectations fly right out the window."

It took a moment for her friend's wise words to sink in completely, but Jenny suddenly knew she was absolutely right. Putting her arm out the window, she let her hand dip and the wind slip-slide around her fingers. The cold air on her face felt bracing, cleansing. As Charlotte raised the windows, Jenny smiled at her. "Let's go find me a pretty dress."

The traffic thinned and the skyscape of Charlotte came into view. "I read online that this city's skyline was named one of the top twenty prettiest in the nation," Jenny mused, wondering why she could remember facts like this but not why she'd walked upstairs to her bedroom.

"I can see why," Charlotte said admiringly as she made one more oh-so-gracious, *please do go before me* hand gesture topped with a friendly wave, and let the red Lexus beside her into her lane. Signaling, she took the exit toward Great South Mall. As she pulled up at a red light, the red Lexus pulled up beside her. A fellow with a big moustache gave her a flirty smile and raised his eyebrows up and down.

"Good heavens." Averting her eyes, Charlotte hurriedly moved her sun visor to the side window and flipped it down. She stepped on the gas as soon as the light turned green. "Maybe I was a little too friendly."

Jenny bit back a smile, and held an inch of air between her thumb and forefinger. "Maybe dial it back just a smidge. You'll give poor men a heart attack."

At the first of the nice department stores, Jenny was dazzled by the gorgeous dresses and tried on several, but none of them worked for her. The bridal consultant, a tall older woman with high cheekbones and an elegant gray chignon, spun her finger around in the air. "Honey, turn around so you can see how stunning the cut of that dress is in the back."

Jenny did as told and drew in her breath. "Wow. They really make these dresses so they look as good coming as they do going." As soon as she said it, she flushed. She sounded like Elly May Clampett at the fancy dress store in Hollywood.

But the woman just laughed. "They'll be admiring the bride as she walks down the aisle and up the aisle."

Feeling almost apologetic that she hadn't found a dress she liked, Jenny thanked the consultant, and they headed on to the next department store at the other end of the mall. No luck there either, and they left again.

"There were so few customers in those nice stores," Charlotte pointed out, a tinge of sadness in her voice.

"I noticed the same thing. I hate that those stores are struggling so and closing."

Charlotte buttoned up her coat as they stepped out into the blustery day. "Mama still talks about going to Ivey's Department Store for lunch with her mama. They had an elegant little lunch restaurant called the *Tulip Terrace*. The two always had the turkey pie and cinnamon ice cream. The ladies all wore dresses." She sighed dreamily. "I would have loved that."

"I know. Even after the heyday of those stores had passed, I remember what an event it was for Mama and me to go to Dillard's to shop for a prom dress. We only looked at the sale racks but still, it was special. They had a fellow playing the piano over the holidays, and the window displays were amazing," Jenny said wistfully. "It's the end of a more gracious era."

Each lost in their own memories, the two were quiet as they traipsed back to the car.

Jenny slumped as she clasped on her seat belt. "That was discouraging."

Charlotte patted her arm. "Buck up, buttercup. Those were only our first stops, and the day is young. Next, we hit the high-end bridal boutiques and then the discount stores."

They parked in front of a store called *Arabella's Bridal* that was painted a pale pink-and-white veranda stripe. "According to reviews on The Knot, this is the most elegant bridal store in town." Charlotte gave a determined nod.

But again, Jenny wasn't wowed. An exquisite young bridal consultant who looked like Natalie Portman discretely followed them around. If Jenny or Charlotte displayed the slightest interest in a dress, Natalie would whisk the dress off the racks and fluff and swirl it around to give them the full effect. Jenny found it unnerving.

Sipping sparkling water from a champagne flute, Charlotte led her to one of the simpler dresses, a graceful bell-shaped number with long lacy sleeves. "I found that lace overlay and sleeves can hide a few slight imperfections," she said sotto voce.

"Like my dimply, tapioca-like upper arms?" Jenny gave a half-smile.

"I had batwings *and* tapioca," Charlotte bragged. Lifting a pinky, she sipped her drink in her best snooty imitation. "What do you think of the dress and of this place?"

Looking around to make sure Natalie wasn't within earshot, Jenny whispered, "The dresses are all too glamorous, too over-the-top, or too young for me." Idly, she looked at a price tag that had been discretely tucked into a long lace sleeve, gasped quietly, and stared at Charlotte. "Why would you, of all people, bring me to a place where a dress costs this much?" She held up the price tag for her always economical friend to see.

"I know this place is pricey," Charlotte admitted. "I just wanted to make sure I wasn't imposing my borderline over-the-top thriftiness on you. It's *your* wedding."

"I get that." Jenny held both hands palms up "But even though we're doing okay money- wise, I'd never pay this much for a dress. It's just not how we spend money."

Charlotte looked at her proudly. "That's my girl. Now let's get out of here before that bridal consultant hunts us down."

At *Brenda's Bridal Barn*, swarms of young women were on a dress-shopping mission with faces as intent as a SWAT team. They came in fours, Jenny decided, the bride-to-be and three henchwomen who would stalk to separate corners of the store to scout the dresses. At the racks, they riffled rapidly through gowns, possessively snatching up ones that might work and tossing them in a cart. When their cart was towering with frothy dresses, they would meet in a corner. The queen bee, the prospective bride, would point imperiously to separate the keepers from the rejects.

"Whew. Quite an operation," Charlotte said drily, as she watched a flint-eyed future bridesmaid almost run over another customer.

Jenny tried to get interested in the sea of dresses and dutifully examined several racks, but between the SWAT-team shoppers and the sheer number of dresses, she just felt overwhelmed.

Not saying much, Charlotte followed her as she drifted around. "You doing okay?"

Jenny rubbed her eyes with her fingers. "I don't get a lot of this. The plunging necklines, the plunging backs, those keyhole peek-a-boo bodices, the strapless styles. Every dress I look at makes me feel more dowdy, fat, and old."

Charlotte put an arm around her waist and walked her toward the door. "Time to get you home."

Stopping at a drive-thru, the two women bought chicken wraps, fries, and iced tea. Jenny's mood rose as her blood sugar returned to normal. She turned to Charlotte.

"Sorry I was being so negative. I just ran out of steam. You did an outstanding job today, and I'm grateful."

Balancing her wrap on her knee, Charlotte slurped her drink as she got back on I-40. "You did great, puddin'. This is only day one of dress shopping, so don't give up now."

Jenny groaned aloud. "I can't handle too many more days like this one. Can't I just order a dress off the internet? Maybe we could find a gown that's made with a lot of elastic so we know it will fit."

"You want a one-size-fits-all wedding gown?" Charlotte's lip curled.

"Well, when you say it that way," Jenny said sulkily, and she stuffed a handful of fries in her mouth.

Her friend gave her a sympathetic look. "Let's simmer down. We'll be out of this traffic soon and back in God's country. You can get cozy in your cabin, put your feet up, hang with your boys, and recover from this day." Charlotte cast a sideways glance at her. "But I have a Plan B."

"Ahhh." Jenny heaved a tired sigh. "How did I know you would?"

"Leave it to me," Charlotte said with a confident nod. "When you've had a chance to recover, we're going shopping again. We're going to find you a dress that you love."

"Okay." Jenny popped the last of her wrap in her

mouth. She still liked the one-size-fits-all elastic dress idea.

Charlotte slowed as a speedy black luxury car forced its way into the small gap in the lane in front of her.

"Good defensive driving," Jenny said.

"You have to be one these days," Charlotte muttered. Frowning, she glanced over at Jenny. "Next week, I'm the featured speaker at the Noontime Rotary Club of Celeste. I'm going to talk about the *Drive with Courtesy* campaign."

"That's exciting." But Jenny saw that Charlotte looked stricken, not excited. "What's wrong?"

"I'm terrified." Charlotte gave a tense smile. "You know I have a teensy-weensy fear of public speaking, right?"

Jenny shot her a skeptical look. "At our *Fabulous You Fit and Healthy Week* last summer, you were calm and so real when you spoke to those women. They loved you."

Charlotte shook her head. "That was different. The group was all women, and I *knew* them all. This Rotary group is mostly men I don't know well, and it's Ashe's Rotary Club. If I bungle it up, people will think his wife is a dolt."

"Anybody who knows you..." Jenny began.

Charlotte interrupted. "Jen, you haven't seen me speak when I get a case of nerves. I forget my point, have long pauses, perspire, and giggle nervously..." She shuddered. "It's really bad."

"Okay." Jenny looked at her friend. "How can I help?"

A note of desperation crept into Charlotte's voice. "Come to the Rotary meeting. You can sit right at the front table and do that little encouraging head nod thing that you do."

"Like this?" Jenny demonstrated the barely discernable nod of appreciation.

"Perfect." Charlotte blew out a sigh of relief. "If you'd come and be my nodder, I'd be calmer."

"I'll be there," Jenny promised as she took a scrap of paper from her purse and jotted down the date.

Back home, Jenny shucked off her clothes and slipped on what she was now thinking of as her athleisure wear—fleece pants and a sweatshirt with a Labrador retriever on it. Immediately, she began to feel better. Heating a casserole dish of tasty chicken vegetable soup she'd made in the slow cooker last week and frozen, Jenny poured herself a glass of wine and sipped it. Yum.

When her text sounded, she debated ignoring it, but worried that a bad thing had happened to a loved one. Sighing, she picked up her phone. Mama's note read:

Darling, Hope you had as much success on your shopping trip as I did today!! Tomorrow, I want to hear all about your dress hunting. I'll show you my fashion finds, too! Your ever lovin' Mama

Jenny smirked and replied.

Couldn't find a dress I liked today but Charlotte has another day of shopping planned. Can't wait to see your new clothes! XOXO

CHAPTER 11

E ARLY THE NEXT MORNING, JENNY spent two hours at her laptop looking at options for the interior of the new cabin. Today, she had to narrow down choices for appliances. Jenny had looked at so many options that her head ached, and she was starting to doubt her choices. Reviews helped, and Jenny made careful notes on a yellow legal pad.

Pausing for a stretch, Jenny fixed herself a tall glass of ice water. Swallowing it down, she stood at the window to admire the lake, an azure blue this morning. From the corner of her eye, Jenny caught movement and peered at the garden she and Landis had tilled up last week. Mama, who was dressed as colorfully as a garden troll, sat on a padded garden kneeler slipping seeds and seedlings into a tray of small peat pots. As she took in what she could see of Mama's attire, Jenny's eye widened and her mouth quirked up. Pulling on a sweater, she stepped outside to investigate.

Her mother had on a blue, extra-long billed visor and

had a ponytail sprouting from the hole in the top. She wore the extra-large wraparound sunglasses that were a favorite of senior citizens in Florida. Pulling off her shades, Claire beamed at Jenny, then stood and brushed the dirt off her knees. "Good morning, love. What a grand almost spring day."

"Morning, Mama." Jenny tried not to smile as she studied her. Mama wore a large green Army jacket with a nametag that read *Bub*, a white T-shirt with Daffy Duck on it, and baggy capris in a snakeskin-patterned polyester fabric that had tears in the knees. On her feet, she wore white socks under pink Crocs. "You're looking comfy."

"Oh, I am," her mother assured her. "And being comfy is the most important thing."

"So true." Jenny stuck her hands in her pockets, trying not to laugh. The large bill of Mama's visor gave her the profile of a Great Blue Heron. "So this is what you found shopping?"

"Yes, ma'am. Yesterday, I met up with a few other wives of the cronies. We found a military surplus store and a shop called *Closeouts and Seconds for Women*." With a mischievous look, she turned around slowly so Jenny could get the full effect. "I think this is athleisure wear."

"I would call it that." Jenny cocked her head. "Has Landis seen you this morning?"

"Not yet," Claire said airily. "He was in the shower when I dressed, but he'll be out shortly to help me take these pots inside."

Jenny shook her head and laughed. "Well, I'll leave you to it. As much as I'd like to stay and watch y'all scrap, I've got a newsletter to write and errands to run."

Mama blew her a kiss.

As she closed the door to the Dogwood, Jenny caught a glimpse of Landis emerging from the Redbud. Jenny drew closer to the window. She just had to watch. In his gray sweat suit, Landis whistled and had a spring in his step as he strode toward the garden. When he saw Mama, he braked hard, gaped, and rubbed the back of his head. Claire looked up and gave him a big friendly wave. Pasting a smile on his face, Landis approached as cautiously as a man stepping on a path where he'd seen a snake the day before.

Dropping the curtain, Jenny shook her head. She couldn't wait to get the full report from Mama. Hopefully, this would be a one-day skirmish, but if Landis dug in his heels, Jenny felt sure Mama had planned a longer strategic offensive and more appalling fashion.

Now, the newsletter. Jenny dreaded starting each one she had ever written, but found that as she got rolling, words came easier, and she ended up happy with the results. Jenny now had seven hundred followers, though she suspected a number would never stay at the Lakeside Resort but just liked the pictures she included and the stories she told. She always got cute email responses from readers when she included pictures of Bear, Buddy, and Levi. She reminded herself to put a recent shot of the three of them on the front page. Garland, the concrete goose that Jenny dressed up in little outfits, also had a lot of fans.

Leaning back in her chair, Jenny tried to think about compelling content but her mind was blank. Drumming her fingers, Jenny brainstormed. Nothing. Sugar lump. She needed to focus. Jenny made herself get on the floor and do ten bridges to stretch her back and jump-start her brain. Sticking her head out the front door, Jenny took several big deep breaths of fresh, cool morning air and slid back into her seat at the computer.

> *Good morning, friends. Spring has almost sprung! Daffodils are poking their heads up from the ground, the birds are chirping and chatting, and the trees are budding green and blooming. It's another beautiful day on Heron Lake.*
>
> *We have exciting plans for the spring and summer here at the Lakeside Resort!*
>
> *Here's our big news:*
>
> *In past years, we have offered active water sports like tubing, wakeboarding, and knee boarding. This summer, we're adding **water skiing**. The sport is coming back. If you have ever watched a skilled water-skier gliding, dipping close to the water, and going airborne as they jump a wake, you'll know why. It's a sport about grace and athleticism. With just a few days of water-ski lessons, you'll likely get*

up on skis and several of you will learn to slalom. Exciting, and of course we'll take lots of pictures of you from the boat for you to post.

For guests staying full weeks during August, we are offering **swimming lessons** for the little ones and for those adults who'd like to improve their swimming skills. Every year, we read too many stories about senseless drownings. Knowing how to swim is the best way to keep everyone safe on the water. Our Red Cross-certified instructor will have your little ones swimming like fish in no time.

As usual, we'll offer the activities you've come to love—**canoeing, kayaking, swimming,** and **lolling about in inner tubes**. The fish will be biting, so toss in a line. **Fishing** licenses available for just $15. Last summer we had a number of prize catches. We'll have **sunset boat cruises** every night at six. Be ready to take pictures, because the light at that time is magical!

Resort guests can kick back, catch up on reading, walk our trails, or just relax and take in the natural beauty all around you. Heron Heights State Park is just a short drive away. The park has miles of lakeside **hiking trails**, places to ride your **mountain bikes**, and **bird watching** galore. Our friend, Ranger Emory, leads nature walks four times a *week and can give you the inside scoop on the animals and birds that call the park home.*

*Those of you who are on the **autism spectrum** or have family members or friends who are, mark your calendars! We have a very special weekend planned for the first weekend in September. More info in our next newsletter! Call or drop us a note if you'd like to learn more.*

Jenny leaned her elbow on the table and rested her chin in her hand. She hadn't yet planned that *very special* weekend. She needed to get her act together. Grabbing a pad of paper, she wrote herself a note in bold print: GET WITH CHARLOTTE AND ASTOR AND PLAN AUTISM WEEKEND!

So, that's our lineup. We look forward to seeing you all. Returning guests have become our friends. We can't wait to catch up on your lives. For those of you who are considering staying with us, but haven't quite decided, please read our online reviews. They should help you make up your mind.

Have a look at pictures of all our accommodations, and book your reservations now. Our cabins are filling up fast and our two vintage campers, the Silver Belle and the Shasta, have become guest favorites.

Bear, Buddy, and Levi send warmest regards and can't wait to see you.

Scrolling through the photo gallery on her phone, Jenny found a picture of Bear, Buddy, and Levi snuggled together dozing in a sunny spot on the cabin floor. Next, Jenny found a good shot of Garland dressed in the little lifeguard outfit that included sunglasses, a red T-shirt that read *Lifeguard* above a white cross, and a whistle around his neck. Inserting those two pictures below her signature, Jenny spellchecked the newsletter, proofread it three times, and sent it on its way. Done.

Errand time. Jenny got ready to leave. Pulling her hair back in a ponytail, she took one last sip of coffee and rinsed her mug. Jenny gave carrot snacks to all the boys, tucked a copy of the cabin plans and her shopping list in her purse, and got going. She'd make the drive and hit two big box home improvement stores and a builder's discount store. With deadlines for the new cabin looming, Jenny needed to do reconnaissance about appliances, cabinets, sinks, toilets, lighting fixtures, and countertops. Then, she'd run them all by Luke.

Hours later, Jenny's cloth shopping bag was heavy with brochures and samples. Her head was spinning as she drove to the Big Rock, a store that carried quartzite, granite, soapstone, and concrete countertops. Gazing at sample books, actual stone samples, and the slabs of handsome granite stacked side by side on the ground, Jenny listened to the salesperson explain the pros, cons, finishes, and features of each choice. She inspected all of the veins, swirls, and colors. Many were too busy, she decided. Jenny was drawn to several dramatic pieces, but worried she'd tire of the look in a few years.

Rubbing the knots of tension on the base of her skull, Jenny realized she was too muddled to make even a preliminary decision about her top two picks. Finally, she just shot close-up photos of the four she liked best and the prices. She'd text them all to Luke and let him make the first cut.

By the time Jenny finished errands and headed home, it was almost full dark. With no street lights, the road that led to the resort was black as tar. Less than a mile from home, Jenny rounded a curve and gasped. A vehicle approached, coming fast and driving well over the center line into Jenny's lane. The driver had high beams on, momentarily blinding her. Jenny's heart hammered as she braked, but there was no shoulder and no place to go. Jenny sized up the road ahead, trying to pick the safest spot to plow her car in the woods. She laid her hand on her horn and kept it there. Would the other driver correct? The speeding vehicle drifted farther into her lane. Jenny could see the big truck and hear the pounding of music. Her hands white-knuckled on the wheel, Jenny was seconds away from driving into the woods when the truck swerved back into the correct lane and roared off.

Cold with sweat, Jenny made herself slowly decelerate and stopped to collect herself. Resting her head on the steering wheel, her breath was ragged as she waited for her heart to slow to normal. The truck that had almost hit her head-on was the same one that she'd seen drive by the cabin that night. Their macho truck guy was back.

Jenny drove to the end of the road, saw the fresh peel-out marks, and smelled burned rubber. Edging around the perimeter of the cul-de-sac, Jenny's high beams hardly penetrated the pitch-black darkness into the woods, but it looked like the driver had taken another joyride through those woods.

The adrenaline receded as Jenny pulled into the driveway of the resort, and she thought about it rationally. The trespassing and damage to the property next door were plain wrong, and she and Landis would report it to the sheriff. But as frightening as the near-collision had been, Jenny was certain that the macho truck guy hadn't deliberately tried to hit her. He didn't even know who she was or what she drove. Also, this was not the first time she'd considered ditching the car in the woods because of an approaching driver drifting into her lane. Drivers enjoyed zipping along the winding country two-lane and got lulled into thinking theirs was the only car on the road. The truck guy probably scared the wits out of himself, too. Feeling calmer, Jenny couldn't help but smile. The pictures from the game camera would tell the story. She couldn't wait until she and Landis checked them.

Back home, Jenny locked her doors behind her and hugged her animals, still a little shaken. With guests staying in two other cabins, she wasn't alone, and that was reassuring. Next door, the Redbud was dark. Tonight was

Mama and Landis's last shag class, and they were going out to supper afterward with their new dancing friends. They'd be late, but that was fine. Jenny wasn't nearly as rattled as she'd been last time.

Pouring herself a tall water glass full of wine, Jenny thought it through. She'd call the sheriff's department to report the trespassing, but she didn't want a deputy to come out tonight to investigate. No need to unnecessarily worry her guests with blue lights and a cruiser. Feeling calm and purposeful, Jenny made the call, texted an update to Landis, and headed to bed.

The next morning, Landis tapped at the door at seven. "So, we had another visit from the truck guy," he said in a matter-of-fact tone and pulled at the brim of his ball cap. "Come on, Jessica Fletcher. Let's see what kind of shots we got." They hopped in his SUV and wheeled over to the property next door.

Hands on hips, Landis surveyed the scene. The driveway was even more deeply rutted than before, and new paths had been cut through the woods by the wildcatting driver.

Jenny spied a familiar blue beer can in the weeds and pointed at it. "At least he's loyal to his brand."

Landis just shook his head, and the two of them strode over to check the game camera.

Jenny peered at Landis as he scrolled though the shots. "Are they clear? Did we get the license plate?"

"Son of a gun," Landis muttered. "The infrared camera

blanks out the license plate. I should have known that." But after looking at a few more frames, he looked at Jenny and broke into a grin. "We may not have the license plate, but I believe we've got enough good shots here for Sheriff Tucker and his team to get well on their way to solving this little mystery."

Back home, Jenny popped the last of her avocado toast in her mouth and sat at the computer as she transferred the pictures from the game camera SIM card to her computer. Leaning closer to the screen, she examined them. There were several good shots of a macho-looking black truck, but they were common enough around here. This truck was distinctive, though, with its jacked-up frame and the extra-gnarly tires. Jenny couldn't see the truck's make or model, but guessed the law enforcement guys would be able to figure that out easily.

Leaning forward to make sure she didn't miss a detail, Jenny scrolled through to the last few pictures. Bingo. The truck must have fishtailed as it came back out of the overgrown driveway, and they'd gotten a grainy picture of the driver—a burly-looking man sporting a moustache and wearing a baseball cap backward. Jenny grinned. Landis was right. They'd gotten enough good evidence for the sheriff's department to try to find a suspect.

Attaching the best photos, Jenny tapped out a short email to Sheriff Tucker and hit SEND. "Take that, macho truck guy trespasser, and don't come back again," she murmured. Jenny tipped her chair back on two legs and let herself enjoy the little victory.

Later in the week, two orange portable toilets for the construction crew arrived at the resort. Jenny directed them to a spot behind four tall and bushy Nellie Stevens holly. As she walked home, she shuddered inwardly, imagining colorful toilets in the background of her wedding photos. The guest count for the wedding was now at seventy-five. They'd need more portable bathrooms for their wedding day. Jenny shook her head ruefully. Maybe she could find a few that looked like charming she-sheds or artists' studios.

The building crew from West Virginia arrived the next morning, pulling up in a caravan. Four pickup trucks hauled tool trailers and another towed a fifth-wheel camper that they'd use as an office, for cooking, and as a general hangout. They'd sleep at the Budget Nights Motel just up the road and head home on weekends. Nice fellows, Jenny decided as she, Landis, and Mama greeted them and let them get started.

The next morning, Jenny stood at her refrigerator feeling giddy and buoyant as she stared at the Horses of America calendar. She hugged herself, scarcely believing the day was finally here. Luke was coming home. Right after a farewell luncheon bash that Zander and his team were throwing for him, he would jump in his truck and drive north. If Luke made good time, he'd be home for supper.

Jenny glanced around and sighed as she took in the clutter — piles of mail she'd opened but had not decided what to do with yet, a stack of catalogs from expensive stores she liked to browse through but never bought from, tumbleweeds of animal hair, and glasses of partially finished iced tea, coffee, and water. Not the warm, inviting space a hardworking man would enjoy coming home to.

Pinching her lip, Jenny glanced at the baggy jeans she'd thrown on to clean cabins this morning. Athleisure wear for sure. She knew what her hair looked like, too, wavy on one side and flat on the other. Between the cabin and her appearance, Jenny had cleaning, polishing, and primping to do before Luke got home. She'd better stop mooning around and jump on the day.

Jenny did a whirlwind tidying of the cabin, neatly folding fleeces, jeans, and sweaters into compact squares so they'd fit in their tiny cubbies and under sofa storage drawers. Finally finished, Jenny spun slowly around. Perfect. The cabin was clean, orderly, and inviting.

Before she hopped in the shower, Jenny turned on the robot vacuum cleaner. All three animals clambered onto the sofa and began to snooze as the whirling orb spun by.

By early evening, Jenny's cabin was spruce and spotless. She'd washed and blown out her hair so it was shiny, applied a light coat of makeup, and put on a soft sweater, her best-fitting jeans, and her favorite red cowboy boots. She looked good for her mileage, Jenny decided.

Pulling the still-sizzling roasted chicken from the oven, Jenny rested it on the counter. She poked a fork in the sweet potatoes on the stove top. They were soft and the brown sugar on top had caramelized perfectly. This supper looked and smelled scrumptious.

Jenny's heart leapt up in her chest as she heard a familiar truck pull up in the driveway. Throwing open the door, she raced outside. Luke stepped out of his truck, and his grin lit the dusk. "Hello, darlin' girl."

Jenny threw herself into his arms. "Luke, Luke," she murmured, blinking back happy tears. "You don't even know how much I missed you."

"Precious Jenny," Luke's voice was low and husky. Lifting her chin, his lips met hers and kissed her hungrily. He kissed her eyes, her cheek, and her throat. When he finally let her go, Jenny felt weak-kneed.

His arm slung casually over her shoulder, they headed toward the house. Toward home.

The next few days were a few of the happiest Jenny could remember. That was saying a lot, because she'd banked a lot of happy days since she'd met Luke that day at his daddy's hardware store.

Jenny and Luke couldn't stop hugging, kissing, and talking. They puttered around together, enjoying doing chores, sharing meals, and taking the boys for long, meandering walks. They visited all the parents. Luke quickly bonded with the West Virginia cabin builders.

Luke was at the grill barbecuing chicken, and Jenny was whipping up a vinaigrette for the salad when she got the text from Ella: *Y'all free for supper tomorrow? Slowpoke's at six??*

Jenny poked her head out the door, enjoyed the whiff of smoke and tangy sauce. Yum.

"Watch this." Luke gave a cocky smile as he flipped his spatula in the air and neatly caught it. "Call me Grill Man."

Jenny laughed. "All right, Grill Man. Is tomorrow night good for us to meet the Parrs for supper and talk about our wedding?"

"Sure." Luke paused and gave her an apologetic look. "I've got to work from home tomorrow during the day. I've got to check in with Zander and his team and work on taxes."

"That's fine," Jenny assured him. "This break has been exactly what I needed, but I've got things to do, too." Giving him a quick kiss on the cheek, she headed back inside. After accepting Ella's invitation, Jenny got busy with items on her to-do list. So much to get accomplished before the wedding!

CHAPTER 12

THE NEXT MORNING, BOTH DOGS had appointments at the veterinarian's office for yearly checkups, and Claire rode along with Jenny to give her a hand. Thankfully, Mama was dressed normally in a knee-length skirt, boots, and sweater. Jenny gave her a grateful look. "Thanks for coming. When Bear goes to the vet without Buddy, he shivers the whole time. When Buddy goes solo, he lifts his leg on everything. I've learned to take them together, but it'll sure be easier with two of us."

"I'm happy to help." Mama reached back to give each dog a reassuring pat.

Jenny glanced behind her. With the windows cracked enough to let air riffle their ears, the boys' noses twitched as they sniffed animal scents. Both looked calm and happy.

Mama held out her hand and showed Jenny her tangerine-colored nails. "I had an incredible manicure yesterday at a new place over by Gus's. This color's called *Orange You in Love With Me Yet?*"

Jenny gave Mama's nails a quick once-over. "They're pretty. Maybe I'll get mine done when things slow down."

Mama gave her a knowing look. "In my experience, things rarely slow down right before a wedding, but you might want to schedule a mani-pedi close to the big day."

"Good idea." Jenny started feeling overwhelmed and drew slow breaths to try to calm down.

"You need to start delegating tasks to me. You can't do all this on your own while you're running a business and building a house," Claire said firmly.

Mama was right. Jenny needed help if they were going to pull off this wedding. "Will you schedule that mani-pedi for me for the nineteenth? Will you to help me pick the caterers and decide on a menu for the reception?"

Claire clasped her hands together, looking delighted. "Of course, my darling girl. I'd be honored to help." Mama hesitated. "While I was at the salon, a nice woman who just opened a new bakery called *Harper's Heavenly Cakes* stopped by to drum up business with little paper plates of cake samples for the customers. Her lemon pound and hummingbird cakes were both divine, light, rich, and just scrumptious. All of the other women getting their nails done were as impressed as I was." Her mother twisted her hands together. "I may have gotten ahead of myself a teensy bit. Have you arranged for a wedding cake yet?"

"Not yet." Jenny glanced over and arched a brow. "How exactly did you get ahead of yourself?"

"I invited the owner to stop by the resort with wedding cake samples." Mama's words came out in a rush. "You said you and Luke would be home all day Saturday. I know I should have checked with you first, but I got caught up in that delicious moment. I can cancel if you'd like me to," she said, sounding apologetic.

Jenny just smiled and shook her head. "It's fine, Mama. One less thing for me to do." She gave Mama a questioning glance. "So her cakes were really special?"

"So special." Mama gave a swoony sigh. "She says brides are picking all sorts of flavors these days."

"Charlotte and Ashe's cake was half-coconut and half-carrot," Jenny reminded her.

"Harper can bake any kind of cake you like. Her cake menu says she makes white chocolate lemon raspberry, red velvet, orange chiffon, and caramel wedding cakes."

"Great choices, and different, too," Jenny admitted. "Saturday cake tasting sounds fine."

On the drive over to Slowpoke's Diner to meet the Parrs for supper, Jenny kept reaching over to touch Luke's hand and squeeze it. "I pined for you while you were gone. Did you pine for me?"

"I pined." With a crooked grin, Luke pulled her hand to his mouth and kissed it.

"We're as sappy as Charlotte and Ashe," Jenny said, a sunny lightness in her limbs.

"So what is Paul going to talk with us about? Is this a premarital deal where the preacher reminds us to communicate with each other and be good listeners?" Luke smirked. "I'm already kind of a pro at both. If I were to rate myself, I'd say I was a ten at communicating and listening."

Jenny barked out a laugh. "Last night, I tried to talk to you twice, but you kept staring at the sink, probably thinking through how to repair the garbage disposal. You just didn't hear me." She looked over at him. "You are an excellent listener…"

Luke gave a smug smile.

Jenny held up a finger. "…when you're not fixing or thinking about how to fix something. You're only five star if you're watching a YouTube video on old motorboats," she said blithely. "You're a four if you're engrossed in a TV show about restoring old muscle cars. When you're focused, I could wave both hands in front of you, and you wouldn't notice me."

"That's a little strong." Luke pretended to look injured. "I *can* be single-minded at times."

Nobly, Jenny let it go. Staring out the window, she thought about it. "You know, I could improve, too, in the communication department. I can talk things to death when I'm anxious. Does that ever bother you?"

Looking wary, Luke glanced over at her to see if this

was a trap. "You're better at communicating that I am, but you can hammer away at things if you're worried."

"I can work on that." Maybe Jenny should keep a journal and put her worries on paper instead of hashing and rehashing them with Luke. "What else could I do better?"

Luke shot her a quick look to make sure the conversation was still friendly. "You're doing better on not giving me advice about business stuff, and I'm grateful. I know you mean well, but work issues can be more complex than you know." Luke hesitated. "You still do it a little. Yesterday when Zander called, you told me I just needed to be direct with him."

Jenny flushed. She'd been working on not giving unsolicited advice, but apparently not hard enough. "I'll keep working on that."

"Anything I need to work on?" Luke adjusted the visor to block the sun.

Jenny thought about it. "You could be a little more expressive about your feelings toward me. I know you're a John Wayne, still-waters-run-deep guy, and I love that about you. I don't want you to turn into a touchy-feely man. I wouldn't like that." She gazed out the window at the passing scenery as she gathered her thoughts. "You could just talk more often about why you love me. You could let me know what's going on in that big heart of yours, like you did before you left for Georgia and when we talked on Valentine's Day."

Luke squinted off in the distance and then turned to look at her. "I can do better."

"Good." Jenny felt relieved. That one was hard to say but needed saying, and he'd responded like a champ.

"Anything else?" Luke pulled up to a four-way stop.

Jenny waited tensely, watching the other driver in the Subaru with her right blinker on trying to size up Luke's intent. Jenny couldn't *not* say it one more minute. "Blinker, honey. Just give the poor woman a hint about where you're going."

Luke turned on his left blinker but not before the woman glared at him as she passed. He gave Jenny a rueful look. "I could work on more frequent use of directional signals."

"That would be nice." Jenny cracked a smile. "Southern men think using a turn signal is a sign of weakness, but it's not. It would make me less of a back-seat driver."

"*That* would be nice." Luke made a show of turning on his blinker a quarter mile up the road from the approaching turn to the diner.

"Excellent signaling," Jenny said drily but cracked a smile.

Luke grinned as he turned into the parking lot of Slowpoke's. Pulling into a spot, he turned off the ignition and paused for a moment to look at her gravely. "One thing I know. I'm sure looking forward to living with you every day for the rest of my life. I'm the lucky man that gets to eat supper with you every night, work beside you every day, and wake up with you every morning."

Jenny stared at him, her eyes prickling. "Wow. What a wonderful thing to say."

Luke held up a hand. "I can be a silver-tongued devil."

"I'm starting to see that," she said lightly and gave him a peck on the cheek. The rare times Luke tipped his hand about how much he loved her, she felt like she was walking on air. She hoped he kept up his promise to do more of it, because it felt lovely. The two held hands as they walked toward the diner.

Luke pulled open the door for her. Inside, the diner was simply furnished with pine dining tables and mismatched wooden chairs. The big fieldstone fireplace crackled and glowed, making the tables closest to it the most sought-after ones. The place was friendly and unpretentious. The menu was simple, but with one or two zippy daily specials, like jalapeno shrimp poppers wrapped in bacon or Asiago chicken breasts on baked grits. Jenny inhaled the scent of freshly baked bread, and her stomach growled. Tilden's kitchen staff made all the breads from scratch daily, and he contracted with local organic farmers for the meat and produce. Everything Jenny had tasted on the menu was always fresh and tasty, including the completely cooked turkey dinner, sides, and pies she'd bought here and taken home to serve for Thanksgiving and Christmas dinners.

Inside, Jenny scanned the room for Paul and Ella.

Spotting them in a booth near the back, Jenny gave a big wave.

With quick hugs all round, Jenny and Luke slid into the booth across from the couple.

"Let's get the ordering over. Then we can relax and catch up," Ella suggested.

Jenny looked at the menu, deciding on a shrimp po' boy on a crusty French baguette.

Luke had told her Tilden got the seafood fresh from the coast on Mondays.

Luke and Paul were leaning toward the Angus beef burger, while Ella decided on the fried chicken platter.

As the waiter brought them a basket of steaming hush puppies and butter and took their orders, Jenny tried to surreptitiously take in Ella's ensemble. Her friend wore a red-and-green plaid turtleneck with little Christmas trees on it and a black-and-white striped French fisherman sweater. She wore a small hoop earring in one ear and a larger hoop in the other, and her curly hair was standing up like a white, puffy dandelion head. Ella examined the menu wearing bright blue readers that were crooked and had two more pairs of reading glasses on beaded leashes draped around her neck.

After the waiter left, Jenny smiled at Ella. "So, you're working on your next novel."

"How does everyone always know when I'm writing?" Ella asked irritably, and looked at her husband.

Paul patted her hand. "You have a certain intensity

about you when you're plotting a murder. It's endearing, though," he assured her.

Jenny leaned closer. "So, what's this one about?"

Ella's eyes danced as though she were relaying a juicy story about mutual friends. "A woman meets a wealthy older man at church. In a month, they're married. Shortly thereafter, he dies in a suspicious boating accident. The widow doesn't seem grief-stricken and quickly marries yet another wealthy widower from the same congregation. He begins to have mysterious health problems. The whip-smart but unassuming church secretary suspects that this church lady may be a murderer and begins to investigate."

Intrigued, Jenny clasped her hands together. "I love it."

"Car chases, I hope," Luke said as he took a bite of a hot hush puppy.

Paul grinned. "When Ella started the book, she was mad at me for something or another, so she made the first murder victim an Episcopal priest. She changed it when we made up."

Jenny laughed and looked at Paul. "So, the Galapagos Islands trip was fantastic. Ella said you took amazing photos, Paul."

"I did." Paul's face lit up, and he detailed what he'd photographed. "When the islanders found out I was a priest, they had me do a blessing of the animals. With as much trouble as they have had protecting those magnificent animals and unique plant life from all the threats like pollution, overfishing, and poaching, I was more than happy to do it. The whole trip was moving and humbling." Paul blinked back tears and paused to polish his glasses with his napkin.

Jenny felt her own eyes mist. Paul was such a nice man.

Their suppers arrived, and they all dug in. Jenny took a bite of spicy shrimp in crusty warm French bread and patted her mouth with a napkin. "Delicious," she murmured.

For a little while, all they did was comment on their meals and enjoy them.

"So, let's talk about the ceremony," Paul said briskly, pausing to sip his iced tea. "Are you interested in a traditional service or do you want to write your own vows and do it your own way?"

Jenny looked at Luke. "Traditional, right?"

"Yes," Luke quickly agreed.

Ella popped a last piece of fried okra in her mouth. "This is my cue to disappear. I'm going to go powder my nose." Sliding out of the booth, she trotted off.

Paul gave Jenny and Luke meaningful looks. "You both are friends of mine. I see no need for any premarital counseling, but I do want to share two important lessons that I learned from my own very happy forty-three years of marriage." The priest cleared his throat. "First. No one ever wants a divorce, but in certain situations, it's the only course of action you can take."

Jenny shot a puzzled glance at Luke. This was inspiring?

Paul flushed. "What I mean is this. You are both mature individuals with good communication skills. You seem extremely well-suited. Because you've both been married before, I assume you've learned important lessons along the way."

Both Jenny and Luke bobbed their heads in agreement.

Paul went on. "When you argue, and you will, my suggestion is that even in the heat of the moment, you never threaten the other with divorce. It's like pouring gasoline on a small, manageable fire. You can turn a simple disagreement into World War III." He gazed at them steadily. "You've both waited so long to find true love again. Don't treat it carelessly. You must decide before you marry that you are in it for the long haul."

Luke looked at Jenny, his eyes intense. "We're in it 'til death do us part," he said gravely.

"I agree." Jenny swallowed a lump in her throat.

"Good." Paul smiled slowly. "Second. You each must place a priority on the marriage. Make time for the other, listen well to each other, and don't let family, work, or any other obligations come before your time with your spouse." He shook his head ruefully. "I can enjoy being the guy everybody calls on when a project needs to be done. A few years back, I was acting like super-priest at work and putting Ella on the back burner. It almost caused irreparable damage." He tapped a finger on the table to emphasize his point. "Your spouse is your best friend who will be beside you your whole life. You must tend to your marriage, nurture your relationship, and keep it as your number-one priority."

The muscle in his jaw working, Luke nodded slowly. "I needed to hear this, Rev."

Jenny reached under the table and gave Luke's hand a squeeze. She looked at the priest. "We will think about all that you said. Thank you, Paul, for sharing your wisdom."

"You're welcome," Paul said simply. His face brightened as Ella returned. "Hello, love."

"All set?" Ella eased into her seat.

"We are," Luke said.

"Good." Ella put on her crooked glasses and picked up the menu. "Who'd like dessert?"

They all ordered coffee and dessert.

Ella sighed rapturously as she tasted her carrot cake. Swallowing, she pointed her fork at them. "I got the scoop on the lot next to y'all's."

Jenny hurriedly swallowed her bite of lemon cheese cake and leaned in. "Wow. Spill, Ella."

Ella took a sip of decaf. "The owner is an older lady, a widow named Pearl Mayhew, who is in her mid- to late seventies. Pearl and her husband attended All Saints Church before Paul became a priest there. Her daddy gifted that property beside you to the couple when they were newlyweds. They built a home on it." She took a large bite of cake and chewed it. "The Mayhews were real do-it-yourself-ers before DIY television made it popular. The two lived there for twenty years before a house fire burned it to the ground."

"How sad." Jenny gave Luke a meaningful look. After a scary late night flare-up of a fire- pit they thought they'd extinguished, they'd gotten even more rigorous about safety. They'd beefed up their protocol for making sure fires were completely out. A chimney sweep inspected and cleaned the woodstoves in each cabin twice a year. All the fire extinguishers got tested regularly.

Ella licked her fork and looked thoughtful. "The fire was devastating to the Mayhews. They moved to Eastover and intended to rebuild but never did. The husband passed away about five years ago. Now, Mrs. Mayhew's living at a continuing care retirement home in Eastover called Gracious Home Senior Living." Ella gave them a shrewd look. "The Women's Guild ladies can spread unfounded rumors, but a lot of times they're dead right. They've heard Pearl Mayhew is making noises about moving in with her daughter and that property might go on the market." Ella gave Jenny a wicked grin. "How's that for reconnaissance from a one-hour Women's Guild meeting?"

"Top-notch snooping, Ella. Thank you for that." Jenny's appetite was gone, though, and she put down her fork. "When I talked with that awful man at the Register of Deeds office, he said another person was researching the property. Maybe the rumor about Mrs. Mayhew selling is true, and word is getting out."

"Could be." Luke's voice was quiet but steely. "If that's so, we'll need to talk with Mrs. Mayhew soon. We can only hope we get a chance to make our case before another person does."

On the drive home, the two of them talked about their best approach.

Luke was quiet for a few moments, but then looked over at her. "How about we call Mrs. Mayhew and just talk with her about it?"

Jenny stared moodily out the window at the passing lights of cars. "What if Mrs. Mayhew feels vulnerable, has a hearing problem, or gets confused by the call? My guess is that a call isn't the way to go."

Luke considered it and nodded his agreement. "A letter might be the best way to get this conversation started."

"That's what I think." Jenny looked over at him. "Neither of us wants Mrs. Mayhew to feel intimidated or manipulated, and if she has a letter she can run it by her children or attorney or a trusted friend."

"We both know I'm no good at writing." Luke shot her a questioning look. "Will you write the letter?"

Jenny groaned and scrubbed her face with her hands. "I will, but it's got to be the best letter I've ever written in my life. No pressure at all."

"You can do it, Jenny," Luke said with a reassuring nod.

Jenny shot him a doubtful look. Good thing one of them thought she could do it.

CHAPTER 13

THE NEXT DAY, THE EARLY morning mist was still rising off the water when Jenny sat down at the desktop. After two cups of a bold French roast, her brain was fresh and firing on all cylinders. Her elbow on the Formica table, Jenny rested her chin in her hand and thought hard about exactly what they wanted to say.

Closing her eyes to center herself, Jenny took several deep breaths in and out. When she felt clear, Jenny opened her eyes, and her fingers flew across the keyboard.

Dear Mrs. Mayhew,

My name is Jenny Beckett, and I own the property next to your beautiful property on Heron Lake. I got your name from my friend Ella Parr, whose husband recently retired as Chief Priest at your old church, All Saints Episcopal.

I understand you may have an interest in selling your property. If this is so, my fiancé, Luke, and I would like to talk with you about buying it.

Here is a little background on us. I inherited my property from my father, Jax Beckett. I'm not sure if you ever met Daddy, but he was a fine man. He had started building eight small rustic guest cabins on his land, but sadly, he passed away before he was able to finish. My fiancé, Luke, his sister, and I finished building the cabins. For over a year and a half now, I have been operating the cabins as a small and quiet resort here on Heron Lake.

After Luke and I marry in June, we'd like to expand the current resort to include eight additional small log cabins.

By way of introduction, here are several things you should know about us.

We are quiet people, and the resort is a tranquil place, not a party place. Guests come to read, hike, play board games, admire the lake, and reconnect with one another.

Family and friends are very important to me. My mama and stepdaddy live in one of our small cabins and help us run the resort. It means a lot to me to have them close by. Our friends have been of immeasurable help to us in restoring and running the resort.

I was an educator before I became an innkeeper. For many years, I worked as an academic tutor for middle school and high school students and enjoyed that work. (I love running the Lakeside Resort even better, though!)

Both Luke and I are nature lovers and animal lovers. Currently, we own two eighty-plus-pound rescue dogs and a spoiled miniature horse named Levi.

Luke is a general contractor and a can-do kind of guy. He has taught me a lot about building, construction, and home repair. I now have basic carpentry skills and am proud to say I can fix toilets, do basic wiring, and install hardwood floors.

Luke and I think your point has one of the most glorious views and prettiest sunsets of any property we've seen on the lake. We'd like to protect it and not let it get developed in a careless way.

May we set up a time to visit with you and discuss this? If you are open to talking with us, please invite your children, your attorney, or whomever you'd like to join us.

We so look forward to hearing from you.

Sincerely,

Jenny printed the letter in a 14-point font and carefully signed it. Under her signature, she neatly printed her phone number and email address. To cover all options, Jenny printed a self-addressed stamped envelope, folded it, and tucked it in the envelope. Whether it was by smoke signals, messenger pigeon, or the US Postal Service, however Pearl Mayhew wanted to communicate was fine by Jenny.

Rereading the letter twice, Jenny was pleased. The tone was direct, clear, and aboveboard. Pulling her photos up on her computer, she browsed around until she found one that Alice had taken of Jenny, Luke, and all the animals sitting on the dock. Jenny smiled, remembering that cold day. Their coats were sprinkled liberally with sawdust, Luke had green paint on his khakis, and the two were holding hands. They were both open-faced and laughing, flushed at the first stages of love, and punch-drunk from working so hard. Levi was leaning into her and Bear and Buddy were swarming around Luke. Jenny printed it and included it in the envelope. If Mrs. Mayhew wanted an accurate depiction of who they really were, the picture told the story.

Closing her eyes, Jenny rested her hands on the letter and sent up a quick prayer. *God, if it's your will, please deliver this land to us. We'd take good care of it and make sure it stays as pristine and extraordinary as you made it. Please, Daddy, if you're on this line, put in a good word for us. Amen.*

Jenny blew out a breath, satisfied she'd done the best she could do. If Luke liked the letter, they'd drive to Eastover and hand-deliver it to the front desk of Gracious Home Senior Living first thing tomorrow.

Her text sounded. Mama wrote:

Sweet girl, don't forget the cake tasting. I'll be by a little before noon. Landis tagging along. He's only in it for the cake. XOXO

Smiling, Jenny stood and stretched. The cake tasting would be fun, but she had work to do. She had cabins to clean, but first, she'd run the letter over to the Silver Belle where Luke was working to ready the camper for their long road trip. Today, he was installing things to keep food and supplies from flying out while the Belle was rolling down the road. Jenny poured a freshly brewed mug of coffee to take over to him.

The sun glinted off the shiny silver aluminum of the old Airstream, and Jenny appreciated its iconic beauty. The wind caressed her face as she remembered how rough a shape the camper had been in when she'd inherited it from Jax, who had never been big on maintenance. He treated the Silver Belle like an old hunting camp that wasn't worth fixing up.

Jenny stepped over a root, careful not to spill coffee. Luke had done a great job of fixing up the camper. Charlotte had pitched in, too. Using her design prowess, she had repainted the interior, reupholstered the couch, and generally fluffed up everything. The Silver Belle was in prime shape.

Jenny stepped inside. "Hey, buddy. Fresh coffee." She smiled and extended the mug.

Luke took the mug gratefully and sipped it. "Ah."

"Will you take a look at the letter?" Handing it to him, she breathed shallowly while he read.

Luke nodded slowly. "It's good. Honest, to the point, not slick. Just like us. We'll run it by tomorrow."

"Whew. Good." Jenny peered around curiously. "How's it going?"

"Check this out." Luke pointed at the wire mesh baskets he'd attached under the table, inside the cabinets and in the miniscule pantry. "I added content-securing bars in the refrigerator and put these drawers under the table, and I found these little babies online." With a flourish, he showed her a spice rack with clips and stacking plate organizers.

"So clever," Jenny said.

A knock sounded on the aluminum side, and a fellow poked his head in. "Good morning, I'm Pete. My wife Jill and I are staying in the Hydrangea."

"Good morning. Sorry about the noise," Luke said apologetically. "I'll keep it down."

The fellow held up both hands palms out. "You're not bothering us a bit. Jill's reading, happy as can be. I don't want to interrupt your work, but I did want to take a quick look. This Airstream is amazing. Did you do the fix-up, or was she in good shape when you bought her?"

"We renovated." Luke waved Pete in. "We patched the subflooring, shored up the frame, and put in new plumbing and electrical. The exterior had to be made watertight, the floors leveled, and the insulation replaced. Come see what we've done in the bathroom."

Pete whistled. "Great use of space. I like that shower…"

The men were so engrossed, they didn't even notice Jenny slip away. She just smiled as she headed home. Between the tiny log cabins and the vintage campers, the imaginative, the nostalgic, and the design buffs had a lot to look at here at the Lakeside Resort.

Around lunch time, Jenny took Luke a ham and Swiss sandwich she'd warmed in the oven and chatted with him companionably while he ate.

Glancing out the window, Jenny saw Mama and Landis walking toward the Dogwood. Jenny glanced at the time. It was 11:50. "Snap. The cake lady's going to be here any minute."

Unplugging power tools, the two closed up the Belle and walked quickly toward the cabin. "Hey, y'all. Come on in," Jenny called. As they drew closer, Jenny did a double take.

Looking determinedly blasé, Mama wore a turtleneck under a baggy floral zip-up house coat, black socks, and scuffed Keds. Claire sent Jenny a meaningful look, and cut her eyes at her husband, who wore a burgundy sweatshirt emblazoned with Cocky, the yellow-beaked mascot of the University of South Carolina. Landis's baggy pants were spattered with paint. He had gray stubble on his face, and his jaw was set as he took an athleisure-wear stand for retired men everywhere.

Jenny widened her eyes at Luke, who looked bewildered. Jenny guessed Mama's odd attire must be part of her goose-and-gander strategy. If Landis looked unkempt, Mama would too. Trouble all around.

Mama and Landis got situated while Luke changed out of his work clothes, and Jenny did a quick tidy-up. A car door slammed, and Jenny looked out the window. Wearing a ruby red car coat, a slim woman tossed back her tawny hair, grabbed an item from her car, and walked toward the house. She looked as classy as the models in the *Vogue* magazines that Jenny flipped through at her hair salon while waiting for Star. Then, Jenny recognized the familiar man-melting, hip-swiveling walk. "Ember," she gasped.

Mama joined her at the window. "Her bakery is called Harper's Heavenly Cakes." But she sensed Jenny's anxiety. "Who is Ember?"

"Ember is Luke's late wife's sister. She's always carried a torch for Luke," Jenny said grimly.

"Gracious." Mama put her hands on her cheeks.

Jenny turned to her mother and Landis. "Last time she was here she made a play for him right in front of me."

In clean jeans and a fresh collared shirt, Luke stepped away from the refrigerator with another half of a ham sandwich in his hand. "Ember's here? Why?"

Jenny swung open the door before Ember could knock. "Well, hello there. You remember me. I'm Jenny Beckett, Luke's fiancée."

Ember stuck out a manicured hand and gave her a limp handshake. "My goodness, it's a small world. I didn't even know I was bringing samples to you all until I plugged that address in my GPS and saw where I was headed. Good to see you again." Without invitation, she bustled inside, carrying a large pink-and-white striped cake carrier with the name *Harper's Heavenly Cakes* scrawled around the side in white.

"Come right in," Jenny muttered to no one, and rolled her eyes as she shut the door.

Ember's brows flew up as she took in Landis's and Mama's attire, but she quickly turned on the charm. "Claire, I can't believe you're Jenny's mama. I would have sworn you were her younger sister. And this big handsome man is your husband. Hello there, Landis." Ember's smile tightened when she got to Luke. The spigot for her charm got turned off. "Good to see you," she said coolly.

No bicep squeezing, eyelash fluttering, and full body embrace for Luke like last time.

Jenny hid a smirk. Ember's ardor for Luke had died when she'd learned he was poor. No money, no honey.

"Hey, Ember." Luke raised a hand and polished off the rest of his sandwich.

Jenny gazed at the woman. "I expected a baker named Harper."

Looking irritated, Ember pointed to herself. "That's my name, Ember Harper. John Dale bought the bakery for me for Christmas. I *do* love to bake, and he thought it'd give me something to do with my time." A flush crept up her face, and her eyes darted around the room.

There was a story there, Jenny thought as she settled in on the couch close to Luke.

"Sorry about your little...business reversal, Luke." Ember's voice dripped with sympathy. "These things happen, though, and you've got to get back up, brush yourself off, and soldier on."

Luke rubbed his chin. "What reversal is that, Ember?' he asked politely, languidly crossing one long leg over the other.

"Why your little...bankruptcy," she said sotto voce. "Your losing the business and having to deliver newspapers on your bike to make ends meet."

"Oh. Huh." Luke pinched the bridge of his nose and gazed steadily at Jenny with a look Ricky would have given Lucy after a crazy stunt.

Both Mama and Landis were quiet, sensing the undercurrents. Landis pulled out his phone and pretended to scroll importantly. Mama excused herself to go to the bathroom, mouthing *I'm sorry* to Jenny over the top of Ember's head.

Rats jumping ship, Jenny decided grimly. No family member would even make eye contact long enough for her to give them a dirty look. "We just don't like to talk about that money pickle." Jenny gave what she hoped was a brave look.

Luke scratched his chin.

"Well, I can bake a cake for the budget-minded bride," Ember said brightly. "I can use day-old cakes from the shop. No one can really tell, although they can be a bit dry."

"That is so kind of you, Ember," Jenny said sweetly. "But Mama and I must have gotten our signals crossed. You see, I'm baking my own wedding cake. It's so much more economical, and nothing says 'love' like a cake you baked with your own two hands." Jenny cringed inwardly as she heard her own fatuous prattle, but better than having Ember bake her a cake with antifreeze in the icing.

"Oh, pooh. I understand the tight purse strings, but I'm so disappointed." Ember actually stuck out her lush pink lower lip and pouted but regained her composure. "Anyhoo," she said with a world-weary sigh. She pressed a stack of business cards in Jenny's hand. "Please give my business cards to any of your guests who decide to hold their wedding here." Glancing around the small cabin, she wrinkled her nose. "Such a darling, teeny-tiny spot. Affordable though, I'm sure."

"I had a good paper route. That helped," Luke said gravely.

"Ah." Ember smiled nervously.

"How's John Dale doing?" Luke called out.

"Busy, busy, busy." Ember did not meet his eyes. She wore a look like she'd caught a whiff of a casserole that had been left in the fridge a few days too long.

"What's John Dale working on?" Luke asked.

"Oh, he's trying to buy a piece of land for a big new condo development. It's just right up the road from here." She pointed airily north, south, west, and east. "Condos on a point,"

Widening her eyes, Ember put a hand over her mouth and giggled. "Whoopsie. I'm not supposed to share things like that. You didn't hear that from me."

"Hear what?" Jenny said gamely and smiled tightly, but her heart starting to gallop. Was John Dale the one sniffing around and trying to buy Mrs. Mayhew's lot for one of his luxury condo developments? Jenny stood suddenly. "Well, we've wasted enough of your time, Ember."

The blonde rose and gathered her purse and cake carrier. "Sorry it didn't work out with the cake. Maybe another time," she said hopefully.

"Of course," Jenny said silkily holding up the stack of business cards like they were bars of gold bullion. When pigs fly.

"Well, I'll be praying for you." Ember swiveled out the door.

After she'd gone, Jenny leaned her back against the door dramatically. "Whew."

Luke rocked back on his heels. "I didn't realize I'd lost everything to bankruptcy and had a paper route."

Jenny gave a sheepish grin. "I forgot to tell you. While you were in Australia, Alice and your mama decided Ember was a gold digger who wanted to get her hooks into you. They told her that your businesses had gone under and you'd had to file for bankruptcy."

"Glad I overcame that setback," Luke said mildly.

Mama emerged from her prolonged stay in the bathroom, red-faced with embarrassment.

"I am so sorry, Jenny. All I knew was that she was a woman starting a new business a little later in life. It made me think of you when you first came to the resort."

"You meant well," Jenny assured her.

"Sorry I was no help. I panicked." Landis gave a guilty hound dog grin. He put his hand on the small of Claire's back and led her to the door. "Let's skedaddle, honey bun. These young people need to sort out a few things."

Jenny and Luke flopped down on the sofa side by side. Luke draped an arm across her shoulder.

Covering her face with her hands, Jenny thought about the beans Ember had spilled about John Dale's plans for a condo development. No other points were nearby. He had to be planning to build next door. Rubbing the back of her neck, Jenny could picture all the trees being cleared. Their wooded views would be gone, and they'd see an asphalt parking lot. The bluebirds would leave when the forest was gone. Boat traffic, noise, and hubbub were part of the deal with a large community boat dock. Her breathing grew shallow as Jenny started to get panicky. Expensive cars would glide constantly up and down their quiet little road.

Jenny fixed Luke with a stare. "If John Dale is trying to get his hands on the land next door, he'll ruin the Lakeside Resort. He'll set a precedent for dense, view-blocking, traffic-causing development on the lake." Jenny's hands were clammy and her heart was slamming. "We'll start a petition. We'll go to the county commissioners or the newspaper or the governor or…" Jenny tossed her hands up, out of ideas.

"Let's take it one step at a time." Luke squinted off into the distance. "First thing, let's drive to Eastover and deliver that fine letter you wrote to Mrs. Mayhew. Then, all we can do is hope and pray she hasn't already signed a deal with John Dale."

CHAPTER 14

MONDAY MORNING, JENNY OVERSLEPT. SHE'D had a fitful night's sleep worrying about the land next door. Drowsily, she glanced at the time and jumped out of bed. It was already seven, and Charlotte was coming soon to pick her up and take her for round two of dress shopping.

As she dried her hair, Jenny reread the text Charlotte had sent yesterday.

Monday, we're going to A TOP SECRET AND UNDISCLOSED LOCATION to find your wedding dress. Already talked w/your Mama about covering resort. Pick you up at eight. Cheerful, positive attitude, please. XO

Charlotte had also inserted emojis of a wedding ring, a bouquet, and a little bride and groom. As she put clips in her hair, Jenny gave herself a talking to about having a good attitude.

Feeling peppier, Jenny did a few quick chores while she kept an eye out the window for Charlotte's car. After she'd thoroughly cleaned and refilled the new stainless-steel pet water fountain she'd bought the boys, she heard car wheels on the gravel drive. Pulling back the curtain, she broke into a smile when she saw the small turquoise-blue hybrid that belonged to Luke's sister Alice, who was one of her closest friends. Alice grinned from the driver's seat, and Charlotte was laughing in the passenger seat. Both women waved wildly from lowered windows.

Grabbing her jacket and purse, Jenny hurried outside and put both hands on her head, laughing delightedly. "One good friend is lucky, but two is a jackpot." Leaning in the driver's side window, she bussed Alice's cheek and blew a kiss to Charlotte. After choosing the side of the back seat without the baby car seat, Jenny buckled in, grinning. "It's a good day already," she announced.

"It's getting even better," Charlotte said with a mischievous smile, and held up a paper bag. "We picked up still-warm baked goodies from *Posy's Sweet Shop*. Do you want a glazed pecan Danish, a chocolate brioche, or a raspberry-ginger muffin?"

"Yes, please," Jenny said in a ladylike tone.

"I thought you'd say that." Charlotte passed around paper napkins and pastries. "I got us extras of each."

As Alice steered toward the main road, she took a bite of her muffin and patted her mouth with a napkin. "Oh, I've missed you all and missed normal life."

"We need to hear every little bit about what's new with you, little mama." Charlotte smiled fondly at Alice.

"How's my goddaughter, Cherry?" Jenny mumbled, sprinkling a few crumbs on her coat.

"Cherry's a little firecracker. She's smart, exuberant, and adorable." Pushing back lank hair that looked a day or two past the due date for washing, Alice stifled a yawn. "For the first few months, all she did was cry, sleep, eat, and poo." She hesitated. "I'm going to tell you a secret, and you must swear on your mama's Bible that you'll never tell another soul. Mike knows, but no one else can know."

"We swear." Charlotte nibbled on a muffin and peered expectantly at Alice.

"Spill, sister," Jenny said.

Alice shot them hard looks to make sure they were in agreement. "I did not like Cherry that much in the beginning. All that business about the instant love and the mother's bond just did not happen for me." Looking guilty, she went on, her words coming out in a rush. "We were just so tired, and it seemed like the baby's wants were just endless."

"All that on top of that hard pregnancy, too," Jenny said sympathetically.

"I remember hearing about this, Al. You couldn't stop..." Charlotte trailed off delicately but made a whirling hand movement under her chin to indicate throwing up.

Alice shuddered theatrically at the memory. "The good news is that I'm finally starting to feel the way

I should. I am finally falling in love with my baby. Our sleep schedule is improving; Mike has been a soldier, and Cherry is starting to turn into this little person. She's real interested in my face now, and pulls my nose and my eyebrows." Alice gave them a wry smile. "All the books say she's too young for facial expressions that mean anything more than passing emotions or gas. But I swear she's giving us these little looks now, like she's tickled pink or just fascinated about everything."

"My goddaughter is advanced. She's probably gifted and talented," Jenny said smugly.

"I saw Cherry just this morning, and she's the smartest, prettiest little baby girl ever."

Charlotte bobbed her head as if it were a fact.

"We think so." Alice gave them each grateful looks. "I'm so glad I told you about not exactly bonding with Cherry. I was afraid you'd think I'm a terrible person."

"We'd never think that, no matter what you told us," Charlotte said staunchly.

"I'm still sleep-deprived, and my baby weight is sticking around for the near future." Alice made a face. "But all in all, I'm happy. And I'm so, so, so happy that Mike's keeping Cherry so I could get out with you gals." Alice held up a finger. "I want to hear all y'all's news but wanted to warn you that one of you may need to drive us home. I'm prone to sudden, hard naps. Not good behind the wheel."

"We've got you covered," Jenny assured her.

"Now, fill me in on every little thing. Charlotte, you've got the floor first, then my soon-to-be sister-in-law," Alice demanded, sounding like her old bossy self. "Details, people. I need details."

And the two women filled her in.

Alice's jaw had dropped when Jenny told her about Ember's offer to bake their wedding cake. "She'd have put Ex-Lax in the chocolate frosting."

"Luke had not heard that story about his losing all his money," Jenny said serenely.

"You told Luke about his paper route? I may have embellished and said he only had a small bike with a banana seat and sissy handlebars." Alice's mouth twitched with amusement.

Jenny giggled. "Ember looked at him like he was muck she'd stepped in and gotten on her shoe."

The three women cackled and finally wound down.

"Am I allowed to know where we're going?" Jenny watched Alice take an exit for downtown Asheville.

"All will be revealed, my little cricket," Alice said in a mysterious tone.

"It's *grasshopper*, not *cricket*," Jenny muttered, but the two women in the front ignored her.

"All right. I'll tell you since we're almost here," Charlotte announced. "Here's a clue. It's my favorite store in the whole world."

"*Flights of Fancy Thrifty Antiques*," Jenny guessed, reminding herself to be open-minded.

"That tobacco warehouse where you got married." Alice looked delighted. "I was so sorry to miss that wedding, but..." she broke off.

"But you were busy upchucking." Charlotte repeated her hand twirl under her chin.

"True. The pics and video were amazing, though." Alice looked in the rearview mirror to catch Jenny's eyes. "Now, tell me more about your wedding plans."

"Let's see," Jenny said. "We're holding it at the resort. We've not taken any bookings for that entire week so a few out-of-town folks can stay on the property. Your mama and daddy have offered a few bedrooms for overflow, and there's always the Budget Nights Motel up the road."

"Exciting." Alice glanced back at Jenny.

"So, we're looking at vintage wedding gowns today," Charlotte announced.

"It's worth a look." Jenny had her doubts, though. She pictured a prissy high-necked dress with leg-of-mutton sleeves, a Dynasty-era gown with shoulder pads like defensive tackles wore, and all the other yellowing castoffs. Would there be the faint whiff of failure in the fabric of the dresses worn in the one in three marriages that ended in divorce? Jenny shuddered involuntarily, gripped by her old fears about weddings and commitment and men who always leave.

Jenny must have gone quiet for a few moments because Charlotte turned around in her seat to scrutinize

Jenny, waving her hands in front of her face. "Cut it out, Jen. I can tell by that look on your face that you're getting worried about marrying. This one is sticking. You picked a stellar guy."

"Except for the girly bike he rides," Alice interjected and sped up to pass a pokey driver.

Charlotte ignored her. "Luke loves you to pieces. He will never leave you. This marriage *will* work. Now, get those thoughts gone." She lowered her window, and Alice did the same. They both made sweeping motions with their hands toward the open window.

"Shoo, bad thoughts," Alice said.

Cold air rushed in Jenny's face, and she broke into a smile "Thanks. I needed that."

"Good." Alice's window hummed back up. "Happy thoughts, happy day, and happy bride."

Walking briskly, Charlotte pulled open the twenty-foot-tall doors of *Flights of Fancy Thrifty Antiques* as if she owned the place. Pausing, she inhaled deeply. "I adore that smell of old wood, beeswax, and a hint of tobacco."

After hugs and kisses with the owner, Charlotte led them through the store past the old oak moonshine barrels from Johnston County and the cut-off front end of an old red Bel Air that a hip person would probably mount on the wall of a loft.

Jenny kept pausing to look at items, and Charlotte kept pulling her on. "We're burning daylight."

"This place is a wonderland." Alice's head swiveled back and forth, not wanting to miss a thing.

At the very back of the store, Jenny saw a room with a fuchsia glittery sign above it that read, *The Bodacious Bridal Cave*. "Mother of pearl," Jenny breathed as she stared wide-eyed at the large room that was filled wall-to-wall with wedding dresses that were arranged by decade and labeled with smaller glittery fuchsia signs. There was The Sweet but Rocking Fifties, The Groovy Sixties, The Swinging and Suave Seventies, The Go-Go Eighties, and The Namaste Nineties.

"We're the only customers back here." Charlotte waved an arm around the room. "No sale types stalking us. No roving girl gangs of bridesmaids like at the *Bridal Dress Barn*."

"Perfect." Jenny tilted her head, examining dresses, feeling a blossoming hope. Maybe vintage would work for her.

Alice grabbed a shopping cart as Jenny eyed the crinoline-skirted ivory number from the Sweet but Rocking Fifties section. Why not? She'd give it a whirl. Alice grabbed several dresses from the Groovy Sixties and Charlotte fisted a hand on her hip as she whipped through dresses in the Go-Go Eighties. Soon her cart was brimming with frothy dresses. Jenny peeled off her clothes in the dressing room, feeling a flutter of excitement that she'd not felt in any of the stores they'd visited in Charlotte.

Her two friends sat in two blue velvet slipper chairs and called out ratings for the dresses Jenny modeled. "I'd give that a nine," Alice called. "You look demure and stacked. Men love that."

It was a gorgeous dress. Jenny tugged up the neckline. Would well-placed safety pins keep it from being so va-va-va-voom? No need to give the wedding guests a peep show, though.

The silky, bias-cut slip dress was too revealing in a different way. This one revealed figure flaws. Though the cut and fabric were flattering, the dress showcased every bump, dimple, and roll. Why had she eaten that chocolate brioche *and* the muffin?

Charlotte pursed her lips. "Seven. That dress isn't working hard enough for you."

"Four. Poor fit," Alice chimed in and tried on a wedding headpiece-veil combo that looked like Napoleon Bonaparte's hat. Turning her head this way and that, she admired herself in the mirrors. "I look hot."

Next, Jenny modeled a Victorian-looking dress with puffy sleeves.

Charlotte gave her an appraising look. "Five. Too much like Mary Poppins."

"I agree." Alice donned a fascinator with a small-scale bird cage on it. "Work it, girl," she said, pouting exaggeratedly and snapping her fingers as she gazed at her reflection.

The slim-fitting column dress with the portrait collar

and the miniskirted dress with the lace bodice both got low scores from the judges.

Wriggling into the last dress on the 'Possibilities' hook, Jenny slipped on the white ball gown with the immense skirt she could wear to a dance at Tara. She flounced out of the dressing room and held up a hand. "I know it's bad. No scores please."

"Okay," Alice said. She was wearing a tall tiara with an elaborate floaty veil. Trying to lighten the mood, she draped the crinoline over her face. "Handy if the mosquitos are bad."

"Nothing is working." Jenny slumped onto the velvet bench beside her friends, holding down the bell skirt that kept popping up. "I am never going to find a dress that I love." She rubbed the bridge of her nose, fighting tears.

"Let's take a break." Charlotte jumped up. "There's a drink machine in the other room. We need caffeine and a new game plan." With a determined glint in her eye, she trotted off.

"Maybe we need to rethink everything." Alice squinted as she stared off into space.

"You're hard to take seriously, wearing that thing on your head," Jenny groused.

"Sorry." Alice slipped off the tiara and veil.

Charlotte returned with cold drinks. The three of them were silent as Jenny and Charlotte sipped their Diet Pepsi, and Alice swallowed her bottled water.

Charlotte gazed at Jenny. "My favorite blogger from

My Phenomenal Fluffy Life is in her mid-fifties. She wanted to marry again but had almost given up on finding a husband. She started visualizing her perfect husband every morning, from his red-brown hair to his big smile and his nice eyes. She did this for two months, prayed, and sent positive energy out into the universe." Charlotte raised her hands in the air and wiggled her fingers, demonstrating the energy-sending.

Jenny listened politely. Although she usually liked Charlotte's original thinking, this morning she was too disheartened for woo-woo talk.

Alice sent Jenny a *where is she going with this* look.

Charlotte's face was animated as her story unfolded. "Then, her luck changed. Her pipes froze, broke, and flooded her house."

"That is lucky," Alice said drily.

Charlotte pretended to not hear her. "The plumber she called was a ginger with chocolate brown eyes and a smile that melted her heart." She threw up her hands. "Just like that, they fell in love, married two months later, and are happy as can be." Looking proud of herself, she took a big swig of soda.

Jenny touched a spot on her temple, not tracking with Charlotte. "Luke might get mad if I found another husband."

Alice broke into a smile. "Charlotte, you can come at things sideways, but you're a smarty. Visualizing is a great idea." She turned to Jenny. "Girl, will you please close your eyes and take deep breaths."

Too tired to argue, Jenny leaned her head back against the wall, shut her eyes, and deepened her breathing.

In a soothing, calm tone, Alice began. "Now, it's the morning of June 20th, your wedding day. You're feeling elated because you're gazing at the perfect wedding dress. Wearing the dress makes you feel beautiful, hopeful, calm, and comfortable. What do you imagine the dress looks like?"

Fighting the feeling that this was hokey, Jenny realized she was indeed picturing the morning of her wedding and feeling thrilled about her dress. Blowing out another deep breath, she let herself be in her cabin, seeing the dress. "It's tea length, floral, fitted, and elegant."

"Anything else you see?" Alice asked in that dreamy tone.

Now, Jenny could actually picture herself wearing it. "It's got blues and greens in it, just like the color of the lake."

"Good," Alice said in a matter-of-fact tone. "You can open your eyes."

Blinking open her eyes, Jenny looked at her friends and broke into a grin. "I can't believe it, but I think that worked."

Beaming, Charlotte jumped up and pointed to another annex that Jenny hadn't even noticed. It was full of bridesmaids' dresses, evening gowns, and cocktail dresses. "Come on, ladies. The hunt is on."

That afternoon, Jenny was at the wheel of Alice's hybrid as they motored back to Heron Lake. Charlotte was beside her in the passenger seat, texting Ashe and giggling like a preteen girl when Ashe texted back.

"I'm just sending him emojis now," Charlotte announced. "Let's see. A heart, a rose, a darling chicken, a cupcake, and a ladybug." She tapped away happily and hooted with laughter when she read his response.

With a half-smile, Jenny just shook her head at their lovey-dovey antics.

Alice was sprawled in the back seat, mouth open, snoring like a chainsaw. Jenny eyed the gown hung carefully on the hook beside her friend and pictured that amazing vintage blue and green floral print dress with the sweetheart neckline and slightly poufy skirt. It was charming, retro, and summery, and she'd found it just minutes after picturing it.

Now, Charlotte phoned Ashe. "I'll be home soon, you big hunka love. Yes, my snuggy- buggy-wuggy, pookie-wookie." Ending the call, Charlotte giggled softly as she slipped her phone in the pocket of her purse.

Jenny pretended to stick a finger down her throat and made a retching sound. "You two are the mushiest newlyweds. I mean it."

"Isn't it divine?" Charlotte gave her a sappy smile.

"It is," Jenny agreed. As the busy city roads turned

into tree-lined two lanes, she thought about how patient and determined Charlotte had been in the dress hunt. "Thank you, girly girl. Couldn't have done it without you."

"I feel honored to help." Charlotte hooked a thumb at Alice sprawled in the back seat. "I know sleeping beauty feels the same way, too."

CHAPTER 15

WHEN JENNY GOT HOME THAT evening, she carefully slipped her tissue-paper-wrapped find into her very small closet, squishing back neighboring clothes to keep them from wrinkling the dress. Still high from her success, Jenny pulled on comfy elastic-waist shorts and Luke's well-worn old Cabin Masters T-shirt and blew out a breath. Mission accomplished.

The day had been so busy that she hadn't had a chance to check her email every two minutes or stare at her phone and hope it rang. Though they'd only dropped off the letter two days ago, not hearing from Mrs. Mayhew was nerve-racking.

With all that had gone on, Jenny was ready for a quiet evening at home by herself. With the help of Alice's husband, Mike, Luke was helping his parents move their bedroom from the second floor of their home to the first floor to make it easier for Frank to get around. Luke being gone suited Jenny fine.

A bowl of veggie lasagna she'd baked and frozen last weekend whirled around defrosting in the microwave. Jennie poured herself a glass of wine and sat at the computer, pulling up the Etsy sites she'd found that sold wedding attire for animals. The blue-and-green striped tuxedo bow-tie collars would look sharp on Bear and Buddy, and the bright blue halter embroidered with entwined wedding rings would be dashing on Levi. The entire wedding party would be color-coordinated.

Her curser hovering over Pay Now, Jenny hesitated and did more searching. Garland, her concrete goose, also needed snazzy wedding clothes. Ah. Leaning forward, she clicked on the small black cutaway tuxedo with the green cummerbund and the jaunty goose-sized top hat. Perfect. Jenny grinned as she put it in her basket. Luke might be dressed more casually for the wedding, but Garland would be dressed to the nines. After that purchase, Jenny had a thought and began clicking around determinedly. Garland needed a bride. Her goose was a good man, a sharp dresser, and faithful. There was no way a guy like that should be lonely.

Jenny could not sleep that night. She'd bought a relaxation app that Charlotte had recommended and gave it a try. Breathing deeply enough that Bear looked worried, Jenny really tried to get into *Guided Meditation for an Easy, Dreamy Sleep.* The narrator's impassive, droning voice just gave her the creeps, and she did not want to *walk down a ladder* or *slowly count backward.*

Jenny gave up and tried to read, but couldn't get into the plots of the three books she tried. Off went the light, and she tried again to sleep but kept tossing from one side of the bed to the other so frequently that Bear huffed an aggrieved sigh. *"You* are sleeping on *my* bed," Jenny reminded him, but he just yawned hugely and stretched his legs out even longer. After midnight, Jenny gave up, turned on the television, and found the *Andy Griffith Show*. This was comfort TV, she decided and quickly became engrossed. Andy and Barney caught the dangerous fugitive on the loose even though the state guys thought the Mayberry deputies were hayseeds. Jenny laughed out loud and started to relax as Aunt Bea kept giving Andy and Barney jars of the pickles that neither of them wanted. Next, she watched an episode of *Homestead Rescue,* a show she loved. Finally, Jenny drifted off to sleep.

Jenny had trouble feeling perky the next morning, still tired from her restless night. She and Mama had the planning meeting for the Special Populations weekend at eleven and she needed her wits about her. Fixing herself a hearty breakfast of a hard-boiled egg and a bowl of oatmeal, Jenny felt marginally more alert and decided fresh air would clear her head. Jenny would leave the phone at the cabin so she wouldn't feel compelled to constantly check it. Stupid phone. Calling the boys, Jenny headed out for a long walk around the lake.

After hiking a trail Jenny knew was two and a half miles, they headed home. Jenny felt more energetic and the muscles in her legs burned in a good way. As she glugged a glass of cold water, she couldn't help but glance at her phone. Jenny's heart leapt in her throat, and she felt breathless. She had a new voice mail message, and it was from a number in their area code. Her hand shaking, she listened.

Good morning. This is Pearl Mayhew, and I'm leaving word for a Miss Jenny Beckett. I'm visiting family in Wilmington for a few days. When I get back to Eastover, I'll be in touch. Thank you and have a good day.

Jenny held the phone in her hand and thought about it. The woman's voice was crisp and intelligent, and her Southern drawl was pronounced. This was no doddering older woman. Feeling equal parts elation and worry that Mrs. Mayhew had been in touch, Jenny leaned back against the sink, questions running through her head. Was this call a bad sign or a good sign? Her gut told her that Mrs. Mayhew wouldn't have called if she had no interest at all in talking with them. But maybe she was old school and polite, and felt it was good manners to respond to a letter, especially since they had the All Saints connection and Jenny was a neighbor. Maybe Mrs. Mayhew was going to break the news to her that their new neighbor was building a mega-development. Jenny rubbed her forehead with her fingers. She was back on the hamster wheel of worry. Squaring her shoulders, Jenny made a decision. She'd let Luke know of the new development, but then she was going to get on with her day and try not to dwell on it.

By ten, the West Virginia boys were drinking Mountain Dew and coffee and working hard on setting logs on the concrete foundation. Jenny was happy to be driving away from the cacophony of construction, the pop-pop-pop of nail guns, the screech of power saws, banging hammers, and the loud voices of eight men working. She turned to her mother, who looked serene as she pulled a knitting project from her large purse and studied it. "The noise is getting to me," Jenny grumbled.

"I know, sweetheart. It won't last forever, and the end result will be splendid." Mama quietly clicked away on the scarf she'd started.

"I've got a lot of folks coming in this weekend and am worried the noise will disturb them. You really can't hear it well from your cabin?" Jenny pictured angry guests stomping out of their cabins with hands over their ears and frazzled mothers trying to hush crying babies.

"You can't hear much at all. The logs on those cabins are so big and thick, I think that helps," Claire reassured her, adjusting her glasses and peering at her stitches.

Her mother was probably being kind, but Jenny let herself be reassured. The Dogwood was closest to the site for the new cabin, so most of the noise was outside her door. Jenny had also explicitly told every guest who'd booked for this spring and summer about the construction. When she'd explained that she was getting married, needed a bigger house, and would take 10 percent off their nightly rate for their inconvenience, all but two couples agreed to keep their bookings.

Jenny had also been touched by the flood of cards, emails, and texts of congratulations and mazel tovs that she'd received from guests. Returning guests or guests who were referred by happy customers were the best. They tended to be kind people.

"Try to think about the racket as the sound of progress. That's what you did when those nice men were working on building that curvy, smooth walkway out front," Mama reminded her.

"You're right." Jenny lowered the window a bit and let herself enjoy the drive. It was a perfect Carolina spring day with bright sunshine, mild temperatures, and the heady scent of honeysuckle in the air. The purple redbuds were blooming their hearts out.

At the Lake County Library, Lily smiled as she approached and hugged them both. "Welcome, welcome, welcome," she said in a lilting tone.

Wearing a pale blue paisley tunic, leggings, and flats, the librarian's skin glowed, and she looked relaxed and happy. Love was becoming to her. Jenny gave herself a mental pat on the back for matchmaking Lily with Tom, the manager of Luke's family's hardware store.

"It's so quiet in here," Jenny said appreciatively.

Lily gave a rueful laugh. "It wasn't fifteen minutes ago. You just missed the chaos of Storytime. The children learned songs about Earth Day and spring and made flower costumes." She threw up her hands and chuckled. "There was a spring flower parade for the other patrons' enjoyment. The daisy got into a fight with a daffodil about their place in line, and there was kicking and pushing. Those flowers can be mean." Lily linked one arm in Jenny's and the other in Claire's and walked toward the small conference room. "The others just got here, and I invited Winnie Wright from Carolina Autism Spectrum Services to make sure we are on track. Winnie is the wife of one of our board members and a Friend of the Library."

The conference room buzzed with energetic conversation. Charlotte gave her and Mama a twinkling smile and a finger wave. She was busy passing around a box of pastries from *Posy's Sweet Shop*. Astor was talking quietly with the man beside her, but her eyes lit up when she saw Jenny. Mama chatted more with Lily and fixed herself a cup of tea.

Excusing herself, Astor hurried over to greet her and gave her an unexpectedly warm hug. The two stepped outside the conference room to talk more privately.

"How *are* you?" Jenny asked. Astor looked open-faced and softer.

"I'm doing better than I have in I don't know how long." Astor gave a half-smile as she pushed back a lock of gleaming blonde hair. "I'm well on the way to being a single lady, and I'm so relieved about it."

"Good." Jenny had talked and texted with Astor several times since the woman's hard weekend at the resort, and Astor and Charlotte were becoming fast friends. "I'm a little surprised at how well-behaved Trey has been during the divorce."

"The upside about divorcing a narcissist is that they are obsessed with keeping their images spotless and shiny. I was prepared to not play nice and tell every soul I knew and perfect strangers about the cheating." Astor gave a wicked smile. "Did you know you can record a FaceTime conversation?"

"You didn't," Jenny gasped, impressed with her friend's resourcefulness.

"I did." Astor shrugged. "I don't know what made me think to record that call with the woman in the hotel room, but I did. It's not admissible, but what if it accidentally got leaked?" Astor put a finger on her chin and gave a look of wide-eyed innocence.

Jenny burst out laughing. "Remind me to stay on your good side."

Astor glanced at her jeweled watch. "We need to get started."

"Thanks for organizing this with Charlotte, Astor. I didn't know how to start," Jenny admitted. "You two are going to need to run with this because I'll be away almost right up to the weekend of the event."

"Gotcha. Charlotte and I make a good team. I'm starting a career in this field, and this gives me more experience," Astor said proudly and patted her arm. The two went back into the conference room.

Jenny slid into a chair beside Mama. A woman with a scarf braided through tumbling gray curls gave Jenny a warm smile and leaned across the table to shake their hands. "So pleased to meet you all. I'm Winnie Wright, and I'm tickled to pieces that you're going to host this."

"It's a team effort." Jenny swept an arm around to the others in the room. "But we're excited. Nervous, too. I'm so glad you're here to lend a hand."

"Happy to help," the woman said with a reassuring smile.

The group quieted, and Jenny stood. "Good morning. Thanks to all of you for coming today to help us plan this special weekend for individuals with autism and their families. Let's keep this informal. Winnie Wright is here from Carolina Autism Spectrum Services, a nonprofit that serves clients on the autism spectrum such as direct caregiver services, job coaching, support for families, and advocacy. Maybe we could begin with her giving us a brief overview of what life is like for her clients on the spectrum."

"Of course." Winnie nodded graciously and stood. "Autism spectrum Ddsorder is a condition characterized by difficulty with communication, understanding social relationships, and building friendships. The symptoms can be mild to severe. Many people on the spectrum are very high functioning and are indiscernible from individuals not on the spectrum. Many are married, have families, and have rewarding work as doctors, researchers, engineers, and all sorts of other professions. Others are more profoundly affected by the disorder and have more limited abilities. Many have challenges cognitively, developmentally, or emotionally. This is the group my agency works with." She looked around the room. "All of the individuals we serve have a lot to offer, want to lead full lives, and want to be contributing members of their communities." Winnie smiled at each of them. "So, that's why I was so excited to hear about the weekend you're planning at Heron Lake."

Winnie held up three fingers. "For our clients, there are three big challenges in making the transition to adulthood. One, they need to find a network of friends. If they lack the interpersonal skills, don't *get* social cues, and their living situation doesn't make it easy to meet others, it can be hard to make and deepen friendships. Many of our folks don't drive, so they can't hop in the car and buzz over to meet a new friend for coffee or a movie."

Pausing, Winnie took a swallow of water. "Two, folks need to find work they like and that suits them. They need to learn and build workplace skills. We still don't have enough employers who understand the value of recruiting for neurodiversity. If any of you own businesses or are married to spouses who own businesses and want to learn more about how to make use of the skills, conscientiousness, and work ethic of our folks on the spectrum, call me." With a thumb and baby finger, Winnie held an imaginary phone to her ear and grinned.

Jenny scribbled notes madly.

Winnie went on. "Three, if they're capable, they need to find a living situation that works for them. It could be independent living, supported living, group homes, or living with family. We don't have enough quality group homes. We don't have enough housing options in general, though organizations like churches and Habitat for Humanity are making inroads with this. If individuals are capable of more, they don't want to sit on their parents' couch for the rest of their lives."

Jenny tentatively raised a hand. "What about a tiny house community? Would that be a possibility?"

Winnie bobbed her head enthusiastically. "That's a great idea and one that we're looking into. We need the organization and the money to back that kind of residential option, and we need to find the right builder." Glancing around to see if there were any more questions, Winnie held up both hands and grinned. "That's all I have to say. I'm going to turn this over to Charlotte and Astor, who have done preliminary planning. They can get us up to speed on what they're cooking up."

Charlotte was midway through a gulp of coffee and began to cough and sputter. She pointed to Astor. "She's the point person here," she choked out.

Looking confident, Astor spoke up. "So, we're going to offer this camping weekend for the clients who have the most challenges. I've talked to each of you, and we're going to focus on two outcomes. Let's give everyone a break from their regular routine and have fun. Let's give the parents a chance to get ideas and support from each other, but stay focused on positives."

Everyone around the table nodded their approval.

Astor continued. "Here's what we've got so far. Jenny and Luke are giving us a big Friends and Family reduction on the nightly rate for the weekend. We'll have the whole resort to ourselves. Winnie has come up with a list of people who might reap great benefits from the weekend."

"We could fill this weekend ten times over," Winnie said with a wry smile.

"Two of the parents own an Italian restaurant in Eastover and would like to donate pizzas for the campers on Friday night. Jenny, Luke, Landis, and Claire are providing the rest of the meals," Charlotte added.

Astor gave Winnie Wright a grateful look. "Carolina Autism Spectrum Services have graciously offered to have four of their trained caregivers join the campers during the day and help lead activities. This will give the parents a break."

"We're happy to help." Winnie clasped her hands together and looked at Astor. "I hear you're getting back in this field. I can write a reference letter that will knock the socks off of a prospective employer."

"I'd like that." Astor grinned and glanced at her notes.

"In terms of activities for the campers, all of us have talked, and we came up with these ideas. We'll leave unstructured time, of course, but how about corn-hole, board games, and a hike with Ranger Emory? Lily has volunteered to lead yoga and meditation classes for the campers and parents. Landis and Luke are taking folks boating and fishing. Any other ideas?" she asked.

Charlotte raised a hand. "My husband goes to all these mayor conferences where they use icebreakers to help people get to know each other. Maybe we could find fun ones that would make it easy for the campers and the parents to talk with each other."

"I like that idea a lot," Jenny said.

"I agree." Winnie bobbed her head.

Mama chimed in. "Can we call it a name other than the Special Populations weekend?" Taking off her readers, she glanced around at the others. "I know that's what it is, but it doesn't sound...well, friendly."

"You are so right, Claire," Charlotte said, pointing at her.

Mama tilted her head, looking thoughtful. "If the emphasis is friendship, fellowship, and fun, how about Lake Buddies? The Lake Buddies weekend."

The others smiled at each other and chimed in with their approval.

"Lake Buddies it is." Astor looked around the table, suddenly looking vulnerable and unsure of herself. "I think that about wraps it up. How does this all sound to you?"

Jenny slowly began to clap, Charlotte chimed in, and soon everyone was applauding.

The Lake Buddies weekend was off to a great start.

CHAPTER 16

J ENNY AND LUKE SPENT THE next day doing spring and summer chores and readying the property for the wedding. Jenny changed the bedding at the cabins and camper, trading heavier coverlets for lighter ones. Luke took the Weed eater to overgrown patches and banks, and directed the fellows delivering mulch to dump piles in the right spots to make it easy to spread.

The two of them hauled the boat out of the water at the put-in and trailered it home. Luke checked oil levels, the condition of the battery, the propeller, and the fuel level. As they worked together washing the boat and cleaning the interior, Jenny realized that chores didn't seem like work when she was doing them with Luke.

Midafternoon, the master gardener who had designed their landscaping plan pulled up in her truck. Jenny was buzzing with exuberance as she and Luke met with her and made final selections. They both waved as she tooled off. The new plants, shrubs, and trees would be in the ground and thriving several weeks before the wedding.

Jenny reached up and kissed Luke. "Best present ever, buddy."

Supper that night was a rotisserie chicken and veggie tots made of broccoli, cauliflower, and cheese. Both of them had worked hard all day and should have been ravenous, but Luke didn't eat much, and Jenny pushed her food around her plate.

Jenny looked at Luke and said what she'd guessed they'd both been thinking. "Pearl Mayhew said she'd be in touch in *a few days*. What is a few days? Two, three, four? Shouldn't we have heard from her by now?" she asked plaintively.

"Honey, I just don't know," Luke said patiently and leaned back in his chair.

Jenny speared a veggie tot and ate it without even tasting it. "We shouldn't call her again, right?"

"Right. Let's just let this unfold, Jenny. We can't control outcomes here." Luke gave her hand a squeeze.

Her phone rang and both of them jumped. Jenny shot out of her chair to get it, but it was a health insurance company with *a very special offer*. With a stabbing finger, Jenny blocked that number. The phone rang again, and her heart ticked up a beat when she saw it was from their area code. "Hello?" she said anxiously. After a second or two, the robocall about the elections started. Again, Jenny blocked that number.

After they'd tidied up, Luke sprawled on the couch watching the shows that he liked to watch when he had things on his mind, *Gold Rush*, *Counting Cars*, and the shows about Lego competitions, fighting robots, and drone racing.

Bemused, Jenny watched him cheer on a robot. When she was younger, she really had believed that men and women were basically alike in most ways. What had she been thinking? Kissing him on the head, she grabbed her tablet and headed upstairs.

Fluffing pillows behind her, Jenny had just gotten comfortable on her bed and was about to slip in earbuds when her phone rang again. She snatched it up. Again, a local area code. "Hello," she said warily.

After a slight silence, a woman spoke in a distinctive drawl. "Jenny? This is Pearl Mayhew. I understand you and your fellow want to come see me."

Jenny's mouth went dry as cornstarch. Pushing both dogs aside, she sat up straight, swallowed, and struggled to sound alert. "Yes, ma'am. We surely do."

"Come see me tomorrow morning, any time after eight," she said.

They were going to see Pearl Mayhew. Jenny's fingers shook as she finished smoothing on a bit of makeup. She still could not quite believe that this was happening. The conversation with Mrs. Mayhew had been so brief that she wasn't even sure why they were meeting, but she and Luke had talked about it. Neither could think why their neighbor would agree to meet with them if she'd already sold her property.

A squadron of butterflies revving in her stomach, Jenny caught her hair up in a tortoiseshell clip. Stepping into a black skirt with a stretchy waistband, she topped it with a sage green, gently used cashmere V-neck sweater that Charlotte had bought for her. Donning black tights and a pair of low but dressy black boots, she stretched her sweater out a bit and smoothed it so it hid her muffin top. Nervously, she checked herself out in the mirror. She looked presentable and respectful, without looking like she'd gone over the top to impress Mrs. Mayhew.

Jenny heard the front door open and poked her head in the living room. "Hey, you. How do things look at the new cabin?"

"Good. They're right on schedule." Luke stuck his hands in the pockets of his khakis.

"Those fellows are in high gear and doing nice work."

Jenny hooked on small gold earrings, gave the mirror one last glance, and turned off the light. In the living room, she slipped her arms around Luke's waist and leaned into his chest. He carried with him a breath of fresh morning air and the faint scent of sandalwood soap that Jenny loved.

Luke gave her a reassuring hug. "Let's get going, Jenny girl."

In the parking lot of the retirement community, Jenny felt nervous again. She turned to look at Luke. "What if we blow this one chance to keep the resort as tranquil and perfect as it is now?" she asked, her voice quavering.

Luke gave her a glimmer of a smile. "All we can do is our best, Jenny. We don't even know if she wants to sell. Her kids may want the lot. If she would consider selling and she loved the land, she might listen to our proposal, but she may also be ready to sell to the highest bidder."

Jenny nodded mutely. She double-checked her tablet and made sure she'd queued up the pictures she wanted to show Mrs. Mayhew if she had the chance. Last night, she'd worked for an hour lining up a slideshow of life at the Lakeside Resort. If she had a chance, she'd love to show them to her neighbor. A picture was worth a thousand words.

Hand in hand, the two walked into the senior living facility.

Outside Room 104, Jenny knocked lightly on the open door. "Mrs. Mayhew?" she called, and tentatively stuck her head inside the door.

"I'm decent. Come on in," a woman's voice called out.

Watching television in a wheelchair, a white-haired woman with a twinkly smile waved them in. "Good morning." She gestured toward her wheelchair. "I'm not as feeble as this thing makes me look. I'm going in for hip replacement surgery soon. Mine has been giving me a fit." In a red-checked flannel shirt and blue jeans, Pearl had bright eyes, pink cheeks, and an unlined face that made her look younger than her mid- to late seventies.

Clicking off the television, she whirled the chair around to face them. "The news shows can drive me batty, but I like keeping up with the world," she announced and waved a hand at two armchairs. "Please have a seat."

Luke smiled as they sat. "I'm Luke Hammond and this is Jenny Becket. We're glad to meet you and thank you for being willing to talk with us."

"Good to meet you." Pearl's eyes swept over them to get their measure.

Jenny jumped in. "In my letter I told you a little about us and what we wanted to talk with you about, but I have a question. How did you end up on that beautiful point?"

Pearl Mayhew got a faraway look in her eyes. "My daddy gave that land to me and my husband, Clark, right after we got married. At one time, Daddy owned that lot, your property, and eighty-seven acres of land around y'all."

Luke gave a whistle of appreciation. "That's a lot of lakefront land. Now, we heard that you put a house on the property that y'all built yourselves."

"That's right. We had no money to do it any other way," Mrs. Mayhew explained. "Clark and I met in a Sunday school class and married right out of high school. My folks hoped we'd wait until we were older, but we were young and in love." Pearl Mayhew threw up her knotted hands and gave a crooked smile. "Though Daddy gave us that land, he made it clear that we were going to have to make it on our own without any more help from him and Mama. So, we both got teaching jobs near here and built our home on the lake one board at a time. We'd come out on weekends and camp in a little pup tent. We'd bathe in the lake and cook over campfires. Those were golden years." She gave a wistful sigh. "Then came the fire, and we had a daughter. Life got going faster, the years flew past, and we never rebuilt. We'd go out on weekends to get away and piddle around but never rebuilt. Clark passed of cancer five years ago, and now I'm here."

Jenny was thoughtful. There was truth the woman's words about doing what you wanted, instead of waiting until the perfect time.

Pearl gazed at them with keen interest. "Now, tell me about you two. You're a little long in the tooth to be getting hitched, but I think that's smart. You both know what you want. Tell me more about your resort and your plans for the future."

And they did. Jenny felt herself relax as she told Mrs. Mayhew the story of how her father had won the land for the resort in a poker game and how she'd come to inherit the property.

Luke chuckled as he added to the story. "So when we met, Jenny didn't like men in general and me in particular," he said in a self-deprecating tone. "But I wore her down."

Pearl Mayhew laughed, her eyes sparkling with amusement.

The two talked about progress they'd made on the property, the events they'd hosted, and the good feedback and loyalty they'd gotten from their guests. Jenny scraped her chair over to sit beside the older woman's wheelchair and showed her the photographs on her tablet. Pearl polished her glasses on her shirt and peered with interest at every one.

Jenny had photos of her and Landis's new organic garden and Garland in his farmer's overalls and straw hat, ready for spring gardening. She'd caught gold-lit sunset shots of the gleaming Silver Belle and the jaunty red-and-white Shasta canned ham. The exterior pictures of the cabins and the lake turned out well, as did the interior shots of the Dogwood, including the robin's egg blue woodstove and Daddy's rustic oak bookshelf still filled with his books by Zane Gray and Earnest Hemingway. The last photo she showed Pearl was the one that she'd used in the recent newsletter and gotten such a positive response about—Bear, Buddy, and Levi snuggled together, dozing in a sunny spot on the cabin floor. "That's our place in a nutshell."

A smile lingering on her face, Pearl took off her glasses. "I have so enjoyed hearing your stories and looking at those pictures." She folded her hands in her lap and her eyes, bright with intelligence, gazed at them. "Now, let's talk about why you two came to see me."

"We heard that you might be moving in with your daughter and that you might be considering selling that land on the point," Luke said. "If that's so, we'd like to buy it."

The corners of Pearl's mouth turned up and she arched a white brow. "That's the rumor going round, is it? I'm not ready to pack it up and go live with my daughter. My baby sister Ruthie lives in Wilmington in an over-55 place. Both of us are no spring chickens but we've got life in us yet." Her face grew animated. "We're both checking out of our old folks' homes and going on an around-the-world cruise that lasts a year. If we like cruising, we'll sign up for more."

From the pocket of her wheelchair, she pulled out a glossy cruise ship booklet and pointed at it with her forefinger. "You heard of those people that make their lives on cruise ships? Eat all that good food that a chef prepared? Get maid service every day? See all sorts of ports of call?" Her eyes sparkling with zest, she pointed a bony finger at her chest. "That'll be Ruthie and me. We'll have an adventure."

Jenny broke into a smile and clasped her hands together. "I love that idea."

"We do, too," Pearl said, looking pleased.

"I was always intrigued reading about those full-time cruisers," Luke said and tilted his head. "But is part of that rumor true? Are you considering selling your land?"

"Doesn't your daughter want it?" Jenny asked and then could have kicked herself. Whose side was she on?

Pearl snorted. "My daughter, Julie, says the land is a

hundred miles east of nowhere. Her husband, Steve, can't be more than five miles from a good golf course." She gave an exasperated sigh. "Even when he's not playing golf, the man wears salmon-colored pants."

"Ah." Luke nodded his understanding.

Pearl looked out the window for a moment and then gave them a canny look. "Another fellow came to see me about that land, and he's keen on buying it. It's seven acres, you know."

Jenny's heart lurched and she eyed Luke, but he just looked calmly attentive, like he had at the bank last week when they'd asked their bank manager about CD rates.

Pearl pointed to a wall of her room. "The other man made me a little computer picture show and shot it on the wall. Fancy," she said, her mouth tight. "I know he intends to build a big and citified place, and I don't particularly want that. I like you all and like your plans for the place."

Jenny held her breath, afraid to be hopeful.

Pearl examined them for a long moment. "But this is a pure business decision. It has to be, or my daughter would be very upset with me. I know land prices on the lake."

Luke nodded gravely. "How much did the fellow offer you?"

Brusquely, Pearl spoke a number that made Jenny's legs and arms turn to water.

Jenny's mind raced. She knew from the appraisal

she'd had done on her property a year and a half ago that lake prices were steep and getting steeper, but the sum they were talking about seemed huge and beyond their reach. She tried to send Luke a warning look that said *Let's sprint out of this room while we still can.*

But Luke just nodded slowly. "May I have a few minutes to talk this over with Jenny?"

"Of course." Pearl Mayhew waved vaguely and wheeled back toward the TV.

Jenny linked her arm in Luke's, pasted a smile on her face, and walked him out into the hallway as Pearl Mayhew turned up the news. "The other interested person has to be John Dale."

"That would be my guess." Luke rubbed his chin and looked thoughtful. "We need to make a better offer."

Jenny stared at him like he'd lost his mind. "Luke, we can't afford it. I know you have more money than me by a long shot, Mr. Bill Gates, but we can't put it all in the lot next door." She threw her hands up in exasperation. "We might as well put it all on red and spin the roulette wheel. I just don't think we can afford it."

"Jenny, you know what John Dale's plans are." Luke gave her a measured look. "We can't afford not to."

Jenny put her hands on the side of her head. She could hear blood thrumming between her ears. In living color, she pictured big wake boat waves swamping their resort's kayakers. Boats would fly by their dock with their radios blaring Luke Combs' *Beer Never Broke My Heart*,

Jimmy Buffet's *Margaritaville*, or thumping top twenty songs. Son of a biscuit. Jenny blew out a sigh, resigned. "I can't believe I'm saying this, but I think you may be right," she muttered.

"It's *seven* acres, Jenny. Seven acres." Luke's voice was low and urgent. "That's almost twice the size of your lot."

Jenny blinked and really thought about it. She'd assumed the lot was about the size of hers. "Seven acres. We could protect the resort forever," she said wonderingly and put a hand on her throat. "Let's make the offer. Our future depends on it."

Luke pulled her toward him in a quick, fervent embrace. "That's my girl."

Back inside, Luke sat beside the older woman.

Pearl clicked off the television and looked at him expectantly.

"We'll offer you $10,000 over what the other fellow offered, and if you ever come back from cruising around, we'd like to invite you and your sister to come to stay with us at the resort for two weeks a year, anytime you want."

"Hmmm." Pearl gave a half-smile and pushed up her sleeves of her flannel shirt. "I'll consider your offer. I need to run this by my daughter and son-in-law and my attorney." She gave a wicked grin and tapped the side of her head. "They all need to make sure they think I'm of sound mind."

"We understand. Take as much time as you need,"

Luke said easily. "We'd be happy to talk with your family and your attorney and get you proof of funds."

Pearl broke into a smile. Her knees cracked when she rose, but she stuck out her hand. Both Jenny and Luke shook it, and she waved at them as they left. "Pleasure to meet you two. I'll be in touch."

"Oh, honey. Why did you say *take as much time as you need*!" Jenny said reproachfully as she hoisted herself gracelessly into the high passenger seat of his truck. "I'll have a heart attack while we wait for her answer."

"No heart attacks allowed." Luke cracked a smile as he slid into the driver's seat.

She stared unseeingly out the window. "What if John Dale gets wind of all this and ups his offer?"

Starting the truck, Luke turned to look at her. "Jenny, I know how much you want this now, and I do, too. More than you know. But John Dale *could* up his offer. If he does, we'll just have to deal with that the best we can. All we can do is our best."

Jenny nodded slowly, knowing he was right. Taking a few long deep breaths that did no good at all, Jenny stared out the window and sent up a prayer to Jax and God. *I really want to protect the resort. Please look favorably on us and help us buy this. We'd be such careful, loving stewards of the land. You know that about us. Please, please, please.* But Jenny reminded herself about the futility of trying to strong-arm God. If she'd have been successful at that, she'd be married to her ex-fiancé Douglas and trying hard to squish her identity into a ladylike, rule-following good girl that didn't suit her. Jenny made an addendum to her prayer. *"If us getting this land isn't your will, God, I understand, and I'll try hard to let it go. But I'll need help on that, so just keep that in mind."* The corners of her mouth twitched. There. Another odd but good prayer from Jenny Beckett, but God must be used to it.

Looking over at Luke, she caught his eyes and gave him a tentative smile. With a tender look, he held out his warm, calloused hand and clasped hers. Jenny held on, comforted. *All we can do is our best.*

CHAPTER 17

TODAY WAS CHARLOTTE'S TALK, AND Jenny was there a half-hour early as her friend had requested. The Noontime Rotary Club of Celeste met in what had been a Mexican restaurant that never made it. After the town of Celeste had bought the building and converted it into a meeting space, they rented it out to community groups to generate income. The faux mission bell and faint scent of chipotle that lingered gave the building a certain exotic feel, Jenny decided, as she sat at the table and chair closest to the speaker's podium.

Jenny spotted Ashe, and he came to greet her with a smile and a hug. "Thanks for coming. Charlotte's making me leave the room when she gives her talk. She says I'll make her more nervous than she already is," he said, sounding worried.

"Okay." Jenny got into damage-control mode. "Did she do her deep breathing beforehand? Did she practice her visualizations about the audience being receptive and thrilled with her talk?"

"Check and check. She did them both last night and in the car before we came in." Ashe rubbed his sweating palms on his pants legs. "I'm nervous *for* Charlotte, but we both decided she had to get more comfortable with this if she wanted to promote her *Drive with Courtesy* campaign."

"I agree. It will just take practice," Jenny said, hoping she was right. "She was so natural and relaxed when she spoke to the women at the *Fabulous You Fit and Healthy Week.*"

"Good." Looking grateful for her reassurance, Ashe explained, "Here's how the meeting goes. After about fifteen minutes of fellowship, we get rolling with the Pledge of Allegiance, then quickly move on to business because we all have to get back to work. The president has the club officers give updates and make announcements, then comes the speaker. We eat and leave. It's just an hour, so Charlotte will need to be succinct."

"Charlotte can do this, Ashe," Jenny said, and watched as a bit of tension eased from his face.

The Rotarians were a friendly bunch. Her tablemates introduced themselves warmly and politely. After the announcements, the president, Daniel Stern, gave Charlotte a bright smile. "And now, for those of you who haven't met her, I'm delighted to introduce Charlotte Perry Long, a talented home designer and wife of our esteemed mayor, Ashe Long. Charlotte is here today to tell us about a courteous driving initiative she's undertaking with community leaders to make our fair town a safer and more pleasant place to live." Daniel pointed at Charlotte with a closed hand and began clapping. The Rotarians joined him as Charlotte stepped behind the podium. In her tomato-red tailored jacket with gold buttons, a crisp white blouse, and black houndstooth check slacks, Charlotte looked polished and professional, but her face was as white as her blouse, and she promptly dropped all her note cards. Daniel and another Rotarian leaped up to help her retrieve them.

Jenny sent up a quick prayer. *Please, God. Send her courage and composure.*

Charlotte shuffled her note cards, looked up at the crowd, and began visibly trembling. "Good afternoon," she said rapidly, but she spoke too faintly to be heard.

"We can't hear you," a Rotarian called from the back of the room.

Outside the glass door of the meeting room, Jenny could see Ashe pacing, his hands clasped behind his back.

Jenny nodded like the little bobblehead dog on a car dashboard, trying to send her friend encouraging looks. "Good afternoon," Charlotte croaked, trying again, but her mouth must have gone dry. Daniel Stern jumped up and poured her a glass of water. "Take your time, now. You're among friends," he said softly, but the mic picked it up.

Charlotte's face just registered terror, and she eyed the exits. She fixed her eyes on Jenny, who was now maniacally nodding. Drawing a deep breath, Charlotte looked at the crowd, and it was like a switch had been flipped. "Hello, friends," she said serenely.

Jenny exhaled, relieved. Charlotte looked like herself, not like she'd just come face-to-face with a ghost.

Charlotte scanned the room, meeting peoples' eyes and nodding at those she knew. "I'm here today to talk with you all about safe driving. Now, unsafe driving is a thorny set of problems that includes drivers who are distracted, impaired, not obeying the seat-belt laws, speeding, and driving aggressively. We can't fix all that. So I'm proposing we try to address just two parts of the problem, speeding and aggressive driving. Let's just talk about how we can make driving safer and a more pleasant experience in Celeste, the town we call home."

Charlotte stepped out from behind the podium and walked around the tables, meeting people's eyes. "The population of Celeste has risen 11 percent in the past year. We have more people living here, more congested roads, and newcomers bringing more aggressive driving styles with them."

Several participants nodded vigorously.

Charlotte went on, looking surer of herself. "Over the past few years, we've experienced an increase in both speeding and aggressive driving in our town." Briefly, she glanced at a notecard and looked back up. "Speed is a factor in nearly one-third of all traffic fatalities. Our local law enforcement is seeing more drivers exceed the speed limit in town and around town. They are also seeing what the state highway patrol is seeing, significant increases in aggressive driving like tailgating, weaving in and out of traffic, unsafe and illegal passing, flashing headlights, not stopping at stop signs or traffic lights, and screaming or gesturing." She tapped a notecard in her hand and frowned. "You all remember the road rage incident last year when a speeding, angry driver ran a pregnant woman's car off the road when she accidentally pulled in front of him?"

Looking disgusted, Rotarians shook their heads and murmured to one another about the senselessness of the incident.

"Luckily the driver and her unborn baby were okay, but it shocked and scared us all. We all pay the price for speeding and aggressive driving. We could be injured and fear our loved ones could be injured. We pay for parts of accident victims' medical expenses. But mostly we pay because, if we accept it sadly and resignedly and think we can't do anything about it, we let slip away the kindness, graciousness, and neighborliness that are part of the fabric of living in the small town we love." Charlotte stood taller and gave the group a meaningful look. "In Celeste, we treat each other the way we want to be treated."

More emphatic head nodding in the group.

"When y'all entered this room today, I noticed something," Charlotte said in a conversational tone. "Sorry I didn't get all your names." Peering at nametags, she pointed at each individual as she spoke to them. "Helen, you were first to arrive, and you held the door open for Heather and Daniel. Daniel, you paused to hold the door open for these two gentlemen." Charlotte pointed at two others and then another man. "And you, sir, just decided to stay there and act as doorman for every other person who came in. Now, I know Rotarians are just plain nice people," she said with an easy smile. "But in the outside world, have you ever noticed how frequently this happens? If you're driving, and a person lets you in a long line of traffic, you are more inclined to let another driver in in front of you." Attendees bobbed their heads. "Here's another thing I noticed. If I make the effort to be extra pleasant to a checkout person at the grocery store, often times, I overhear the person behind me being extra pleasant, too." Charlotte held out both hands palms up. "So, the rudeness can be contagious, but the kindness and courtesy can be just as infectious."

Jenny's tablemates looked absorbed as they listened.

Charlotte's eyes swept around the room. "You all are the business leaders and the influencers of our town. So, I'm here to ask your support for the *Drive with Courtesy* campaign I'm proposing we adopt in Celeste." She paused to sip her water. "It's a two-part deal. First, we'll launch a big public awareness campaign. We'll be all over social media, in the paper, and on billboards in town and on the outskirts. We'll enlist volunteers to speak to community groups, the TV stations, and our schools. In a big way, we'll get the word out about our safe driving campaign."

Charlotte gave them a businesslike look. "Second, our sheriff's department is 100 percent behind this initiative and will be on the lookout for offenders. If you speed or drive aggressively in Celeste, you will get pulled over and given a friendly reminder to drive with courtesy. The second time you get caught for speeding or aggressive driving, you'll get a ticket. No sweet talking, no excuses."

A smattering of applause came from the group. Daniel Stern tugged at his necktie and called out in a sheepish tone, "I'm going to need to slow down." Other folks chuckled, admitting that they needed to do the same.

The talk was going so well. Jenny breathed normally for the first time since she'd arrived at her table and relished watching her friend explain the details of the campaign. Engaging, articulate, and relaxed, Charlotte owned the room.

As she concluded her talk, the Rotarians smiled and gave Charlotte a rousing round of applause.

Turning pink with pleasure, Charlotte dimpled as she stood at the podium. "Before you leave, I have little parting gifts for each of you." She began passing out the *Drive Nice, Darlin'* bumper stickers.

Catching Charlotte's eye, Jenny gave her a radiant smile, holding two thumbs up.

Jenny was still marveling at her friend's performance as she pulled in her driveway. She'd just stepped out of the car when the text signal dinged. Jenny smiled as she read it. *May Landis and I stop by? I've had a brilliant idea!! Hugs and kisses from your lovin' Mama*

Jenny had just greeted the dogs when she heard the rat-tat-tat of Mama's familiar knock and swung open the door. "Hey, you two." Jenny bit back a smile. Claire and Landis must have reached detente on the athleisure wear war, because both of them were dressed neatly and, thankfully, normally, in jeans and cotton shirts.

Jenny waved them in and they all sat. Mama gave her a twinkling smile, "You told that awful woman that you'd decided to bake your own wedding cake. I hope you didn't mean it. A bride has too much going on before her wedding to take that on." Mama touched a hand to her chest, her jaw set in determination. "*I* am going to bake your wedding cake."

Landis stepped back out of view of his wife and widened his eyes as he pantomimed a look of terror and mouthed the word *No.*

Jenny pinned a smile on her face, feeling a little panicky. Mama wasn't much of a cook, but unfortunately, she kept trying. Last summer, Mama had baked two loaves of a "healthy" zucchini bread using millet flour and flaxseeds. The bread came out of the oven dense as bricks. After her expensive serrated knife would not cut them, Mama admitted defeat and put them outside in the compost pile. The loaves had not decomposed much in the compost turner and the dogs and the deer wouldn't touch them.

Jenny realized she was wringing her hands and made herself stop. "Mama, I couldn't let you do that. I have so many more important things I need your help with. We need to make arrangements for out-of-town guests. I haven't even thought about flowers, and Charlotte said she needed your help with the caterers."

Looking pleased, Mama smiled tentatively. "Well, I do like to be helpful, and maybe my talents are stronger in areas other than baking."

Leaning forward, Landis bobbed his head in agreement. "Good. Now it's all decided."

Mama turned to him and smiled sweetly. "Darlin, don't think I can't see you from the corners of my eyes. With all those facial expressions, you ought to be on Broadway."

Jenny chuckled and Landis gave a sheepish grin. He put his arm around Claire and squeezed her. "Sorry, shug."

On the way back from the store, the back of Jenny's car was packed with groceries. In her head, she was reviewing all that she needed to get done for the wedding. The baker in Shady Grove had laughed out loud when Jenny'd asked if she could bake a wedding cake for a

June 20th wedding. *Darlin', my Junes are crazy hectic. For a whole year now I've been booked solid for that month.* Jenny drummed her fingers on the steering wheel. She hadn't heard back from two other bakers she'd contacted, and the only other one that lived less than an hour from the resort had sketchy reviews on Yelp and Google. Darn it. Maybe she would have to bake the cake herself.

Jenny saw the sign for Gus's Gas-N-Git and on a whim, pulled in. An iced coffee would hit the spot and give her the oomph that she needed to get groceries put up and the rest of her day's work done. As Jenny stepped into the bakery, she inhaled the aroma of freshly ground coffee and baked sweets. She touched her forehead and broke into a smile. Why hadn't it occurred to her? Maybe, just maybe, Posy also baked wedding cakes.

The young baker approached. She looked like Pippi Longstocking had grown up to become a biker chick. With her hair in two braided pigtails, she wore a short skirt, tights, and platform tennis shoes in a leopard print. Quirking her mouth up in a smile, she held up a full coffeepot and tilted it back and forth. "Hey there, Jenny. What can I get for you?"

Jenny gave a crooked smile. "How about a wedding cake for seventy-five people?"

Jenny put groceries in her kitchen cabinets and hauled paper towels and toilet paper to the laundry shed to store them until she had more storage. Yup, a bigger kitchen, more cabinets, and tons more storage space would be the big bonus of living in her new cabin. As Jenny wedged the last of her meats and vegetables in her always crowded freezer, Charlotte texted.

Can I stop by and take a walk with you tomorrow at five? I have to run to the lake to deliver new pieces of local artwork to my client, the woman whose ex-husband is the 'lying, cheating sack of worms.' Ashe said my talk today went well. Did you think so, too?

Jenny replied. *Rotary went swimmingly. You were a mega hit! Amazing! Walk tomorrow, YES.*

The next day, the late afternoon sun was starting to sink in the sky as Jenny and Charlotte hoofed it down the road swinging their arms like power walkers because Charlotte had read a blog post that said it toned arms and burned 15 percent more calories than regular brisk walking.

"What's new with you, chicky? I've been me, me, me lately, but I've turned a corner now that my talk is over." Charlotte huffed, her arms pumping.

Jenny filled her in on the goings-on in her life.

"So, I wonder what the holdup is with Mrs. Mayhew? Waiting must be driving you mad," Charlotte said knowingly.

"It is," Jenny made a face. "I ate a whole sleeve of

chocolate cookies yesterday before I even thought about it."

"Oh, dear." Charlotte shot her a sympathetic look. "I sure hope she calls you soon. It's hard to not know anything."

"It is and, of course, I'm imagining the worst." Jenny threw up her hands. She looked at Charlotte. "Now, tell me. What's new with your campaign?"

Charlotte gave a confident smile. "The town council is entirely on board. The police chief is not at all sure this will work and may have used the word 'wacky,' but I believe he'll come around."

"What makes you think he will?" Jenny looked at her doubtfully.

"Ashe scrounged up the money to hire a new officer, and he's real pleased about that. Also, I've planned two law enforcement appreciation days this year. Those officers work hard. Celeste is a small town, but we've got our share of problems with drugs and crime," Charlotte said, her voice tight with frustration.

Jenny shook her head. "Law enforcement is such a tough job. Every day, we should be appreciating the police."

"I agree," Charlotte said firmly.

Jenny tripped over a root but caught herself. "What else?"

"Ashe's people got us spots on the news stations in Roanoke, Blacksburg, and Martinsville, and we'll have regular pieces in our little bitty town newspaper. You know, a splashy article and then regular updates on progress we're making. We're also adding the slogan to the Welcome to Celeste sign you see as you come into town."

Jenny realized she was panting. "Can we slow down, please?"

Charlotte grinned and slowed her pace. "Sorry. I get excited talking about it, and next thing I know we're sprinting."

Jenny looked at her thoughtfully. "After this campaign is a smash hit, maybe you could work on getting people to be nicer to each other in general, not just driving. I don't know if it's that people aren't raised right or if it's the media that make people think meanness is normal." Jenny grimaced. "The little things can get to me. Last week, I was behind a woman at the only open line at the grocery store. She had a cart full of groceries. I had two avocados. Wouldn't you have said graciously, 'Oh, you go ahead?' No! She worked real hard to just pretend she hadn't seen me and unloaded all her groceries." Jenny got mad again just describing it.

"I'd like to take it even further." Charlotte gave an enthusiastic skip. "A friend who lives on the coast told me that her little town's motto is, *Kindness Grows.* She says it's working, too. Isn't that encouraging?"

"It is. I love that," Jenny said.

"We could try that in Celeste. I have two other campaign and bumper sticker ideas I'm working on up here."

She tapped the side of her head with a forefinger. "One is *Make common courtesy common again.* Then, this one's for the politicians on both sides and for the media people. *More cheering, less sneering and jeering.* Both are a little wordy, but it's percolating."

"You'll get there." Jenny glanced over at her, admiring the way Charlotte's creativity worked. "Maybe you could start in Celeste, and it would catch on. You could go statewide and regional and next thing you know, you've got your own TV network show like Chip and Joanna."

"You know how I adore those two." Her friend put a hand to her heart. "But I have all that I want right now, a quiet life, great friends, work that's fun, and the man I love."

"You *do* have it all, girl," Jenny said sincerely. She paused. "I haven't lived with a man full-time in a long while. Any tips of cohabiting happily? Pitfalls to avoid? Habits to break?" Jenny asked lightly but cringed inwardly as she mentally reviewed her quirks. She always had to keep the downstairs neat as a pin because that's where guests checked in. When Luke wasn't around and no guests were checking in or out, the cabin could look like the slobby dermatologist and his wife lived there. Yesterday, she'd found her mouth guard on the kitchen counter beside the coffee maker. Jenny also wore her own version of athleisure wear. Add all that to the multivitamin gnawing, and it wasn't an attractive picture. Yikes.

Charlotte paused to retie her shoe and thought about

it. "We had to learn how to fight productively, and that was a biggie. But for the most part, it's been easy living with Ashe. Both of us were single for a long time, so we aren't joined at the hip. We both read. We have two televisions so we can each watch our own shows. He messes around in the garden. I like my Pinterest time," Charlotte said. "Last weekend, I went to hear a blues band with him even though it's not my thing. It was fun. We give each other space, but try to spend time together, too."

Jenny persisted, thinking about the nose strip she wore to bed to help her breathe when her allergies kicked up. "Have you changed any habits that you had when you lived alone?"

"Not really. We just are comfortable with each other and act like ourselves." Charlotte twirled a lock of hair and looked off into the distance. "I'm trying to listen to him better. I'm a good talker, and Ashe is an introvert, but I've been working on not dominating the conversation." She squinted and thought harder. "I'm taking shorter showers so the hot water won't run out on Ashe. I read an article that said eating supper together regularly made for a stable and happy marriage, so I'm trying to cook meals a lot of evenings, even if they're simple ones." She lifted both hands, palms up. "Those are my best tips about marriage."

Jenny sighed at that domestic picture. "Sounds lovely." But she *would* try to be tidier.

When she got home, Jenny added spinach, artichoke,

and fresh sliced tomatoes to a frozen pizza and slid it into the oven. Luke would arrive any minute, and after they ate a simple supper, the two had a lot more planning to do for their honeymoon camping trip.

After they ate, it was dueling computers. Luke settled in on the couch with his laptop, chatting online with members of various RV communities. Jenny slid into her kitchen chair and began exploring advice and tips from the Facebook camping groups and blog communities.

Carefully, Jenny took notes on what more experienced campers identified as being essential to take, what they should leave home, what to buy along the way. Both of them were determined to pack light. Every guidebook and YouTube video she and Luke watched stressed the importance of this, especially if their route took them up and down mountains, over bridges, or on long straight stretches of highway where they could encounter high winds. One camper compared trying to keep an over-loaded camper on the road in a torrential rainstorm as being like *trying to steer one of the bulls running at Pamplona*. Jenny shivered when she thought about that.

The bloggers at *Practical Airstream Gals* offered easy menu ideas for cooking while camping. She copied, pasted, and printed two weeks' worth of tried-and-true recipes just to get her started. Ready for a break, Jenny stood, stretched, and started emptying the dishwasher.

Luke pointed at the screen looking pleased. "Three couples already responded to my questions about the best campgrounds and sites for boon docking between here and the coast. About ten other folks wrote me with their favorite routes out west, and the Airstream Camping groups are real responsive and give a lot of Airstream-specific tips. A few of them wanted to meet up with us for supper."

"Good." Jenny put the last two glasses up in the cabinet. It was comforting to think about making new friends. As much as she enjoyed spending time with Luke, she was still a little worried about being lonely so far away from her girlfriends and mama.

Luke's phone rang. He looked at the number, looked at Jenny, and grimaced. "Zander," he said as he picked up.

Of course it was. What was the crisis of the day this time? With more vigor than was necessary, Jenny clattered a pan away in the cabinet.

Luke answered and the two men talked for a moment. "So, you didn't get the patent and your two top guys walked out. Do you know why?" Luke said in the ultra-calm voice he used when he was trying to get people to calm down.

Jenny caught his eye, threw up her hands, and closed her laptop. If this call resulted in another rescue mission to Athens, Australia, or any other faraway place that began with *A*, she'd just give up. Maybe they should make a guest suite for Zander in the new cabin so he could come live with them. Jenny grabbed her tablet, called the dogs, and headed upstairs. She'd let these two men chat the whole rest of the evening if they wanted to. Jenny was going to put in her earbuds, snuggle in with a dog or two, and find a nice Hallmark movie.

Forty minutes later, Jenny was engrossed in her movie, occasionally nibbling on the emergency chocolate caramels that she kept in the top drawer of her dresser underneath her socks. Lanky Buddy was stretched out beside her, snoozing with his warm head resting on her leg. The heroine, who had recently been fired from her job in a big city, was back in her hometown trying to help her parents make a go of a historic family inn that was close to going under. The heroine's smooth-talking boyfriend arrives, intending to propose and move the heroine back to the city, but Jenny was rooting for the woman to fall for the next-door neighbor, a widower with a heart of gold and two small children who were still sad about losing their mama.

Hearing the creak of the stairs up to her loft, Jenny paused her movie and removed an earbud.

Luke poked his head into the room, looking wary. "Jen, everything all right?"

"Yes, it is," Jenny said crisply, but rubbed her eyes with her fingers as she recalled their talk with the priest, Paul. *Your spouse is your best friend. Tend to your marriage. Nurture your relationship.* She blew out a sigh. "Okay. I'm worried about Zander having ongoing new crises and your jumping every time he calls." Jenny fixed him with an imploring look. "Please tell me you're not going away again."

Luke leaned against the railing, his posture hunched. "I've done that to you one too many times, haven't I?" Looking chagrinned, he rubbed the back of his neck. "Jenny, I really did think about what Paul said to us, and I've made a decision."

Jenny sat up, put aside her tablet, and took out the other earbud. "Tell me," she said, trying to sound calm even though she was hardly breathing.

"I talked with him just now about my working on a real exit strategy. I'm leaving my role as silent partner at the end of next month. Zander has asked to buy my remaining shares, and I'll be available to check in with him on a quarterly basis, but that's it. Zander's also agreed to hire an experienced consultant to act as a sounding board. I'll phase out, and we'll still get contingency payments on profits over the next twenty years." He gave her a crooked smile. "How does that sound, Jen?"

"Oh, Luke. That sounds wonderful." Blinking back happy tears, Jenny rushed over and threw her arms around his neck. Just as Luke grasped her hair with his fingers and kissed her long and deep, the phone rang.

Elated and feeling breathless from their kiss, Jenny pulled away as a muffled ring tone came from the bedding under Bear's rump. She shot a puzzled look at Luke and felt around until she found the phone. Glancing at the caller ID, she widened her eyes and shot Luke a look. "It's Pearl Mayhew." Hurriedly, she picked up.

"Hello, Mrs. Mayhew," Jenny said.

"Hello, Jenny. I have talked with my family and my attorney about your offer," Mrs. Mayhew announced. "Can you all stop by tomorrow morning around ten?"

"Of course," Jenny said, trying to sound calm even though she was thrilled. Looking at Luke, she mouthed, "She wants to meet."

Luke's brow was furrowed. "What?" he asked quietly, and cupped a hand behind his ear.

Jenny put a finger to her lips to shush him.

"I have a few conditions I'd like to discuss with you," Pearl said crisply. "We'll look for you tomorrow."

Jenny had a sinking feeling in the pit of her stomach. If the woman wanted to up the price, she and Luke just couldn't afford it. "We'll see you soon."

Ending the call, she turned to Luke, who had his reading glasses pushed up onto his head and was looking at her steadily. "Mrs. Mayhew wants to meet with us tomorrow morning. She didn't say she accepted our offer. She says she has conditions she wants to discuss with us." Jenny rubbed her forehead with her fingers, her thoughts whirling. *What if her kids decided they want the land? What if John Dale Harper got wind of our interest and offered a whopping higher bid?*

With a look that told her he knew she was thinking the worst, Luke circled her with his arms and leaned his forehead into hers. "Stop worrying, Jen. Let's just let this unfold."

Jenny blew out a shuddering breath and gave him a wan smile. "I'll try."

But not worrying about a decision so important was easier said than done.

When Luke and Jenny arrived at Gracious Home Senior Living, Mrs. Mayhew was sitting on the sunny patio in her wheelchair. In the chairs beside her were a sweet-looking woman in her mid–fifties wearing a green linen dress and a man in salmon-colored plaid pants.

After introductions were made, Pearl's daughter, Julie, looked squarely at Jenny and Luke. "We have talked with Mama about what she wants. We are in full agreement with her plan, and as you well know, she is in full possession of her mental faculties." She gave them a wry smile. "Sharp as a fox and ornery as all get-out. So, we'll let you all chat." The two walked off to sit on another part of the patio to give them privacy.

As she and Luke sat down, Jenny realized she was holding her breath.

Luke leaned forward and gazed at the older woman. "Well, Mrs. Mayhew, Jenny and I are anxious to hear what you've decided."

Mrs. Mayhew pursed her lips and broke into a disarming smile. "Because I don't want the land to go to a developer, and because I see more than a little of my late husband and myself in the two of you, I want you to have the land."

Happiness flooded in. Jenny put a hand on her chest and blinked back grateful tears, her heart swelling with a heady mix of elation and relief. "Thank you so much, Mrs. Mayhew. You don't know how much this means to us."

"I think I do," Pearl Mayhew said softly. She held up a finger. "I have two conditions, though."

"What would those be, Mrs. Mayhew?" Luke asked politely; his face was lit up with barely contained exhilaration.

"I'd like for you to take the fieldstone that Clark and I used to build the chimney and foundation of our house that we lost, and use them in the new cabins you build." Pearl's eyes misted, and her vice quavered. "I'd like for the house that gave us so much joy to live on in a way at the resort."

"We'll do that," Luke assured her.

"They'll look amazing on the cabins." Jenny could just picture it.

"Also, I'd like to take you up on your offer to my sister and me to come stay at the cabins two weeks every year. I want to see if anyplace can be as pretty as those pictures you took."

"Done." Jenny heart beat wildly. She couldn't quite believe her dream was coming true.

Mrs. Mayhew's mouth lifted on one side. "Then we've got ourselves a deal."

Jenny put both hands on her heart, happy tears trickling down her face. "Oh, Mrs. Mayhew, you have made us so very happy. I can't even tell you what wonderful news this is."

"We'll take good care of the land, Mrs. Mayhew," Luke promised with a smile that could not be contained.

Jenny hesitated, not sure whether to bring this unpleasant topic up or not. "Mrs. Mayhew, you've had a trespasser driving his truck around your lot, cutting ruts and making a bit of a mess. The sheriff's department is working on finding whoever did it."

Pearl Mayhew just shook her head, looking disgusted. "I spoke with Sheriff Tucker just yesterday. They've found the fellow."

"Oh, I'm so glad." Jenny blew out a sigh of relief. "It was a little scary, and we didn't want anybody damaging your place."

The older woman suddenly looked weary. "That was my nephew. Jimmy's had scrapes with the law ever since he was old enough to cause trouble."

Jenny let out a huge breath, so relieved. The whole episode had really frightened her. She had to ask. "Why was your nephew doing that?"

"Jimmy had heard the rumors, too, about my possibly selling the property and was under the impression that he and his family had a right to it. This is the boy who never visits me and can't keep a job. " Pearl Mayhew rolled her eyes. "So, partly, he was just cutting up with his new truck, but he was also mad because he thought he was about to get cheated out of what he believed was his rightful inheritance."

Luke nodded his understanding. "These things happen in families."

"They do." But Mrs. Mayhew's eyes glinted with steely determination. "I told the sheriff to tell Jimmy I'd press charges if he ever did it again. The boy's walking a thin line now anyhow, so I don't think he wants that to happen."

"Hopefully, that will be the end of it," Jenny said.

Pearl waved her daughter and son-in-law over. "We're all in agreement. The land is going to these fine folks."

"Congratulations." Steve grinned and pumped both of their hands.

Julie broke into a smile and shook their hands as well. "I'm so glad the property is going to y'all. We wish you all the best and hope you make many happy memories there."

Jenny linked her arm in Luke's and beamed at them. "We will. I promise we will."

CHAPTER 18

I T WAS JUST AFTER 5 AM on Saturday, and Jenny sat in a rocker on her porch in her cotton nightgown and robe. Sipping hot, strong coffee she enjoyed watching the mist rise and the sky brighten over Heron Lake. Jenny felt serene and so buoyantly happy and light that she might just float out of her rocker. Today was her wedding day.

Jenny had hardly slept last night, excited about this new chapter in her life. She still couldn't quite believe that so much goodness had come to her so quickly. Just a year and a half ago, Jenny had been dumped by her fiancé, evicted from her chicken coop cottage, and convinced that love was just not in the cards for her. Leaning back, Jenny pushed her foot on the porch floor and started rocking, remembering too clearly how bleak she'd felt, imagining she'd be the single gal for the rest of her days.

Now, here she was on the morning of her wedding to a kind, funny, smart man that was so good-looking he made her pulse quicken whenever she saw him. Jenny shook her head, marveling at how fast her world had changed.

Her eyes swept the property. Thanks to the landscaper, the resort looked stunning. New bushes flowered pink and apricot; the flower beds were brimming with blue and purple hollyhock, salvia, and lavender. The daylilies and black-eyed Susan's added cheerful yellows to the scenery, and the pink dogwood Luke had gifted her was blooming.

Two bluebirds swooped in to check out the empty nesting box beside her. Closing her eyes, Jenny sent up a prayer. *Good morning, Daddy and God. Thank you for your protection and guidance and for sending this wonderful man to me so I could marry him. Thank you for Mrs. Mayhew selling us the land. I'm eternally grateful for everything. If you get a chance, please try to pair up other lonely people who want to find their soul mates but haven't had any luck. Remind me to keep trying to leave a bit of good in this world. Daddy, I know you'll be with us today, but I wish you were going to be here in person. I'll be on the lookout for you. Thanks again to both of you for this glorious day.* Jenny opened her eyes just as a bluebird winged by. Bemused, she shook her head and broke into a smile. "You're right on time, Daddy. Ready for the big day?" she asked softly.

The boys skidded onto the porch, panting, puffing, and smiling their doggy smiles. Levi trotted into view and clip-clopped up to join them, sidling up to Jenny for a bit of morning love. After she had scratched his back and rubbed his handsome head, Jenny gave Bear and Buddy their share of attention and the four of them headed inside. Time to get this splendid day underway.

After she showered, Jenny looked out the window and saw Mama walk toward her cabin, a lightness in her step. Opening the door before Mama could knock, Jenny beamed and embraced her.

"What a glorious day," Mama caroled, pink-cheeked with anticipation.

"I can still hardly believe it's finally happening," Jenny burbled excitedly.

"The men should be here in an hour to help set up the tents and chairs. Landis is all gung ho about helping. He's as excited as we are, I think." Mama's eyes sparkled as she pushed up the sleeves on her mulberry-colored dress.

"You look so pretty." Jenny studied her and put a hand on her hip. "I forgot to ask you how the great athleisure wear war ended. How did you get Landis to see reason?"

Mama gave a mysterious smile. "I just showed him the mother-of-the-bride dress I'd picked up at the *Closeouts and Seconds for Women* shop. It had a camouflage print in a comfy velour and had quite a bit of beading and sequins. Festive and comfortable," she said airily.

The two of them laughed.

"Anything I can help you with now?" Mama asked.

"I'm worried about the weather." Jenny walked Mama over to the window and pointed out the low gray clouds in the far distance and picked up her phone to show her the graphic of the forecast. "Everything looked clear earlier in the day, but there's that stormy system that could head our way." She pointed to the yellow area around the jet stream.

Mama peered at the screen and nodded. "I hope it amounts to nothing or blows on by, but you've got the tents coming." Grabbing a mug, she poured herself a cup of coffee.

"I wish Kent's Tents would have gotten us set up yesterday, but Luke said they had a big event last night for the Carolina Panthers." Chewing her lip, Jenny glanced at the clock. "They're supposed be here by nine."

"They were on time and reliable when they helped us at Christmas," Mama reminded her. "You've made room in your refrigerator for your cake?"

"I have." Jenny looked out the window as a battered white van pulled in the driveway, Celtic music blaring out the open windows. Turning to her mother, she clasped her hands together in excitement. "That's Posy with the cake."

Propping open the front door, the two of them scurried outside to help the young baker bring in the layers of the wedding cake. Taking small, careful steps, the three of them walked the layers inside. "Let's slide them on the counter first," Posy instructed, sounding sure of herself. Soon, all the pieces of the cake were in. Posy made one last trip to the van, fetching a large serving platter and a ceramic bowl filled with buttercream frosting.

Pushing up her sleeves, Posy washed her hands thoroughly. Her hair pulled back in a floral scarf, her dangly silver earrings jingled as she worked, while she kept up a stream of chatter that was soothing to Jenny. "I know many bakers deliver their cakes already put together but I had one incident with a cake falling to pieces when I drove across railroad tracks." The young woman rolled her eyes at the memory. "It took a boatload of icing to glue that cake back together again. Never again, I told myself. So I always err on the side of caution."

Jenny and her mother watched with fascination as Posy deftly assembled the cake.

Biting her lip with concentration, Posy finally slid the top layer on. "Ta-da," she murmured under her breath. Working quickly, she added a swirling pattern, icing rosettes, and the sugared violets that Jenny had requested. "There we go," the baker said proudly.

Jenny put a hand to her mouth. "That's the prettiest cake I've ever seen."

"Simple and elegant," Claire said approvingly and gave Jenny a quick hug. "Posy, dear, you did an outstanding job."

Wiping crumbs from the counter with a clean dish towel, Posy ducked her head and blushed bright pink. "Thank you, ma'am."

A text sounded on Mama's phone, and she gave them

each an apologetic smile as she read it. "The caterer will be here in less than three hours. She'd given me her work-space requirement for warming and serving, so I need to get our kitchen spic-and-span and organized so they can work." Brushing Jenny's cheek with a kiss, she whirled off.

"Usually, the little bride and groom topper goes there," Posy pointed to the empty place at the top of the cake. She grinned and held up a white box. "Here's a surprise. Your friend, Charlotte, and your future sister-in-law, Alice, picked a special topper for us to use. I think you'll like it."

"Oh, my gosh." Jenny was touched by her friends' thoughtfulness.

"Close your eyes while I put it on." Posy held up the piping bag of frosting.

Jenny did as told and squeezed shut her eyes.

"You can take a look now," Posy announced.

A tiny bride and groom leaned in toward each other in a chaste kiss. Behind them was a miniature Airstream. Tiny tin cans trailed off the back with strings made of ic-ing. Across the side of the camper, Posy had written in icing *Just married!* and *Off on their honeymoon!* Jenny burst into delighted laughter. Leaning over, she gave the young baker a quick hug. "You are amazing."

Taking baby steps, they lifted the cake and carefully slipped it into Jenny's refrigerator.

After Posy drove off, Luke arrived in khaki shorts, a

T-shirt, and tennis shoes. Looking relaxed and jitter-free, Luke had a cup of coffee in one hand and the last bite of his breakfast biscuit in the other. After quick play tussle with the boys, he swept Jenny into a fervent embrace and kissed her thoroughly. When he finally let her go, his voice was gravelly and his eyes glittered with intensity. "Hello, my almost wife."

Her arms still around his neck, Jenny tried to catch her breath after that lightning bolt of a kiss. Tilting her head, she grinned up at him. "Hello, almost husband. I'm not supposed to see you on my wedding day, you know, but I need your help setting up."

"Put me to work, darlin'. Let's get this day going so I can finally marry you."

Jenny flashed a smile and pointed at him. "I can't see you again, mister, until we walk down the aisle. Can you change clothes in the Shasta?"

"I will. My clothes are in the truck." Luke leaned in for one more scorcher of a kiss and headed out the door.

The crew from Kent's Tents arrived precisely at nine. From inside the Dogwood, Jenny could see that Landis had joined Luke and that the two of them and the head man were pointing, nodding, and striding around, probably confirming the best placement for the tents. They must have agreed on their plan because the crew began erecting and staking down the tents like the well-rehearsed team that they were.

Jenny slipped her beautiful dress from the bag and

hung it up on the door sill to relax any wrinkles. Hands on hips, she gave the blue-green floral gown a last appraising look, feeling fluttery delight as she admired the flattering neckline and excellent cut and fabric. With its classic, early fifties, Doris Day vibe, Jenny adored the dress. Luke would, too.

As the Kent's Tent's trucks lumbered off, Jenny got a text. Luke wrote: *Kent of Kent's Tents is amateur meteorologist. He predicts good weather will hold today.*

Ah. Jenny blew out a relieved sigh. If a man who owned a tent company didn't know about the weather, who would? She tapped out her reply. Emojis of a smiling sun, red heart, a diamond ring, and a popping bottle of champagne.

After showering, Jenny towel-dried her hair and slipped on sweats. Fishing in her jewelry box, she found her grandmother's pearls and her own small dangly pearl earrings and laid them on her dresser. Slipping off her engagement ring, she slipped it into a bowl of warm water and dishwashing soap. After it soaked, she'd polish it with a soft brush until it shone.

In her top dresser drawer, Jenny found the jewelry box that contained Luke's wedding band. Opening it again, she stared at the simple gold band, and felt a swell of emotion. Luke would wear the ring for the rest of his life. Her husband. After a moment, she closed the box and put it on the dresser with her other jewelry so she wouldn't get flustered and forget it.

At eleven, another visitor arrived. Jenny's hairstylist Star, the owner of Sassy Southern Gal Salon, was a hair magician, amateur psychologist, and motivational speaker wrapped up in one. She stepped out of her pink Escalade and wheeled a large suitcase full of styling and beauty supplies up the walkway. Jenny opened the door and hugged her. "I still can't believe you came all the way out here to help beautify me."

"My stars and garters! I wouldn't miss it for the world," Star exclaimed. With her perfect long fingernails, she fluffed out Jenny's hair and looked at it appraisingly. "Looks like I got here just in time because your hair is catawampus. We'll do a tiny trim, blow it out until it's as smooth as glass, add a little backcombing, and spray it all down to keep this humidity from doing its dark work. You'll be ready to say your vows with that fine lookin' man of yours."

Jenny sighed happily. "Star, I'm so glad you're here."

Star chuckled. Slick as a matador, she flipped a cape around Jenny's shoulders. "You are one knockout of a bride, and you're an inspiration to all the single gals over the age of thirty-nine."

After Jenny was poofed, smoothed, and sprayed with clouds of special extra-hold hair spray, Star helped her with her makeup.

"I want to keep it fairly natural-looking, Star." Jenny worried she'd look too glam.

"I know you, sugar," Star chided her affectionately,

and shook a bottle of primer. "Just a light touch and we'll enhance your prettiness."

Jenny's makeup station, the kitchen table, faced the window, so as she was getting primped, she got a bird's-eye view of all the happenings outside. Luke and Landis busily hurried here and there. Mike, Alice's husband, showed up and was soon part of the roving pack of busy men. Lily's beau, Tom, arrived, and Jenny saw an older fellow with the erect posture that one got from years in the military. It was Coy, the now-enlightened member of the fighting couple who was now Landis's buddy. She and Luke had invited him and his wife, Neecy. He was chuckling as he helped the others move chairs, set up the bar and serving tables, and confer with the caterer. "This is like watching a good action movie," she told Star as the woman stroked a pale luminous shadow across her eyelids.

Star sighed affectionately as she carefully lined Jenny's eyes. "I love watching men work together. There's nothing cuter."

Luke and Landis took turns with a post-hole digger on the side of the bluff overlooking the lake. The pack of roving men carried a heavy-looking structure over to where they'd been working. Jenny's eyes widened as they tipped up a white wooden arbor with trellises on the sides and secured it in place. It was a gracefully curved, romantic archway, the perfect place to say their vows. She hurriedly tapped out a text to Luke: *Is that what I think it is? It's gorgeous!*

Luke paused and looked toward the cabin and replied. *A surprise for the bride from me and the West Virginia boys.*

Star stopped applying blush, and the two stood at the window marveling at the arbor. "That's charming as can be, and your guests will love it, too. You know how people are with taking pictures these days. It'll be the perfect photo op." Star waved a hand at the structure. "Plant yourself a few roses, clematis, or confederate jasmine, and get them growing up those trellises. Color makes everybody look their best in pictures."

When Star finished her ministrations, Jenny stared at herself in the bathroom mirror. She put a hand to her mouth, scarcely believing what a little subtly applied makeup did for her. Jenny looked softer, younger, and practically dewy. Jenny gave Star a tremulous smile. "I'd hug you but I'm too primped at the moment to risk mussing everything. You did a remarkable job. Thank you so much, Star."

"Why, you are so welcome, honey." Star eyes twinkled. "I'm wishing you two all the happiness in the world." Star packed up her tools of the trade, waved, and headed home.

It was one-thirty now, and guests were arriving and finding their seats. Jenny checked and rechecked her hair, afraid to touch it. A fluttering feeling in her stomach,

Jenny fixed a cup of honey-chamomile tea to calm the butterflies.

A knock sounded at the door. Jenny beamed as she opened it. The women she loved most in the world had arrived, and their faces were wreathed with smiles. Charlotte, Lily, Alice, and Mama piled inside, laughing and talking. With a toothy grin, Charlotte held up a bottle of champagne. Mama had stems of flutes woven though her fingers.

The women chattered excitedly and raved over Jenny's hairdo and makeup.

"Any second thoughts, Jen?" Alice said with a mischievous look as she took a sip of bubbly. "My brother can be a handful. He used to elbow me in church but looked so angelic that my parents thought I was making it up." She narrowed her eyes and shook her head at the memory.

Jenny laughed. "No second thoughts, but I'll keep an eye on his elbows."

After they finished their champagne, the women called out their best wishes and filed out to join the other guests at the wedding. Charlotte was the last to leave.

Grasping both of Jenny's hands in hers, Charlotte gave them a squeeze. "Honey girl, I am so very happy for you. You and Luke have a joyful future ahead of you." Her eyes misted, and she gave a little laugh. "I'm being selfish, too, because now the two of you and Ashe and I can all have adventures together for the rest of our lives. We'll grow old together."

"I love you, girl," Jenny said quietly.

"Love you back." Charlotte pulled her hands away and waved them in front of her eyes. "Now, I'm going to go before we both start boo-hooing."

"Wait." Jenny grabbed the box containing Luke's wedding ring and pressed it in Charlotte's hands. They weren't having bridesmaids or groomsmen, but Jenny needed a hand. "Can you keep this until I need it?"

"Of course." Charlotte tucked the ring box into her small purse and blew a kiss as she left.

Carefully, Jenny slipped on her dress and jewelry and glanced at the clock on the stove. It was two o'clock.

They'd decided on recorded music as the guests arrived but a string quartet would play the processional and the recessional and at the reception. Jenny smiled as she heard the opening bars of Frank Sinatra's, *It Had to Be You*. That was her cue.

Outside, Jenny took a deep breath. She wanted to remember every moment of this day. The sky was a dazzling pale blue, and the indigo lake sparkled and danced in the sunlight.

Luke stepped out of the Shasta wearing a beautifully cut black tuxedo with a winged collar and black bow tie. As he approached, his eyes lit up. "You look like an angel. I'm marrying the most beautiful woman in the world."

Gently stroking her cheek with a finger, Luke gazed at her intently, his blue eyes radiating love.

Jenny blushed and laughed delightedly, putting a hand to her heart. "You look pretty beautiful yourself, all dressed up."

"You wanted a man in a tux." Luke grinned and straightened his bow tie. "We aim to please."

"You look more devastatingly handsome than any one of the Bonds," Jenny told him.

His eyes fixed on hers, a smile played at Luke's lips as he held out his arm. "You ready, darlin'?"

"I am," Jenny said, her voice choked with welling emotion as she linked her arm in his.

The string quartet began playing Pachelbel's *Canon in D*. The expectant crowd turned to greet them, sighed happily, and murmured to one another. Mama dabbed at tears, and Landis mopped at his face with a big white handkerchief.

In the back row, Mike cradled a sleeping Cherry in a sling on his chest, and a grinning Alice held the dogs and Levi until they began the processional. Beaming, Alice released the three well-dressed animals, and the boys wove around Jenny and Luke as they walked slowly down the aisle.

Smiling radiantly, Jenny and Luke stepped toward their families, their beloved friends, and the dancing, glittering waves of Heron Lake.

A Special Invitation

Dear Reader,

Thank you so much for reading *Wedding at the Lakeside Resort* and spending time with me at Heron Lake. I hope you loved this book as much as I loved writing it for you.

I'd like to ask for your help. Reader reviews are powerful tools for making my books successful. While the story is fresh on your mind, would you please go to Bookbub and your favorite online retailer and write a review?

As always, I am so grateful for your support.
Susan Schild

For alerts about new releases, follow Susan on BookBub at **https://bit.ly/2tHuDzu**

ABOUT THE AUTHOR

USA Today Bestselling author Susan Schild writes heartwarming novels about heroines over age forty having adventures, falling in love and finding their happily ever afters.

A wife and stepmother, Susan enjoys reading and taking walks with her Labrador retriever mixes, Tucker and Gracie. She and her family live in North Carolina.

Susan has used her professional background as a psychotherapist and management consultant to add authenticity to her characters.

A NOTE TO MY READERS

I am so grateful to you all for the appreciative comments and reviews. So many of you have said how much you love Heron Lake and the Lakeside Resort story. Some tell me you wish you could book a cabin and come stay for a while! Here's what I think my readers have in common:

You enjoy reading about heroines your own age having adventures, falling in love, and building a happy life. We women over forty are pretty interesting!

You also liked the fact that Jenny and Luke, their friends, and family care about other people and try to do the right thing. Many of you do too, although the news from the world around you might sometimes make you think you in are in the minority. So keep the faith and know that there are a lot of other kind, caring, good people out there just like you!

ACKNOWLEDGEMENTS

My sincerest thanks to:

My lovely readers who inspire my writing with their comments, reviews, and stories.

My wise, encouraging writer friends, Scarlett Dunn, Susie Haught, Barbara Solomon Josselsohn, and Judith Keim. Have a look at their books. I know you will enjoy them.

My walking friends, Barb, Gin, Linda, Barb, Tony, Genela, Kim, Melissa, Kevin, Carol, Gail, Wendy, Charlyne and her husband, *Love ya honey* John, for their kindness, humor, and fashion tips. (Yes, ma'am, you do cut a hole in your sneaker if your toe rubs!)

A special thanks to the North Carolina Autism Society for the support they offer our family.

My husband Bryan, who steadies me, hardly ever complains about frozen dinners during deadlines, and thinks I should put more car chases in my books.

To my stellar editor, Debra L Hartmann, and her team at The Pro Book Editor for their remarkable competence, hard work, and keen-eye.

OTHER BOOKS BY AUTHOR SUSAN SCHILD

If you enjoyed this book, you'll be sure to enjoy the other books in *The Lakeside Resort* Series!

Christmas at the Lakeside Resort

(The Lakeside Resort Series Book 1)

Love and Adventures after 40

Forty-two year old Jenny Beckett is dreading the holidays. Her fiancé has just called off their Christmas wedding, and she's been evicted from her darling chicken coop cottage. When her estranged father dies and leaves her eight rustic guest cabins on Heron Lake, Jenny seizes the chance to make a new life. She packs up her dogs, her miniature horse and her beat up Airstream trailer and moves to the lake.

Short on time and money, Jenny and her contractor, widower Luke, work feverishly to renovate the cabins in time for the festive holiday event she's promised her very first guests. When an unexpected blizzard snows them in and jeopardizes the resort's opening, Jenny and Luke work to save the event and, along the way, find true love... and the magic of Christmas.

Summer at the Lakeside Resort
(The Lakeside Resort Series Book 2)

Ready for more love and adventure after 40?

Forty-three year old Jenny Beckett has just renovated eight rustic guest cabins on beautiful Heron Lake, North Carolina. Brand new to the inn keeping business, she is struggling to make The Lakeside Resort profitable. Wrangling guests like The Fighting Couple, persnickety attorneys, and the curvy gals from the Fabulous You Fitness Week keep her on her toes.

Jenny's business isn't her only problem. Her mother and stepfather have just moved in for an extended stay. Startling developments with her possible fiancé, Luke, make Jenny question his commitment to her. An all-gal camping trip in her old Airstream lifts her spirits, but Jenny still has doubts about whether she and Luke can make their love work. After all the heartache she's had, can Jenny learn to trust love again and finally find her happily ever after?

Mistletoe at the Lakeside Resort
(The Lakeside Resort Series Book 3)

Ready for a feel good read that will ease you into the Christmas spirit?

Join forty-three-year-old newbie innkeeper Jenny Beckett at the Lakeside Resort on beautiful Heron Lake. Jenny's dreading Christmas. With almost no cabins booked for the holidays, she's accidentally made promises on social media about dazzling Christmas festivities happening at the Lakeside Resort. Trouble is, the holidays are fast approaching, Jenny's not begun to finalize plans, and she keeps running into roadblocks.

Stretched tight, Jenny scrambles to book a decent Santa Claus, a horse-drawn wagon for Currier and Ives-style sleigh rides, and the Christmas choirs she's so enthusiastically described online. To complicate matters, Mama has a frightening fall, Charlotte and Ashe are at odds about their upcoming wedding, and Jenny's getting the jitters about marrying and building a cabin with her fiancé, Luke.

When Jenny shares her fears with Luke and her best girlfriends, she starts to feel the wonder of the season.

Friends gift her a new vintage camper, Mama and Landis make a startling announcement, and friends and family pitch in to help her deliver the dazzling Christmas she'd promised. Jenny realizes she already has all she needs for a magical Christmas and a happy future.

With cozy romance, classic carols, horse-drawn sleigh rides, and happily ever afters, Christmas joy is always on tap at The Lakeside Resort.

And check out my Willow Hill series as well!

Linny's Sweet Dream List
(A Willow Hill Novel Book 1)

Set in the off-beat Southern town of Willow Hill, North Carolina, Susan Schild's moving and witty novel tells of one woman who loses everything—and finds more than she ever expected.

At thirty-eight, Linny Taylor is suddenly living a life she thought only happened to other, more careless people. Widowed for the second time, and broke, thanks to her cheating late husband, Linny has no house, no job, and no options except to go back home. There, in a trailer as run down as her self-esteem, Linny makes a list of things that might bring happiness. A porch swing. A job that nourishes her heart as well as her bank balance. Maybe even a date or two.

At first, every goal seems beyond reach. But it's hard for Linny to stay in the doldrums when a stray puppy is coercing her out of her shell—right into the path of the town's kind, compassionate vet. The quirky town is filled with friends and family, including Linny's mother, Dottie, who knows more about heartache than her daughters ever guessed. And as Linny contemplates each item on her list, she begins to realize that the dreams most worth holding on to can only be measured in the sweetness of a life lived to the fullest…

Sweet Carolina Morning
(A Willow Hill Novel Book 2)

Life down South just got a whole lot sweeter in Susan Schild's new novel about a woman whose happily-ever-after is about to begin…whether she's ready for it or not.

Finally, just shy of forty years old, Linny Taylor is living the life of her dreams in her charming hometown of Willow Hill, North Carolina. The past few years have been anything but a fairy tale: Left broke by her con man late-husband, Linny has struggled to rebuild her life from scratch. Then she met Jack Avery, the town's much-adored veterinarian. *And she's marrying him.*

Everything should be coming up roses for Linny. So why does she have such a serious case of pre-wedding jitters? It could be because Jack's prosperous family doesn't approve of her rough-and-tumble background. Or that his ex-wife is suddenly back on the scene. Or that Linny has yet to win over his son's heart. All these obstacles—not to mention what she should *wear* when she walks down the aisle—are taking the joy out of planning her wedding. Linny better find a way to trust love again, or she might risk losing the one man she wants to be with—forever...

Sweet Southern Hearts
(A Willow Hill Novel Book 3)

Welcomes you back to the offbeat Southern town of Willow Hill, North Carolina, for a humorous, heartwarming story of new beginnings, do-overs, and self-discovery...

When it comes to marriage, third time's the charm for Linny Taylor. She's thrilled to be on her honeymoon with Jack Avery, Willow Hill's handsome veterinarian. But just like the hair-raising white water rafting trip Jack persuades her to take, newlywed life has plenty of dips and bumps.

Jack's twelve-year-old son is resisting all Linny's efforts to be the perfect stepmother, while her own mother, Dottie, begs her to tag along on the first week of a freewheeling RV adventure. Who knew women "of a certain age" could drum up so much trouble? No sooner is Linny sighing with relief at being back home than she's helping her frazzled sister with a new baby...and dealing with an unexpected legacy from her late ex. Life is fuller—and richer—than she ever imagined, but if there's one thing Linny's learned by now, it's that there's always room for another sweet surprise...